When We Were Young is a captivating ... with delightful humour. The characters ... escapades reveal the intricate tapestry of the human heart desperately in need of forgiveness, both given and received, and the ties that bind and free us. It is a compelling first novel that leaves the reader eager for more from this author.

— Avril van der Merwe,
Author

A fun adventure story that not only captures the essence of adolescent struggles, but takes the reader through a suspenseful journey of a family facing a looming divorce that pushes the characters to search together for truth and understanding. Throughout the book, Jon Troll brings the reader closer to the characters' internal world of faith and fear; a story that unfolds how a family struggles when faced with adversity; a story with witty humor and heartfelt moments for teen and adult alike.

— Dr. Janet R. O'Donnell
Child Psychologist

Like a river that flows swiftly and deep, readers of this extraordinary book will find themselves caught in a current of mystery and intrigue that they can't pull away from.

Exciting, riveting, and reflective. I highly recommend Troll's book.

— Dr. William Herkelrath
Marriage and Family Therapist
Director, Masters in Counseling –
MFT Program, Palo Alto University (former)

A very unique approach that sheds light on how things affect us and ways we all struggle to some extent. A thought-provoking masterpiece. Get lost in the story and learn something that may help you in your own relationships!

— **Natalie and Daniel Herrington**
Founders of The Something Club
Compassionate Hope Foundation

WHEN WE WERE YOUNG

A NOVEL

By

Jonathan Troll

Deep River
BOOKS

Unless otherwise noted, all Scripture references are from the New International Version®.

Holy Bible, New International Version®, NIV® Copyright ©1973, 1978, 1984, 2011 by Biblica, Inc.® Used by permission. All rights reserved worldwide.

ISBN – 13: 9781632695383
Library of Congress Control Number: 2021916293

Printed in the USA
Cover design by Joe Bailen, Contajus Designs

Deep River Books LLC
PO Box 310
Sisters, Oregon, 97759
541-549-1139 (message)
info@deepriverbooks.com

Ordering Information:

Quantity sales. Special discounts are available on quantity purchases by corporations, associations, and others. For details, contact the publisher at the address above.

Table of Contents

Thank you . . .

To my parents, Robert and Kathy Troll, for your support, encouragement, advice, and godly example. To my brother, Chris Troll and to Jeanette Harney, for reading through and editing the first draft (I probably owed you both more than breakfast at Shawn O'Donnell's). To my friends and family who have been by my side throughout the different seasons of my life—I'm grateful for each and every one of you. To my high school English teacher, Mrs. Tyner, for encouraging me to pursue writing and for leading by example in your own writing pursuits. And to my Lord and Savior, Jesus Christ, the author of all things good in my life.

Prologue

"Merry Christmas, Mom." The boy quietly set a small present on the console table near the front door. "I got this for you."

The woman stood in the doorway for a moment. Snow and frozen air blew in from outside past the gift. She turned, stepped back into the house, and went to the small table. Like a precious metal or family heirloom, she touched the present gently with her fingertips.

"Promise me something." The woman tapped the gift with her fingers.

The boy stood, eager to receive and fulfill the request.

His shoulders lowered upon hearing her words. The woman slid her hand from the gift to a set of nearby keys.

A moment later, the gift remained and she was gone.

1: Out Cold

Logan tugged at his tie, loosening the half-Windsor knot. "Stop that," Rebecca said, as she nudged her brother's shoulder. "We're almost there." She shivered. "Can we go inside now?"

"Why? Forget to add something to your diary?"

"No, it's just freezing out here. And it's not a diary; it's a journal."

"What's the difference?"

"One's full of silly hopes, dreams, metaphors, and exaggerations; the other is fact-based, realistic."

"Sounds like a real page-turner." Logan looked out into the darkness. "You don't ride a ferry and not stand out on the deck. You just don't."

"Even at night when you can't see anything?"

Logan ignored his sister's logic. "I still don't get why we have to wear these stupid clothes. We're going to a Christmas party, not a funeral."

"You know it's not *just* a Christmas party." Rebecca then glanced over at her brother. "How's your eye?"

"It's fine. Probably looks worse than it is." Logan leaned forward to look at his sister. "How's your neck?"

Rebecca quickly cinched her coat collar.

"Seriously, are hickeys even a thing anymore?"

"It's not a hickey."

"Well, you didn't have that birthmark this morning. Is that why you skipped second period? To be with your new boyfriend?"

"He is not . . . ugh, never mind. Wait, how did you know I skipped second period?"

Logan breathed in the icy air. "Aren't you glad we're finally in high school together?"

The two stood in silence as waves lapped against the vessel.

"Are you going to tell me what happened to your eye?"

"Are you going to tell me who your boyfriend is? Dyson? Bissell? Roomba?"

"Fine. Don't tell me."

Rebecca looked over at her brother again. Her attention focused. "What's that in your ear?"

"What?"

"Hold still." Rebecca grabbed Logan's head and brought it toward her face. "What is that?"

"What's what?"

"Is that . . . poop?"

"Where?"

"Right there."

"Believe it or not, I can't actually see my own head."

Rebecca took Logan's hand and guided his finger to his right ear. "There."

Logan looked at his finger. "Hmm."

"Hmm? That's all you have to say?"

"I'm sorry, I didn't prepare anything."

"Where'd it come from?"

"I'm no expert, mind you, but I'm going to go with dog." Logan wiped his finger on the handrail. "Is there any more?"

Rebecca inspected Logan's ear. "No." She then took a disinfectant wipe from her purse. "Here."

"Are there many juniors at school with disinfectant wipes in their purses?"

"Are there many freshmen with fecal matter in their ear?"

"I walked into that one. I see it now."

"You walked into something."

Logan wiped his ear. He looked to his left and then to his right. He then looked behind him.

"Give it," Rebecca finally said, holding out her hand.

Logan shifted uncomfortably in his clothes. "You have to be eighteen to vote and twenty-one to drink. There should be an age limit on ties too." Logan looked at his sister. "You can't tell me that you actually like wearing that skirt."

"Well, I'd be a little more comfortable if I was inside, out from the cold." Rebecca flipped up the collar of her wool coat.

Logan loosened his tie farther. "No boy under the age of eighteen should be forced to wear these things."

"I have an idea; let's give talking a break for a while. A little silence might be nice for a change."

"Silence gets old after a while. Trust me."

"What's that mean?"

"Nothing. I'd think someone on the debate team would like talking more."

"Maybe I'm debated out."

"Is that why you're still wearing that thing around your neck? So no one talks to you about it?"

"It's called a medal."

"I don't think you're supposed to wear it like jewelry."

"And I don't think you're supposed to wear glasses without a prescription, but that hasn't stopped you."

"It's a style."

"It's ridiculous."

The two stood side-by-side. The sound of water crashing against the bow of the ferry made for the only sound on the observation deck. The peace and calm were a welcome change to an otherwise noisy day. Rebecca closed her eyes as she enjoyed the moment of quiet.

"You ever hear the one about the pirate captain and the red shirt?" Logan asked.

"Oh my gosh. Seriously?"

"So there was this pirate ship out in the middle of the ocean . . ."

The ferry's horn sounded as it approached the lights of Bainbridge Island. "Almost home." Rebecca lifted her suitcase. "You can tell me the rest later. Or not. Whichever."

2: Not Just a Christmas Party

The ferry gently bumped into place as it came to a stop at the landing. Walk-ons and bicyclists were the first to leave. Rebecca and Logan took their cue and disembarked with the masses. At the end of a long corridor, passengers met loved ones with open arms and Christmas greetings.

"Do you see Dad?" Rebecca asked.

"No." Logan laid his suitcase on the floor and stood on it in an attempt to see over the crowd. The added height, however, only made his vantage point equal with that of his sister's.

"Here, let me try." Rebecca steadied herself with her brother's head.

"Hey."

"Hold still." Rebecca's heels upon the suitcase gave her the needed height to see over the room of heads and hats.

"See anything?"

Rebecca stepped down. "No."

Logan looked at his watch. "The party hasn't started yet, has it?"

Rebecca looked at a large, circular clock on the wall. "Not yet. Maybe he's just running late. It's been almost an entire week." She looked at her brother. "He'll be here."

Classical music and overlapping conversations filled the grand room as dresses and tuxedos moved about the open space. A member of the wait staff walked the floor offering hors d'oeuvres to the various clusters of people.

"Mr. Stevens, may I interest you in a salmon mousse tartlet?"

Matt turned from his conversation with a smile. "Another? How many appetizers does a single party need?"

"Three, sweetheart. This party needs three different hors d'oeuvres." Mrs. Stevens approached and placed one hand on the small of Matt's back; the other hand she used to support her weight against a cane.

"Honey, I'd like for you to meet Mr. Cartnight. My boss."

"The acclaimed ballet dancer Grace Stevens," Mr. Cartnight said. "Pleasure to finally meet you. And please, call me Nicolas."

"Formerly acclaimed ballet dancer. But thank you." Grace shook Nicolas' hand and smiled. "So you're the one making my husband work such long hours."

"Guilty. If only he wasn't so good at building that beautiful Seattle skyline," Nicolas said, as he pointed to the bay window. "Your husband's made me a lot of money." Nicolas motioned around the room with his glass. "And it looks like he's done alright for himself in the process."

"We have everything that money can buy."

"You don't have your own jet," Nicolas said with a smile. He then snapped his fingers. "That reminds me; have you gotten your pilot's license yet?"

"Still working on it," Matt replied. "I had to put it on hold for a while. Something came up."

"Well, keep at it." Nicolas turned to Grace. "One thing I know about your husband, he finishes what he starts. He doesn't quit."

Grace smiled politely. "It's one of his strong points."

"It certainly is," Nicolas said. "And as a thank you for your dedication, Matt, I want you to have these."

"Sir?"

"They're keys to a seaplane over at Fairview Marina. Consider it a bonus."

"I don't know what to say. Wow, thank you."

"Ah, honey," Nicolas said to a young woman. "Come over here a minute."

Matt twisted the keys into his keychain. "Don't embarrass me," Matt whispered to Grace.

"This is my wife, Tiffany," Nicolas said.

"Pleasure to meet you," Grace said.

"OMG. I just met the governor. This party is cray," Tiffany said.

"I'm glad that you're enjoying yourself," Grace said.

"Serious note." Tiffany placed her hand on Grace's arm. "When I read what happened to you after that terrible car wreck, I literally died."

"And who says miracles don't happen."

"Right? Oh, the heartbreak feels I had were palpable."

"Well, some of us fared better than others."

"I sent out some serious positive vibes that day. Did you feel them?"

"I'm sorry. Feel what?"

"The positive vibes. I know I wasn't the only one sending them up like Chinese lanterns."

"That's it. That must've been what I felt."

Tiffany smiled. "You're welcome. On a similar note, I sprained my wrist opening a bottle of Chardonnay last month. I wasn't able to tweet, post, or check in for . . . what was it, bae? A week?"

"Two weeks, I think."

"Two. Whole. Weeks. Have you ever tried texting with your left hand? It was literally a nightmare."

"I'm beginning to know the feeling," Grace said.

"You have no idea. But that was just a wrist. I don't know what I'd do if I couldn't use my leg. But then again, I'm also one of those crazy health nuts, you know? I just don't know what I'd do if I couldn't make it to the gym."

"Well, it sounds like there's a lot you don't know."

"Dear?" Matt said.

"Yes?"

"Do you miss it?" Tiffany asked. "Performing?"

Grace slowly tightened her grip on the handle of her cane.

"At first. Like you not being able to tweet, I suppose I was sort of lost. But you try to move on. You just keep waking up, morning after morning, hoping and believing things will get better."

"So they have then?"

Grace smiled. "What about you? What is it that you do, Tiffany?"

"I guess you could call me a social media personality. A lot of posting, tweeting, vlogging. It's a place for me to express and share my thoughts."

Grace pressed her lips together as she held back a smile. "Both of them?"

"I just got roasted by Grace Stevens. I love it! Loveitloveit-loveit." Tiffany let out a laugh, which soon faded; her smile was replaced by a look of concentration. Tiffany then bent her knees a little and began to bob.

"Are you alright?" Grace asked.

"Do you have a little girl's room that I could use?"

"Of course. Right this way."

"Don't be gone too long," Nicolas said. Tiffany responded with a smile which turned to slight panic as her heels tapped quickly across the hardwood floor.

One of the wait staff approached. "Another scotch, sir?"

"You read my mind," Nicolas said, handing over the empty glass.

"Another ginger ale for you, sir?"

"Please," Matt said.

Nicolas took a drink. "Matt, my boy, when I look at you, do you know what I see?"

"No, sir."

"Myself—albeit a younger version with better facial hair. I see ambition."

"That's certainly something that I pride myself on, sir."

"It shows. You're driven and I like that." Nicolas began walking toward the edge of the room. Matt took that as a cue to walk with him. "Do you remember that project over in Belltown?"

"That was our first; quite the undertaking if I remember correctly. You gave me my first real shot with that build. It was an opportunity of a lifetime."

"And you finished on time and under budget. I knew then that you were something special, son. How would you like a second opportunity of a lifetime?"

"I'm listening."

"Small picture: I'm looking for an architect to oversee all my forthcoming projects. Big picture: I'm looking for a protégé— someone to eventually take over the company. You're good at what you do, Matt. But as I look to my company's future, I need more than just good. I need that X factor. I need that extra bit of something that isn't found in a book or classroom, and I believe you have it."

"Ambition."

"We all have that one thing that drives us—that thing that pushes us to go further than we think we can go. For some, it's the money; for others, it's the prestige. I don't know what drives you exactly, but whatever it is, it's made you unstoppable. I've never seen anything quite like it. I need that kind of ambition on my team. I need that kind of ambition to ensure the future success of my company."

"I don't know what to say."

"Answer me this: what drives you?"

"This is starting to sound like an interview."

"Of sorts."

Matt thought for a moment. "You know the saying: living well is the best revenge?"

"Why do you think I own three yachts? Revenge is a great motivator—one of life's greatest. But then again, I'm preaching to the choir, aren't I?" Nicolas handed Matt a business card with handwritten information. "If living well is what you're after, meet me and my business partner this Monday at A&D's steakhouse on Pier 30. We'll give you the chance to get even with her, once and for all."

"Her?"

Nicolas laughed. "It's always a woman."

Matt flipped the card over. "Monday at 11:30 a.m.? That's Christmas morning."

"Is it? Well then, consider it an early present. Guess that makes me Saint Nic." Matt looked past Nicolas to the other side of the room where Grace stood.

"That isn't a problem, is it, son?"

Matt's focus returned to Nicolas. He ran his hand over his beard. "No. Monday will be fine."

"That's what I wanted to hear," Nicolas said with a smile. The waiter returned with filled glasses. "Now," Nicolas took his glass and raised it up. "To living well."

"Yeah. To living well."

3: Black and Blue Christmas

"Sorry I'm late," a man said, as he rushed into the ferry landing waiting room. Rebecca quickly stood and smiled. A woman sitting on the opposite side of the room embraced the man and the two walked out. Rebecca sat back down next to Logan. The door closed with a metallic bang leaving the two alone with only silence.

"Come on," Rebecca sighed as she took out her phone. "I'll get us an Uber."

Grace was in conversation with a well-known ballet director and two of her old ballet counterparts when Tiffany reentered the room. Grace looked over at her and quickly away as their eyes briefly met. Tiffany raised her hand to wave at Grace; she quickly retracted it with slight embarrassment when Grace returned her focus to her conversation. After a few moments, Grace looked back over at Tiffany as she stood on the outskirts of the room trying her best to pretend that she was having a good time. She sipped her drink and looked around as if trying to find someone, anyone, with whom she could talk.

"Will you excuse me for a moment, ladies?" Grace said, as she stepped away from her conversation.

"Are you enjoying yourself?"

25

Tiffany turned and smiled. "I'm having a great time, thank you."

"No, you're not." Grace repositioned her weight against her cane. "It's okay. Neither am I."

"Why?"

"See those women over there?" Grace motioned to the small group she was speaking with.

"Yeah."

"Sometimes I get the feeling that they tolerate me, you know? Like they only accept me because of who I was."

"Sort of like people being nice to you just because they know who your husband is?"

"I'm sorry about what I said earlier. It was wrong of me to joke like that."

"I go to a lot of these kinds of parties—the high society type. I'm the one people like to whisper about—the trophy wife that never went to college. Whatevs. What you said was the first honest thing I've heard in a long time. Sort of made me feel like I was talking to one of my girlfriends back home—before the jewelry, jets, and fancy social gatherings."

"So how does it not bother you?"

"All the haters? I never said that it didn't. But being married to someone that I truly love helps. Nicolas helps me weather the storms. As I'm sure your Matt does for you. You two seem happy."

"We do seem happy, don't we?"

"How did you meet?"

"Oh, you don't want to hear that boring story."

"I understand. You probably need to get back to your conversation over there," Tiffany said, as she looked across the room. The three women looked away.

Grace looked down for a moment; she tucked her fallen bangs behind her ear before looking up. "I had just finished my first lead in a professional ballet."

"I'll bet you were amazing."

"I was a disaster. Everything that could've went wrong that night, did. It was my first big performance and I blew it. Missed cues, slips. During the third act I even fell. When it was all over, I literally hid until everyone left. Only after the janitor assured me that everyone was gone did I finally sneak out of the building. And there was Matt, standing outside the door with flowers. He gave me this beautiful bouquet as if I deserved it, and then handed me a small gift." Grace smiled. "It looked like a child wrapped it."

"Men, right? What was it?"

"This necklace, actually," Grace said, motioning to the small chain and pendant around her neck. "He said that he had waited a long time to give it to me. He wasn't kidding. He was out there half the night. He must've been so cold waiting outside until I finally had the courage to leave." Grace looked at her glass. "I began to cry and he put the necklace on me. I was a mess and a failure, but he made me feel so special."

"Anyway, we started to walk toward the lights of downtown. I rested my head against his shoulder. He took me by the hand, and then our fingers entwined. And that's when I knew."

"Shut. Up. When he held your hand like that?"

Grace nodded.

"I'm on the verge of tears over here. For real." Tiffany widened her eyes and fanned them with her hand. "Say, I don't know the proper etiquette. Making friends isn't as easy as it used to be. So whatever, I'll just come right out and say it: do you want to—I don't know—hang out sometime? I'm in town for the next few days. I'm thinking about doing some shopping at Pike Place if you'd like to join me."

"Ten minutes ago, I'd have been surprised to hear myself say this: I wish that I could, but I actually can't. It's just important that I spend time with my kids for the next few days. Rain check though?"

"No worries. Of course. Like I said, I'll be in Seattle for the next couple of days if things change for you. Here, give me your cell number." Tiffany quickly typed the digits into her phone and called it. "If you change your mind, let me know."

"Speaking of kids." Grace looked at her watch. "Excuse me a second." Grace approached Matt and the small group of people he was speaking with. "Matt, dear," she said discretely. "Where are the kids?"

"The kids?" Matt looked at his watch.

"Right here," Rebecca said, as she and Logan approached from behind. "Surprised to see us? Because you look surprised to see us."

"Kids. Mr. Cartnight, I'd like for you to meet my children," Matt said. "This is my daughter Rebecca."

"Pleasure to meet you," Rebecca said with a forced smile.

"And this is my son . . . hey, Cory Hart. Do you mind taking those sunglasses off?"

"I'm guessing that's another one of your jokes that no one gets."

"All the same. Glasses off."

Logan gently removed his sunglasses. "And this is my son . . . Logan, what happened to your eye?"

"Oh my goodness," Grace said, as she inspected Logan's eye more closely.

"What?" Logan said. "Seriously, is there something wrong with my face? Please, not the money maker!" Logan quickly looked at his reflection in a nearby hanging mirror. "Jeez! When did that happen?"

"This isn't funny," Grace said.

"You're right. You should see the other guy's fist," Logan said. "His class note-taking is really going to suffer, which, I think we can all agree, will make him the real loser here."

"If you'll excuse us for a moment," Matt said to his guests. "Logan."

"Yeah."

"Kitchen."

"Not hungry."

"Now." Matt stepped away from the group. "Rebecca, this is Isaac Barstone, the Secretary of the Department of Social and Health Services." The two shook hands. "Didn't you have one of your little debates about the foster system? I'm sure Isaac wouldn't mind humoring you for a little bit while we take care of your brother," Matt said, as he, Logan, and Grace walked toward the kitchen.

"Is that a debate medal?"

"It is." Rebecca pulled it out from inside her coat. "First place."

"Well then, please go easy on me." Isaac smiled at those in the circle.

"No promises."

Matt opened the freezer door. "Here." Matt placed a bag of frozen peas on Logan's face.

"We have icepacks, Matt." Grace put the peas back in the freezer. "Here, use this." Grace gently placed a wrapped gel pack on Logan's eye. "What happened?"

"He got in another fight," Matt said. "That's what happened. I swear, this must be some sort of record." Matt looked at his cell phone. "Is that why the school called earlier?"

"Maybe they called with good news."

"Schools don't call parents with good news. Yours certainly never has."

"Well, there's a first time for everything."

"I don't have time for this. I'm making the deal of a lifetime and you coming in here looking like this doesn't exactly project an image of success or competence."

"I've been meaning to work on my projections."

"What kind of deal?" Grace asked.

"Nothing. Just another opportunity with Mr. Cartnight. As for you, Logan. Upstairs. We'll talk more about this later." Matt anxiously cleaned the lens of his glasses.

"Can't wait."

"Alright then." Matt checked himself in the reflection of the microwave. He straightened his bowtie, adjusted his glasses and checked his hair.

Then one voice passionately rose above the low collective murmur of the conversations outside the kitchen door.

"What now?"

"Now that's projecting," Logan said with a smile.

Rebecca spoke with her hands as much as she did her mouth. Party guests couldn't help but put their private conversations on hold to watch the young woman state her case, and do so with such passion.

"Did you know, Mr. Secretary, that in 2017 there were an estimated 442,000 kids in foster care? And of those 442,000 kids, over 23,000 aged out?"

"There are some who are emancipated from the foster system, yes."

"That's just a nice way to say that when they turned eighteen, they were kicked to the streets."

"That's a little—"

"I'm not finished, Mr. Secretary. In this state alone, studies have shown that upward of one-third of all minors who age out become homeless. That's well above the national average."

"Yes, homeless youth in this state is a very serious matter; one that my office is working with the governor to correct."

"How?"

"Well, for example, we upped the age of emancipation from eighteen to twenty-one. And on top of that—"

"Yes, but it's estimated that only twelve percent actually decide to stay in the system after their eighteenth birthday. Most feel that they've done their time; others simply don't qualify. Long story short, one in three of those who age out in Washington will become homeless. And that only adds to the homeless youth epidemic that this state is already enduring. Forty thousand. Do you know what that number is?"

"It's the number—"

"On any given night, there are 40,000 homeless students in this state."

Rebecca removed her coat.

"And of those 40,000, it's estimated that over 5,000 don't have any kind of parent or guardian to keep them safe."

Rebecca noticed the Secretary smiling, which distracted her, but she kept going.

"And do you know how many of them there are right across the water in King County?"

Those gathered around were now smiling and whispering to each other. "What, you've never seen a girl with an opinion before?"

"Alright," Matt said, as he gently put his hands on Rebecca's shoulders. "Rebecca! What is that on your neck?" Rebecca quickly covered the hickey with her hand. "I'm sorry, but if you'll excuse her."

The kitchen door swung open.

"You two are unbelievable," Matt said.

"I honestly wasn't expecting flattery," Logan said with a mouth full of tartlets.

"That wasn't a compliment." Matt looked at his children. "Upstairs. Both of you. I don't want to see either of you for the rest of the night."

"And here I thought we were being punished," Rebecca said to Logan.

Matt turned and walked toward the party. "You two really need to grow up."

"You first."

Matt stopped, hand on the door. Rebecca waited in anticipation for his comeback. Her rebuttal was already forming in her head. But Matt just shook his head and exited the room.

4: Seattle Burning

Rebecca looked down at the party from the second floor. The upper half of a massive, perfectly decorated Christmas tree helped shield her from the guests below.

"Want another salmon puff thingy?" Logan asked.

Rebecca looked into one of the tree's glass ornaments. The distortion from the ornament's reflection revealed Logan and the rest of the small library in a rounded view. Rebecca inched her way from the ledge, out of sight of the partygoers. Logan sat against a bookshelf holding a tablet in his hands; his tie had worked its way north and was now snuggly wrapped around his forehead; a half-eaten tray of hors d'oeuvres sat next to him.

"You're going to make yourself sick," Rebecca said, as she took one off the platter.

"Right?" Logan said with a full mouth.

"Add it to the list."

"What. Which word?"

"Riiiight?" Rebecca said, overemphasizing the question. "That word has become a catchall response to virtually every passing comment and observation. Not to mention it's a cliché. Surely you can come up with a slightly more thoughtful response than 'right'?"

"I'm actually not sure that I can."

"You're contributing to the slow disintegration of thoughtful discussion and small talk, just so you know."

"I know, right?" Logan smiled. "That was literally 200 percent more thoughtful. Besides, no one likes small talk."

Rebecca shook her head. "At least you used 'literally' correctly. But you can be a little more assiduous when it comes to your word choice."

"Add it to the list."

"Which one?"

"Assiduous."

"You can't just add words when you don't know what they mean." Rebecca picked the ice pack up off the floor and tossed it onto Logan's stomach. "You need to put that back on your face. You know, there may come a time when I won't be here to take care of you."

"Well, until that day comes"—Logan promptly popped another salmon puff into his mouth—"I'll literally be on pins and needles . . . and assiduous. I'll be literally assiduously on pins and needles."

"That's not how you use it."

"Which part."

"All of it."

Rebecca looked at Logan's tablet. "What are you watching?"

"Here, check this out."

"What."

"Come here."

"Fine."

The screen showed a bird's-eye view of the party not too dissimilar from the vantage point Rebecca had moments earlier. Logan maneuvered the view with his finger.

"How are you doing that?"

"It's a drone."

"When did you get that?"

"I don't know. A while ago." The camera then focused in on a man's thin comb-over. The camera zoomed in until the entire screen was filled with stringy strands of hair atop a shiny white dome. "You're meant to be bald, man. Don't fight nature."

"Where's Mom and Dad?"

Logan scanned the room. "There they are."

"Is that Tiffany Mom's talking with?"

"I didn't get a chance to look over the guestbook."

"She's like one of the most followed people on Instagram."

"And you're one of them?"

"So I'm trying to become a little more cultured."

"I'm not sure football and Instagram qualify."

Rebecca and Logan watched the screen for a moment.

"Dad's sleeping in the guest room again," Logan said.

"You shouldn't be such a snoop."

"Just sayin'."

"Me too."

"At least Christmas is almost here, right?"

Rebecca smiled. "At least we'll have one nice day together. Hopefully, this year it'll last. Cool toy." Rebecca walked away and flopped onto the room's only couch.

"Hardly a toy," Logan said, as he maneuvered the drone into the room and landed it at Rebecca's feet. "This thing has a two-mile range, high-def camera, and over a mile altitude hold." Logan folded the propellers.

Rebecca took a book off of the coffee table. "Is this the book you've been reading?"

"Uh-huh," Logan said, as he popped another puff into his mouth.

"What is it?"

"Seattle architecture."

"Gross. Why?"

"Uh, it's not gross, and because I'm going to be an architect someday."

"Talking with your mouth full is gross. Again, why?"

"Come here." Logan walked across the room to the nearest window and threw open the curtains. "That's why."

The snowfall had ceased. Across the Puget Sound, a small Seattle skyline sparkled. Even the Seattle Great Wheel was visible if one knew where to look.

Rebecca stood silent for a moment. "Aren't you tired of that view?"

"Tired of . . . what's with you tonight?"

"I just don't see the appeal."

"You're telling me that you don't like this view?"

Rebecca walked away.

Logan followed his sister. "Did you know downtown Seattle once burnt almost completely to the ground?"

"Good."

"I'm going to pretend I didn't hear that." Logan waited for a moment as if expecting his sister to change her response; Rebecca was perfectly happy with the one she gave. "Aren't you going to ask me how it happened?"

Rebecca dropped back down onto the couch. "How'd it happen?"

"I'm glad you asked." Logan retrieved his book from the table. "It actually all started in a cabinet shop."

Rebecca gave the best "I'm interested" expression that she could muster.

"You see, a pot of hot glue boiled over and caught fire to the wood chips and turpentine covering the floor. Oh, and it was 1889, so there were wood chips pretty much everywhere. So the poor guy tried to douse the fire with water, which only further ignited the flames. Turpentine, remember? By the time the fire department arrived, the flames were out of control and soon completely devoured a nearby liquor store and two saloons; they all exploded. Saloons were like Starbucks back then—one on every corner."

"The firefighters tried to put out the growing blaze, but the more hoses that were added, the more the water pressure dropped. Before long, all the hoses became useless, and the fire continued to rage. Now you see, the fire chief was in San Francisco attending, wait for it. You ready for this?"

"I'm on pins and needles."

"Ding, ding, ding. That's right, a fire convention. So the mayor took control of the situation. Well, sort of."

"So what did he do?" At this point, Rebecca couldn't help but be mildly interested.

"He blew up Colman block."

"Blew it up?"

"An entire block. Boom. Gone. "

"Why?"

"So that the fire wouldn't have any more fuel to burn. Like when they do a controlled burn to put out a forest fire."

"Did it work?"

"Not even close. The fire was too big. It jumped Colman block and spread to the waterfront and up the hill."

"So when was it finally out?"

"Not until 3:00 a.m. the following day. And when it was all said and done, twenty-five blocks were either damaged or destroyed." Logan set the book on the end table. "Which brings me to the best part of the story. Instead of rebuilding, *architects* came up with a plan that would solve two problems at the same time. Like a boss, they built the new downtown on top of the old one."

"Add that phrase to the list."

"With all your banned words and phrases, pretty soon I won't be able to say anything."

"And that'd be a bad thing because?"

"Funny."

"Alright, so why did they build on top of the old downtown?"

"Well, between plumbing issues and regular flooding, raising the city above sea level made the most sense."

"So what happened to the old city?"

"It's still down there. Over thirty blocks. A small portion is used for tourism—three blocks, maybe. But the rest? Well, the rest is completely restricted to the public. But that's getting off point."

"And the point is?"

"The point is that architects did something amazing to save the city, which literally laid the foundation for what we see today. If that's not a good enough reason to like that view at least a little bit, I don't know what is. Plus, Dad's an architect."

Rebecca stood.

"It is interesting though," Logan said.

"What is?"

"How all that devastation started with a simple pot of glue." Logan closed the book. "Where are you going?"

"Not everything is your business."

"What exactly do you do in Dad's office anyway? The one room in the house that's off-limits."

Rebecca picked the icepack up off of the floor again and tossed it to Logan. "And don't eat any more of those," Rebecca added as she walked toward the door.

Logan placed the icepack on his face and promptly ate another salmon puff.

"Whatever you say."

5: Off-Limits

Rebecca walked down the rear staircase toward the kitchen. She purposely skipped the creaky eighth stair (despite the fact that no one in the house could possibly hear) and then tiptoed the rest of the way. With her parents fully engaged in their Christmas party, there was very little reason for secrecy. That being said, any time Rebecca snuck into her father's study, she knew that it was best to be discrete. At the bottom of the stairs, Rebecca walked softly away from the commotion of the dinner preparation and down the hall toward the large, cherry wood door that separated her father's world from the rest of the house.

With a twist of the cold, cast-iron handle, the heavy door came to life and slowly swung toward Rebecca. There, standing on the room's threshold, the soft glow of two low-lit lamps illuminated Rebecca's face as they did the room's most prominent features. Perfectly placed books adorned much of the room's ample wall space, each one assigned appropriately by category and then subcategorized alphabetically. To Rebecca's direct right, a drafting table. Rolls of blueprints were neatly placed inside a custom oak drum beside an angled workstation; rulers, pens, and other architectural paraphernalia were in their place along the table's edge. At the far end of the room, a large oak desk was positioned near a stone fireplace. Behind the desk, there was a leather seat upon which a sports coat hung.

Rebecca entered. She walked slowly along the side of the room as she ran her finger along the bookshelf's edge. She tilted her head reading the titles as she casually moved forward. Though breaking the rules, she was in no hurry to break them quickly. Every so often, she pulled a book from its place to read its table of contents and thumb through its pages. Without fail, each book opened with a subtle crack as if newly purchased; not one sentence underlined, not one page dog-eared. For some time now, Rebecca had wondered if her father even read the books he so meticulously displayed.

Rebecca continued to glide her finger along the shelf's edge. She paused. She moved her finger back and stopped in front of a particular series of books. Rebecca then removed five titles from the shelf and set them gently on the floor. In the empty space, an old ring binder was exposed behind where the books were. Rebecca slid the binder out from secrecy and opened to where she had previously left off. The binder was full of old letters written to her father—letters that read of life, sorrow, regret, and hope for the future. Rebecca hated that her dad kept old love letters, but couldn't help but read just one more.

Rebecca finished her one selected letter for the evening and then returned the binder to its hidden space. As she placed the five books back in their respective, alphabetically organized spots, she couldn't help but wonder if the two ever made amends—if the writer and reader ever found a way to restore the love they lost.

Eventually, Rebecca found herself at the front edge of her father's desk where three small picture frames faced his leather chair; she took the middle picture and walked to the back of the desk. Rebecca then sat in her father's chair causing the sports coat to slide to the floor. She looked down at the picture and stared at the image of her and her father. Rebecca always thought that she was making a weird face. She held the picture with care, not because it was her father's; she held it with care because of a single certainty that it brought. For Rebecca, it seemed that the older she got, the less certain she was—about everything. But one thing she knew for sure: her father couldn't fake a smile like that. He was really happy in that moment with her. She loved what the picture proved. And during those moments of uncertainty, that picture saved her every time.

A book lay open in front of Rebecca. Step Nine was the title of the chapter yet to be read. Rebecca casually placed a pen into the book's crease and closed the binding. She then slid the book *Twelve Steps and Twelve Traditions* to the side and set the picture in its place.

"So I won my debate," Rebecca said to the smiling picture of her father. "Ms. Thomas, the debate coach, thinks that I have real potential. She said that if I keep working on it, I might even get a college scholarship. My teammates couldn't believe that I'd never debated before; they said that I was a natural. I don't know about that. I think anyone with a younger brother has an unfair advantage when it comes to debate.

"I know that you wanted to be there, so it's okay that you missed it. I think you would've been proud of me though. But like I said, it's fine. I have another debate after Christmas break. Maybe, if you're not too busy, you can make it to that one.

"Logan's doing alright. As well as can be expected, I guess. He got into another fight today. Came away with a pretty awful black eye. You know that already. But there's something that you don't know."

Rebecca looked down. "I screwed up." Rebecca looked back at the picture. "Dad, I made a big mistake. I'm not sure that I can ever forgive myself." Rebecca wiped her eye. "Logan misses you, you know. He wishes that you weren't gone so much. Wishes that he could talk to you after days like today. He has this crazy thought. He thinks that even when you're home, you're not really here. Like you're somewhere else. I tell him that it's just his imagination—that he's not being logical." Rebecca smiled. "Like I have to tell *you* he's not logical."

Rebecca leaned back in the chair. "But I'm not sure that he believes me anymore. I think that he thinks that you've changed; that you actually aren't the same person that you used to be. I hope that he's wrong." Rebecca held the picture. "I know that you're still in there. Somewhere."

The sound of approaching footsteps interrupted Rebecca's conversation. She quickly placed the pictures back in place and threw the coat back over the chair. An envelope and letter fell out of the coat's side, which she quickly stuffed into the belt of her skirt. By the time the cast-iron handle turned, Rebecca was under the desk.

A man entered and closed the door. Rebecca sat hugging her knees trying not to make a sound. A familiar voice spoke.

"Hey, Beth. Is this a bad time to call?" Matt closed the door behind him.

"I've been racing around a bit today, but I can always spare a few minutes for my brother."

"Still racing. Some things never change."

"Once a sprinter, always a sprinter. Aren't you throwing your big Christmas party right now?"

"Yeah. But I wanted to say that I appreciate you watching the kids last week."

"Of course, but you could've called me tomorrow."

"Yeah, I know."

Matt leaned against the desk.

"Is everything alright?"

"Just one of those days."

"Have you had a drink?"

"No. But I'd be lying if I said that I didn't think about it."

"You should probably talk to your sponsor."

"I'd rather talk to you."

"You already know what I'm going to say."

"I know, it's just an escape, and it doesn't solve anything; it just masks the pain."

"Right."

"Right. So the kids weren't too much trouble? They can be a handful sometimes."

Rebecca rolled her eyes.

"They were fine."

"They didn't do or go anywhere that they weren't supposed to, did they?"

"No, Matt, they didn't go upstairs, if that's what you're getting at. They don't know."

"Good."

"I wouldn't call it good, but what do I know? What about you and Grace? Did you two get a chance to talk?"

"Yeah, it went about as well as could be expected, I think. Sort of feels like we're actually on the same page for once. There's irony for you."

"Have you told the kids yet?"

"No, we decided to wait until after Christmas to tell them about the divorce. No sense in ruining the holidays, you know? Besides, we need to figure out the best way to break it to them."

"And you feel like a divorce is still your best option?"

"It's for the best—for all of us. We're much better people when we're apart. And if I'm being honest, it feels like a weight's already been lifted off of me."

"Hmm."

"What's that mean? Hmm."

"Nothing . . . except that avoiding conflict is a bit of a pattern with you."

"Here we go."

"Tell me I'm wrong."

"So divorce is just another escape now?"

"Isn't it?"

"Hardly."

"I'm not saying it's easy, but when was the last time you faced even one of your demons?"

"I face my demons all the time, and then I have a drink with them."

"See? Avoidance."

"Speaking of demons, how's Mom?"

"I'm not going to dignify that question with a response. You got the letter, didn't you?"

"I did. And speaking of which, tell that caretaker to stop trying to contact me. She really needs to mind her own business."

"She just cares."

"A little too much. It's getting weird."

"I'll tell her to give you some space."

"A lot of space."

"Fine. But if you received the letter, then I think you have a pretty good idea how Mom's doing. But if you really want to know, you should ask her yourself."

"I think I'll pass, thanks."

"Figured you would. Well, I actually have somewhere I need to be in a little bit."

"Oh yeah? Where?"

"Bible study."

"Do you think that's such a good idea? I mean, with everything that's going on?"

"Is that concern I detect?"

"No, it isn't. And for the record, just because you run to the Bible and not a drink doesn't make your crutch any better than mine."

"And how's that working for you?"

"Couldn't be happier." Matt opened the *Twelve Steps* book on his desk.

"Please, when was the last time you were actually happy?"

"Right before calling you."

"Then why did you?"

Matt switched the phone to his other ear. "Starting to wonder that myself."

"Seriously though, when was the last time you were truly happy?"

Matt moved his hand from the book to one of the desk pictures.

"It's impossible to embrace the present if you never let go of the past."

"Sounds like advice from a fortune cookie."

"Doesn't make it any less true."

"You mean face my demons."

"Matt, we all have shadows in our past, those places where we keep our pain—pain we'd rather just leave in the dark because dealing with them hurts too much. But if we never bring them to light, they can turn into something else, something much worse. If we don't deal with our past, we run the risk of staying there."

Matt now held the picture in his hand.

"Resentment, bitterness, unforgiveness, hate, all grow in the shadows. And left unchecked, these poisons will continue to grow and spread until eventually they infect everything we love. Matt, I get it. If anyone does. But trust me, you'll never find peace until you find the light. You'll never find rest until you stop running."

Silence.

"Matt?"

"Looks like time's up."

"That's usually my line."

"I should really get back to the party. Bill me for the session."

"Matt, think about what I said. It's not too late to make things right."

"Who said I want to make things right? Look, you should get to your study. Of all people, wouldn't want to keep God waiting."

Beth sighed. "Are you going to be alright?"

"Once I accept Mr. Cartnight's offer, I will be."

"Well, I hope that you find what you're looking for in the deal."

"I'll drink to that."

"I'm sure you will. I'll pray for you nonetheless."

"Then make it a silent prayer. I don't want my story to end up in the church bulletin."

"It's not like it hasn't already been in the newspaper. Matt, I'm sorry, I didn't mean—"

"I should really get back to the party."

"Matt."

"Goodnight, Beth."

Matt placed the object back on the desk. The office door then opened and the dress shoes faded back into the dull roar of the party.

How long she remained on the hardwood floor, Rebecca couldn't say; but the fact that her legs were asleep when she finally moved told her that it had been a while. She pushed the chair away and crawled out from under the desk. The prickly feeling throughout her legs and feet prompted her to quickly sit. She stared out over the desk. Two framed pictures stood side by side, a third lay on its face.

Rebecca took the picture in her hands. In the picture, her mother and father, quite a bit younger, stood high above a city. Like the picture Rebecca cherished, this one captured an honest moment. Matt was looking at Grace with a smile no one could argue was forced. Grace looked at the camera, excited and happy, proudly displaying an engagement ring. Rebecca quietly placed the picture back on the desk in line with the other two frames. When the tingling sensation faded from her legs, she stood and softly left the room the way she entered.

6: Hate

Rebecca closed the office door and turned with a startle as she almost bumped into her father. She would have screamed had that been the greatest shock of the evening. All she could do was try to catch her breath as she took a step back.

"What have I told you about going into my office without permission?" Rebecca stood speechless.

"How long were you in there?"

"I . . . I just went in for a second."

"You're away all week and this is how you behave? First you embarrass me in front of my guests, and now you purposely disobey me?"

"I . . . I didn't mean to—"

"So you accidentally embarrassed me and accidentally snuck into my office?"

"No, I just meant—"

"What did you just mean?"

Rebecca tightly twisted her toes feeling that she might start to cry.

"What's that?" Matt asked, as he looked at Rebecca's belt.

Rebecca's heart skipped as she remembered the letter and envelope she took from her father's jacket still remained tucked against her side.

Matt took the letter from Rebecca's belt. "Why do you have my mail?"

"I didn't read it."

"That's not what I asked."

Rebecca couldn't think of a response.

"At some point you'll need to stop acting like a child. Sneaking into places and taking things that aren't yours." Matt shook his head. "It's about time that you—"

"Be more like you?"

"Grow up. It's about time that you grow up." Matt sighed. "I need to get back to the party."

"I won."

"Won what?"

"M–my school debate."

"Maybe if you put as much effort into doing what I ask as you put into your silly debates, we wouldn't have these kinds of arguments."

"If we didn't have these kinds of arguments, I don't think we'd speak at all."

"Tonight, that sounds like a win-win."

No amount of distraction—toe twisting or otherwise—could hold back the tears any longer. Rebecca quickly turned to leave.

"Rebecca."

Rebecca stopped. The first tears now escaped.

"That didn't come out the way I wanted," Matt said.

"I hate you and wish you were out of my life." Rebecca turned and smiled through her pain. "That came out exactly how I wanted."

Without an additional word, Matt entered his office and closed the large wooden doors behind him. The soft glow of the office light faded from Rebecca's face until she was left alone with nothing but the chill of the darkened hallway.

~~~

Rebecca returned to the room where Logan sat.

"So," Logan began, "there was this pirate ship out in the middle of the ocean . . ."

Rebecca didn't stop; she simply rushed toward her bedroom.

Logan hesitantly approached Rebecca's room. "Bec? What's wrong?"

Rebecca lay with her back to the door, silent.

Logan sighed. "Okay. I'm here though." Logan turned and was suddenly embraced by his sister. "Now I know something's wrong."

"Something is wrong. Something big is happening, and I don't know what it means exactly—how it's all going to end up."

"Bec, what are you talking about?"

Rebecca began to tell Logan all that happened in the study. She left nothing out. And after she finished telling Logan the saddest news that she had ever heard, and after the unanswerable "whats," "whens," "whys," and "hows" were met with "I don't knows," both decided that a single day should only be allowed so much pain. Exhausted, the two went to bed with the thin hope that things would somehow be better in the morning.

7: The Gift

Long after Rebecca and Logan drifted to sleep, and after the last party guest left, a sliver of hallway light pierced Rebecca's room. Grace looked at both of her children fast asleep: Rebecca in her bed, Logan on a mattress on the floor. With the help of her cane, Grace approached both her children and kissed the tips of her fingers and transferred her "good night" to their foreheads.

"Kids are asleep," Grace said, as she entered the kitchen. "What's that?"

Matt set a neatly wrapped package on the countertop. "Found it outside just now."

Grace pinched the bridge of her nose. "Logan's sleeping in Rebecca's room."

Matt inspected the package. "Really?"

"He dragged his mattress in there. They didn't even change out of their clothes. I can't remember the last time the kids slept together."

"Maybe it's the storm," Matt said, as he removed his bow-tie and let it hang loosely around his neck.

"So what are we going to do about Logan?"

"We'll talk to him in the morning," Matt said, as he untied the box's ribbon.

"I hate that he's being bullied."

"I know. Me too. I remember what it was like."

"And how did you make it through?"

"You learn to deal with it. You figure it out."

"Is that the advice your parents gave you? Figure it out?"

"Like my parents were around to give that kind of advice."

Grace removed one of her shoes and rubbed her foot. "Even your dad?"

Matt shrugged at the question as he raised the box's lid. "Now would you look at that?" Matt lifted an old bottle from a bed of packaging straw.

"Well, I certainly wouldn't want to relive those childhood days either."

"Oh, come on, prom queen. I'm sure you'd manage fine."

"Perhaps in my senior year, but not at Logan's age. Back then it was Brace-face Grace. Not someone I'd be too eager to meet again."

"Brace-face Grace," Matt said to himself as he inspected the bottle a little more closely. "Brace-face Grace. How have I not heard that before?"

Grace shook her head. "I was so awkward and clumsy at that age. I had a big growth spurt going into my freshman year, which not only left me three inches taller than every boy in my class, but almost ruined my dreams of becoming a professional ballet dancer. And I did this thing where I snorted if I laughed too hard."

"I'm sure it wasn't that bad. I mean, obviously things eventually changed."

"After my braces were removed, I thought that maybe the name-calling would go with it."

"Did it?"

"No, they just called me Disgrace instead. You wouldn't think that some stupid names would get to you. Anyway, it wasn't long after that I promised myself I would start living up to my name again. And I never looked back."

Matt was silent.

"So what's the vintage on the bottle?"

"Um, I'm not sure actually," Matt said, as he rotated the container on the countertop. "In fact, I'm not entirely sure *what* it is. It certainly looks old though." Matt wiped away a layer of dust from the label. "Let's just hope it was stored properly." Matt began fishing through one of the kitchen drawers.

"You're not going to drink it, are you?"

"The thought had crossed my mind."

"Shouldn't you call your sponsor then?" Grace walked over to Matt's tuxedo jacket draped over the counter. "Will you never hang your jackets properly?" Grace said, as she moved Matt's jacket from the counter to the back of one of the kitchen island chairs. Grace pulled a piece of folded paper from the side pocket.

"What's this?" The cursive on the letter, as if written with arthritic hands, was both beautiful and tired.

Matt took the letter in his hands. "Now I know where Rebecca gets it."

"What does that mean?"

"Nothing." Matt closed one drawer and opened another. "Where's the corkscrew?"

"So what is it?"

"A metal curlicue tool used for opening corked bottles."

"The letter, Matt."

"Oh, this?" Matt held up the letter with his free hand and placed it back on the counter. "It's from my mother." He removed his glasses and inspected the writing on the bottle more closely. "She's, uh, dying."

Matt's response took Grace by surprise. She had never heard someone give such serious news in a way one might report the day's weather or what one had for dinner.

"She's dying?"

"Uh-huh."

"Matt."

"It's alright."

"How long does she have?"

"Doesn't sound like long. The letter said a week."

"May I?" Grace asked, motioning to the paper.

"Be my guest."

Grace unfolded the letter and read it. "Matt, this letter was dated over two weeks ago."

"Well, she's not dead yet. Not sure what she's waiting for. We do still own a corkscrew, don't we?"

"Matt, this is serious."

"Tell me about it. There's no way I'd find an open store this time of night."

"I can't believe you right now."

Matt refocused his attention to the adjacent drawer reserved specifically for random junk.

"Why do we even have this drawer?" Matt said, as he sifted through scraps of paper, tape dispensers, and old kitchen appliance manuals. "Look at all this." He then pulled the drawer completely off the track and dumped its contents onto the countertop.

"Found it."

Matt retrieved two glasses from the cupboard.

"You only need one glass. I'm going to bed."

Matt returned to the bottle and twisted the corkscrew into the cork. "Just because we're getting a divorce doesn't mean we can't have a drink like civil people."

"What would your sponsor say?"

"Didn't I tell you? I graduated."

"Even if you did, I'm pretty sure you don't celebrate with a drink."

Matt held up the two glasses. "What should we drink to?"

"Besides to mental stability?"

"How about . . . to the future."

"I'd rather drink to the past."

Matt raised his glass and looked at Grace. "In that case, may the best of our past be the worst of our future."

Grace raised her glass. "I can drink to that."

8: What Child Is This?

Rebecca twirled her father's envelope between her index fingers as she lay in her bed. A thud from upstairs caused her to pause. Her eyes moved from the envelope to the ceiling. A ray of sunlight shone into the room and was quickly extinguished by a passing cloud. Rebecca turned on her side and looked at her brother; his black eye looked worse than the night before. Rebecca remembered, though, from her own unfortunate run-in with a blunt object (in her case a softball), that a black eye always looked worse as it got better. Rebecca looked at her clock.

Nothing.

Power must be out, Rebecca thought. She rolled back and stared at the ceiling again. Like the passing cloud, the excitement of a new day was quickly overshadowed by the darkness of reality. In the quiet of the moment, she remembered something obscure one of her English teachers once said: "Your life is your story. How will you write it?" Rebecca sneered. She was fairly certain that this part of the story was being written *for* her, not by her. And if she had any say in the matter, she would leave today's chapter out altogether.

"You awake?" Logan asked.

Rebecca sighed. "Yeah."

"What are you thinking about?"

"Mom and Dad, I guess."

"Like what?"

"I guess for starters, all the bull they said: 'Don't lie. Be a person of your word. Don't break a promise.' Why even label anything right or wrong if when push comes to shove you just do whatever you want?"

"Do you think we'll all still spend time together?"

"If Mom and Dad wanted to spend time together, they wouldn't be getting a divorce."

"Yeah, I guess that makes sense."

"We'll most likely spend half the time with Mom, and then the other half with Dad. Holidays and birthdays will be split up too. That's how it works with my friends at school anyway."

"So we're not going to be family anymore?"

"We'll still be a family. Things will just be different."

"But you're not going anywhere, right?" Rebecca turned to her side and faced her brother. "I mean, we'll be there for each other, right?"

"Of course."

"No matter what?"

"No matter what."

Logan turned onto his back. "I wish this wasn't happening."

Rebecca tried to think of something reassuring to say— something to comfort her brother. Nothing came to mind.

"You know. Your face still looks terrible."

"I got punched. What's your excuse?"

Rebecca smiled. "We'll be okay."

A second loud thud from the floor above redirected Logan and Rebecca's attention.

"What is going on up there?" Rebecca said.

Logan pulled his covers back over his shoulders. "They may be up, but I'm in no hurry to start the day."

Rebecca rolled onto her back and held the envelope above her head again. "Yeah, I'm fine putting off any more surprises for as long as possible."

Just then, a scream from upstairs cut through the house.

Matt slowly awoke face down in his pillow. His head throbbed. He reached over to the nightstand. His hand flopped around like a fish out of water until it landed on his glasses. Matt slid the spectacles on his face and opened his eyes. Everything in the guest room was blurry and out of focus. Matt slipped his hand under the lenses and rubbed his eyes. He repositioned his glasses and opened his eyes again. If anything, his vision seemed worse. Matt slowly lifted his glasses from the bridge of his nose; the lenses and frame passed from his eyes and the world came into focus.

Matt lowered the glasses back into place. The world blurred.

He lifted again. The world cleared.

He lowered. Blurred.

Lifted. Cleared.

Matt set his glasses back on the nightstand and then looked at his hands; he moved them back and forth, near and away, from his face. He laughed.

Is this possible? Matt thought. He hadn't seen clearly without his glasses in years. He threw off his comforter and quickly jumped out of bed. He landed hard, face down, on the floor.

"Ow!" Matt picked himself up off the floor. He rubbed his neck and looked around the room. Something was different but he couldn't put his finger on it. The dresser looked a bit larger than he remembered, as did the loveseat. In fact, everything in the room looked slightly larger: the window, the door, the Persian rug. Everything.

Matt scratched his chin as he thought. His hand dropped. He immediately walked to the guest bathroom. He turned on the light and looked in the mirror. What he saw was impossible. His hand slowly reached toward the smooth-faced teenager staring back at him.

◦◦◦

Grace woke to the buzz of her phone. She looked at the screen.

"Notice anything . . . weird?"

Grace looked at Matt's text for a moment. She then looked at the blank digital clock on the nightstand.

"Power's out. Not that weird," she responded.

"Besides that."

Grace looked around the room. "Everything seems fine."

"So you're still . . . older?"

Grace read the last text a second time.

"Sorry. Didn't mean it that way," Matt quickly wrote.

"Yes, I'm sorry to inform you that I'm still old."

"Take a selfie and show me."

"You're a jerk when you drink."

Grace tossed the phone beside her. She stared at the ceiling for a moment. *Notice anything weird?* She thought to herself. *Besides you?* Her eyes slowly moved from contemplative to surprised. She did notice something unusual—on the inside of her lips. A coarse, somewhat abrasive sensation ran the length of her mouth. She instinctively ran her tongue across her teeth; she then felt them with her fingers. She quickly retrieved her hand as if pulling it from a spider or bug with too many legs.

Grace slid her feet out over her bed and dropped to the floor, landing harshly on the rug below. She took a moment as she absorbed the pain of the impact. She grabbed for her comforter and accidentally pulled it off the bed; her phone bounded on the floor beside her.

Grace looked at her phone and cautiously took it in her hands. The screen still had Matt's last text: "Take a selfie." She closed out her texts and turned on the camera app. She hesitantly moved her finger to the selfie feature. Then, with the lightest of touches, she reversed the camera, displaying her image on the screen.

Grace quickly covered her mouth when she screamed. When she felt herself calm a little, she lifted her hand from her lips. Grace looked at her palm and then at the back of her hand. Her wedding ring was missing. She searched only for a moment before she found it lying in the fold of the comforter. Grace took the band in her hand and placed it back on her finger; it dropped loosely into place. She inspected the space between the ring and her finger—far too loose to wear and not lose.

Matt, already standing outside the bedroom, knocked. He waited for a moment with his ear against the door. "Grace? You alright?" Matt was surprised by the sound of his voice.

Grace got up off the floor. "Uh . . . just a . . . second," she replied as she connected her ring to her necklace. Grace stumbled a little but she steadied herself—arms slightly stretched for balance.

She then turned and was face-to-face with her reflection in a standing mirror. A familiar yet forgotten girl stared back. A girl she left a long time ago looked plainly back at her. Grace slowly approached and stopped at a safe distance. She pulled on her uncontrollably curly hair and watched it spring back in knots. She clenched her teeth to view her protruding braces. Her shoulders quietly dropped.

Her eyes then focused on the reflections of her legs. She ran her hands down her knee to her shin. The eight-inch scar was no longer there. Grace slowly placed all of her weight on her left leg and then shifted it to her right. She rocked back and forth for a moment, unhindered by her injury. She looked at her cane next to her bed. She smiled in disbelief as she went a step farther and jumped and twirled.

A gentler knock broke her attention. "Grace?"

Grace stopped. She walked to the door. "So that's you?"

"Yeah."

"Doesn't sound like you."

"Doesn't sound like you either."

"What's happening?"

"I don't know."

"How . . . how's this possible?" Grace asked, as she looked at her hands.

Matt placed his hand and forehead to the door. "I'm still not sure that this actually *is* happening."

Grace pinched her forearm in an attempt to wake herself.

"How old are . . . or, I mean, how old do you think you are?"

"Why don't you just open the door?"

Grace hesitated. "I don't think . . . not just yet."

"Sure."

Matt sat on the floor with his back to the door.

Grace did the same on the opposite side.

"Whenever you're ready."

The two sat in silence.

"I'm guessing somewhere around fourteen or fifteen," Matt finally said.

"Yeah, me too."

Silence.

The door finally unlocked. Matt quickly stood, suddenly nervous. The knob turned slowly and the door opened.

"Hi," Matt said.

"Hey."

A voice shouted from the other end of the hall. "Who are you and what are you doing outside of my parents' room?"

⁓

"Now hold on just a minute," Matt said. "First, why not put down the baseball bat, Rebecca."

"How do you know my name?" Rebecca quickly turned her head toward the staircase. "Logan! Get up here. Now!" Rebecca regripped the handle. "And the bat stays."

"Listen, I don't know how to explain . . ."

Logan reached Rebecca a little out of breath. "What's going on?"

"I'm not sure," Rebecca said.

"Who's that?"

"Don't know."

"Who are you?" Logan yelled down the hall to Matt.

"I'm trying to explain."

"Are those my dad's pajamas?" Logan asked.

"They are."

"What a freak. Dad?" Logan yelled as he pounded on the nearby guest room door. The door swung open; the bed and room empty.

"Matt?" Rebecca yelled. "Matt? Mom?"

Grace stepped out into the hall.

"And who are you?" Rebecca asked.

"I'm, uh . . ."

"Is that my mother's necklace?" Rebecca asked, as she took a step forward, baseball bat firmly gripped. "It is! Logan, quick; give me your phone. I'm calling the police."

"I don't have my phone," Logan said in a loud whisper.

"Why not?"

"I don't know. I just don't. But it is downstairs. Let me go get it."

"Don't you dare leave me here with them," Rebecca said, as she grabbed Logan's collar.

"Well, *I'm* not staying here alone with them."

"So what do we do?"

Logan thought for a moment. "Hit them both on the head and then we can get the phone."

"Yeah." Rebecca nodded her head. "Yeah, okay." Rebecca looked at Matt and then Grace. "Which one first?"

"Alright, no one's hitting anyone," Matt said.

"Him," Logan said. "Do him first."

"Okay. Alright." Rebecca tightened her grip and assumed the batter's stance. "One . . ."

"Just a minute," Matt said.

"Two . . ."

"Just hold on."

"Three!"

"We're your parents!" Grace finally said.

"You'll have to do a lot better than that," Rebecca said.

"We are," Matt said.

"They're lying," Logan said. "Tee 'em up."

"Ask us something only your parents would know."

The suggestion created a short pause.

"Either of you?" Logan asked.

"Anything at all."

Logan and Rebecca exchanged glances. "Alright. Fine," Logan said. "This one's for the young lady. There's a first-place ribbon on the corkboard above my dresser. What did I get it for?"

Grace thought for a moment and smiled. "That's a trick question. You don't have any first-place ribbons."

"Well, I can't say that didn't hurt a little. I actually do, and it was for the art exhibit at school last year. Alright, let's try again. Again for the lady. Who did I take to the eighth-grade dance?"

"Now that one *is* a trick question. You went alone."

"Bernadine. Her name was Bernadine." Logan turned to his sister. "Your turn, Bec. It's a little painful but sort of fun."

"Alright." Rebecca thought for a moment. "You," Rebecca said, pointing her bat at Matt. "When I was in the sixth grade, what was the name of my baseball team?"

"The sixth grade?" Matt thought for a moment. "That year's, uh . . . a little difficult to remember. I think I remember your seventh-grade year a little better."

"I only played the one year. Nice try."

"Again, for the lady," Logan said. "What's my favorite food?"

"Chicken," Grace replied.

"Sloppy Joes."

"What's my favorite color?" Rebecca asked.

"Pink," Matt replied.

"Jade."

"Fidget spinner or fidget cube?" Logan asked.

"Spinner."

"Cube."

Logan looked at Rebecca. "They don't know anything about us."

"I know."

"I think they may actually be our parents."

"Just a second," Matt said, as he rushed into the master bedroom. "Here." Matt held an album in his hands. "Just a . . ."—Matt flipped through the pages—"second. Ah, here! Look." Matt slid a picture from the plastic sheath. He took a few steps forward and flicked an old Polaroid to Rebecca's feet.

"Get it," Rebecca said to Logan.

Logan picked it up. "Um, Rebecca? Look."

Rebecca slowly lowered the bat. She held the photo up for a side-by-side comparison. The woman in the picture was an exact match to the one standing down the hall. "Okay, that's weird." She lowered the picture and looked at Matt. "What about you? Where's your picture?"

"You'll just have to trust me."

Rebecca thought for a moment. "Alright, there's a picture on your desk downstairs—a picture of me and my father. Where was it taken?"

Matt smiled. "That picture was taken at Green Lake on your eighth birthday—life jackets on, paddles in hand." Matt took a step forward. "You wanted so badly to try paddleboarding but the weather had been absolutely terrible all month— rain, wind, you name it. We checked the forecast for your birthday and the report said that it would be just more of the same. But you insisted. You said that you were sure it would clear up by the weekend. And you were right. In fact, not only did it clear up, but it was one of the warmest days in March on record. And as for paddleboarding, you were a natural."

Rebecca and Logan looked at each other. Rebecca lowered the bat and looked at the two young teenagers at the end of the hall. "What's going on?"

9: Clues

The house was frigid. The biting winter weather had crept inside during the dead of night taking full advantage of the electrical outage. The four sat silently looking at each other. Cross-legged and under throw blankets, each one tried to understand the situation as best as he or she could—each one ready to put into words an explanation or solution once one came to mind. Rebecca looked across a driftwood coffee table at Matt and Grace. Suspicion still lay paramount on her mind. Logan blew a large puff of warm breath into the air.

"You know, Rebecca, you can put the bat away," Grace said.

Rebecca just looked at her and continued to spin it vertically against the carpet. "How about you walk us one more time through everything you remember about last night."

"Why do I feel like I'm being interrogated by my own children?" Matt asked.

"Just answer the question," Rebecca said.

Matt began, "Like I said, we just woke up this way."

"And you did nothing out of the ordinary?"

"No."

"Nothing unusual happened?"

"Like what?" Grace asked.

"I don't know, like make a deal with the devil?"

"Wait, that's it," Matt said.

"So did you invite Satan to the party last night, or did he just show up unannounced?" Logan asked.

"No." Matt went to the kitchen and returned with an empty bottle.

"What's that?" Rebecca asked.

"It was a gift given to us last night."

"And what was in it?"

"I'm . . . not sure."

"Well, who was it from?"

"Uh, not sure about that either."

"Is there anything that you do know about it?"

"Of course . . ." Matt started. "Well . . ." Matt looked to Grace for a little help.

"Did anyone else at the party drink any of that?" Rebecca asked.

"No."

"The two of you just decided to polish off an entire bottle on your own?"

"I only had half a glass before going to bed," Grace said.

The three looked at Matt.

"So I had a little more than half a glass."

Logan took the bottle. "Geez, it's a wonder you didn't wake up as a fetus." He looked at the strange writing. "Wonder what it says?"

"Here, look it up," Grace said, as she tossed Rebecca her phone.

"Hmm."

"What?"

"Signal just dropped."

"Must be the storm."

"Was there anything else in the box?"

"I don't think so," Matt said, as he took the package in his hands. He opened the lid and turned it upside down on the coffee table. There among the packaging straw, a small business card rested.

"Esoteric," Rebecca said, holding the card in her hand.

"What's that?" Matt asked.

"That weird shop on the pier?" Logan asked.

"I think so."

"You mean the one with the real-life mummy, shrunken heads, and a fortune-telling machine?" Matt asked.

"That's the one, I think."

"Great," Matt said.

"So we make for the pier then," Logan said.

Matt was silent.

Rebecca looked past the business card toward the pile of packaging straw. A small tail-like cord peeked out from the mess. She lifted the cord up out of the straw until a stopwatch hung suspended above the table. Rebecca took the small digital clock in her hand and watched as it counted in reverse: thirty-nine hours, fifteen minutes, fifty-three seconds . . . fifty-two . . . fifty-one . . . fifty. Rebecca showed the watch face to the others. "It's counting down."

"Counting down to what?" Logan asked.

"To zero," Rebecca said.

"No, really?"

"Is there anything else?" Grace asked.

Matt spread the packaging straw across the table. "Nothing."

Grace looked at the business card. "At least it's something."

Rebecca took Logan's arm and looked at his watch. "Alright, it's 9:15 right now." Rebecca walked to the kitchen and pulled a ferry schedule from the refrigerator door. "The next ferry leaves in five minutes so we'll miss that one. That gives us about a half-hour until the next one leaves."

"If it's even running," Logan said. "Wouldn't be the first time they shut down the ferries because of bad weather."

Rebecca returned to the living room window and took a pair of binoculars from an end table. She adjusted the viewfinder and looked out over the water. "There's one of the ferries," Rebecca said, looking at the Bainbridge terminal. "One unloading and the other . . ." Rebecca panned across the Puget Sound toward Seattle—"on its way!"

Grace opened one of the coffee table drawers and retrieved a small battery-operated radio. A spattering of static sounded as she turned the station knob until landing on a local news broadcast.

"And if you thought the storm that hit us late last night was bad, then get ready because we're not out of the woods just yet. A second, larger system is quickly approaching. Expect high winds, frigid temperatures, significant snowfall. The Doppler indicates that the city may see upward of eight inches of snow by this time tomorrow morning. We haven't seen a weather event like this in over twenty years. Now for traffic on the elevens, here's Kelly."

"Thanks, Rich. Last-minute shoppers are certainly out and about earlier than normal today as the threat of this second storm looms. Starting at Northgate, it's a slow move into downtown. There's a fender bender at the Mercer Street exit, which certainly doesn't help the situation. All things considered, however, it isn't much worse than one would expect for this time of year. The spokesperson for the Department of Transportation said that all modes of public transportation are operating under their regular schedules with the exception of the ferry system. High winds across the sound have already limited travel and threaten to halt travel altogeth . . . this . . . ets any . . . orse . . . Please stay tuned . . . latest . . ."

Static overtook the station. Grace moved the antenna around trying to catch the signal.

"It's not exactly a journey to Mordor," Rebecca said. "We should be able to make it there before lunch. But from the sound of it, we need to leave as soon as possible. If they shut the ferries down, it'll be virtually impossible to get to the city." Rebecca looked again to the ferry. "She's rocking pretty good."

"I'm in," Logan said.

Matt was silent.

"We're not getting any younger," Grace said with a slight grin. "Could be the last boat off the island."

"Alright," Matt said, "I'll leave in ten minutes. The three of you should stay here."

"We're going," Rebecca said.

"It would be safer for the three of you to wait here until this is figured out."

"You wouldn't have even known where to go," Rebecca said. "You may have helped build the city, but you obviously don't know it very well. Besides, any separations should really wait until after Christmas." Rebecca looked at Matt. "Right?"

"This isn't up for debate," Matt said.

"You're right; it isn't. Because you see"—Rebecca walked toward Matt—"there's a height requirement to tell me what to do."

"Oh, snaps!" Logan said.

"Add that one to the list."

"Add your face to the list," Logan mumbled.

"So we do this together then," Rebecca said.

Everyone waited for a reply.

"We do it together," Grace said.

"Fine. But, we can't go out there looking like this," Matt said, referring to the oversized clothes he and Grace wore.

Logan stepped toward Matt observing his height. He then looked at Rebecca and Grace. "I think we may be able to help with that."

༄࿐

Matt and Logan were the first out of the front door. "Nice hat," Logan said. "You know that was part of my Halloween costume, right? Oh wait, you probably didn't."

Matt straightened the bill of his newsboy cap as Grace and Rebecca stepped out of the house.

Matt looked at Grace.

"What?" Grace asked.

"Nothing," Matt said.

Grace looked down at her jeans and furred boots and then at Matt. "Well, it's not really my style," Grace said.

"No, you look. You look nice."

"Well, you don't look bad yourself, Oliver Twist."

"Alright, so we're ready then?" Logan asked, as he cinched up his backpack.

"Everyone warm enough?" Grace asked. A biting gust of wind nipped at the four. Logan wrapped his scarf around his neck. Rebecca adjusted her wool beanie.

"Still holding onto that bat, I see," Matt said.

The Louisville Slugger was strapped snuggly to the side of Rebecca's backpack.

"Batter safe than sorry," Logan said.

"I can't believe you just said that."

"We don't have time for this," Matt said, holding up the stopwatch. "Literally."

"Yeah, yeah," Logan said. "It's all pun and games until someone gets curt."

"Serious?" Matt said.

"Not if I can help it."

"Children," Grace said with a smile. "We really should get going."

"He started it," Matt said, as he flipped his jacket collar up and cinched up his backpack. "Everyone ready?"

Everyone replied with nods.

"Here we go." Matt turned and the group took a step forward.

And stopped.

The Mercedes SUV faced the four travelers as if taunting them to try and drive her.

"Hm." Sitting in the driver's seat, Matt peered between the steering wheel and the dashboard. "I think my growth spurt happens next year," Matt said, as he moved the seat all the way forward.

"We don't have a year. We have fifteen minutes," Logan said.

"You need a booster seat?" Rebecca asked.

"Don't look at *me*," Grace said. "I haven't driven since . . . well."

"Rebecca, haven't you passed driver's ed yet?" Matt asked.

"If by 'passed' you mean failed for a second time, then yes; she passed with flying colors," Logan replied.

"I understand how to drive . . . it's just the actual driving part that I haven't quite gotten down yet. But don't think for a second that I'm going to drive on icy roads."

"They're not icy. Just a little snowy."

"It only takes five minutes to drive there, so we're still okay for time. We'll take Firncliff Drive instead of the highway. That'll bring us right to the public parking. Plus, we'll avoid having to drive past the police station," Matt said.

"But we obviously won't be able to drive on board," Grace said.

"True, but it really won't matter much if we can't even leave the driveway." Matt stretched his legs as far as he could, desperate to reach the gas and brake pedals. "You're going to have to work the pedals."

"You've got to be joking."

"If you have a better idea, believe me, I'll take it." Matt looked at Grace. "Like you said, this may be our last chance to get off the island."

Grace took a breath. "Logan. Rebecca. Seatbelts."

"If you want to wreck the car, you should really just let Rebecca drive."

"That wasn't my fault," Rebecca said, as she fastened her seatbelt.

"The other car was parked!"

"Blatantly, more than twelve inches from the curb. It was practically in the middle of the street."

"Well, your driving instructor and that nice officer saw it differently."

"Alright, that's enough," Matt said, as he adjusted his seat to its highest position.

Logan secured his belt. "She's just upset because I'm probably going to get my license before her."

Grace lay across the floor placing one hand on the brake, the other on the gas. "This is really stupid. Rebecca? You sure you don't want to try?"

"No way," Rebecca and Logan said at the same time.

"Ready?" Matt asked.

"I think so," Grace replied.

Matt popped the SUV into gear. "Alright, give it a little gas." The vehicle slowly rolled forward. "So far, so good," Matt said, as he approached the end of the driveway. "Okay . . . now, stop." The vehicle stopped suddenly. Matt turned his blinker on. "Alright, don't go."

Grace pressed the gas.

"Stop!"

A passing car swerved around the protruding SUV, narrowly missing it from the left.

"You said 'alright, go.'"

"I said 'alright, don't go.'" Matt caught his breath. "I think we may need to work on our communication."

"Now he wants to work on communication," Grace said to herself.

Matt looked both ways. Rebecca and Logan did the same. "Alright. Give it some gas."

"Are you sure?"

"Yes. I'm sure."

The SUV rolled forward. With a slight turn of the steering wheel, the vehicle was soon on the roadway, and the four slowly raced to leave the island.

10: Pol-ice

"I think you can go a little faster," Matt said, as he looked at the speedometer. The needle was just below twenty miles per hour. The needle rose to twenty-five miles per hour. "Good," Matt said. "That's good."

"We're never going to get there," Logan said.

Though the road was clear of heavy traffic, branches and small limbs were spread about like confetti while additional debris fell from the sky like a ticker-tape parade.

Pieces of frozen evergreens and firs crunched and cracked beneath the SUV's tires as it made its way east toward the first of two stop signs in an otherwise unobstructed path to the waterfront.

"Stop sign coming up," Matt said. The vehicle jerked to a sudden stop ten feet shy of the intersection. "Close enough."

"What's that?" Rebecca asked.

"What's what?" Grace asked, as she rose from the floorboard.

"Great."

On the other side of the intersection, a massive tree lay stretched across the road. Accompanying the downed tree, power lines were spread about like a coiled mass of snakes.

"Less than ten minutes," Logan said.

"Well, that doesn't leave us much choice," Matt said, as he flipped on his turn signal. "We're going to have to take the highway."

"You sure about this?" Grace asked.

"Nope. But we're going to have to go faster than twenty-five anyway if we're going to make it to the ferry before it leaves."

Grace returned to the pedals.

"Alright, give me some gas."

Matt made the turn and drove toward the highway.

"More gas," Matt said, as he approached the highway intersection. "Stay green," Matt ordered the traffic signal. "Stay green."

"It's yellow," Rebecca said.

"Brake?" Grace asked.

"There's no time," Logan said.

"Brake?"

Grace released the gas.

"Gas!" Matt said.

The SUV sped into the intersection despite a now obvious red light. Matt pulled the steering wheel hard to the left. Horns of other cars blared as Matt barely missed the cross traffic. Matt corrected the turn until the SUV was again traveling in a straight line. Logan looked out the back window to see the aftermath. No wrecks, just angry drivers.

Matt looked out the rearview mirror and let out a sigh of relief. "Alright, in about a half-mile, we're going to have to make a left in front of the police department. When this happens, I want everyone to duck out of sight. Rebecca and Logan, I want you to wrap your faces with your scarves. With any luck, we'll just glide by unnoticed. The public parking lot is down the street from the station." Matt looked at his watch. "This is going to be close."

A large wave of vehicles approached as the SUV rounded a gradual bend in the road and drove onto a large bridge.

"Ferry traffic," Logan said.

"Let's hope it was a full load," Matt replied.

The ferry then came into view as the bridge crested.

"Would you look at that?" Rebecca said. "Even the overflow lanes are jammed. You'd think the island is sinking."

The next intersection came into view. "Alright, Grace, brake lightly. Looks like some road flares ahead. Grace? I need you to brake."

"I am."

"We aren't, uh, slowing down."

Grace applied more pressure. The view from behind the windshield slowly began to veer to the side. Matt's head tilted with it. The SUV gradually rotated on a sheet of ice until Matt could see the ferry through his rearview mirror.

"What's going on?" Grace asked.

"Let go of the brake," Matt said, as the SUV passed a road flare. The vehicle completed its 360-degree rotation and began spinning into a second one when it entered the intersection on the other end of the bridge. The tires gripped dry pavement and violently jerked the SUV to the right. Grace was tossed from the brake and onto the accelerator. The vehicle roared back to life; it sped diagonally through the intersection. The SUV jumped the curb and barely missed a group of people waiting to cross the street. Grace hit her head beneath the dashboard. Rebecca and Logan were tossed in their seats as the vehicle barreled toward the police station.

The uniformed row of cherry blossom trees and unsuspecting shrubs were next in the SUV's warpath. The landscape was no defense as the vehicle tore through the manicured flower bed with unadulterated force. Grace covered her head as best she could. The vehicle screamed toward the front door of the police station.

"Brake, brake, brake," Matt yelled.

Grace tried to find the pedal amidst the assault, but couldn't.

"Hold on!" Matt yelled.

The sound of shattering glass and twisting metal exploded around the four as fury and mayhem erupted with deafening force. The SUV came to a sudden stop as it made contact with the building's inner door.

The engine hissed as pieces of glass bounced off the roof and hood. Rebecca opened her eyes. "You okay?"

"I think so," Logan replied.

Grace rose from the floor. She and Matt looked out through the cracked windshield. Past the steam rising from the engine, half a dozen officers stared back at the two.

Grace raised her hands. Matt looked at Rebecca and Logan through the rearview mirror.

"You know how sometimes in movies someone, usually law enforcement, says, 'don't make any sudden moves'?" Matt unbuckled his seatbelt. "We need to make some sudden moves." Matt popped the rear hatch. "Run!"

The four grabbed their packs, scrambled out the back of the SUV and ran toward the parking lot. The SUV wedged itself like a cork inside the station's entryway, making any exit from the front doors of the building virtually impossible.

"Don't look back," Matt yelled as the four raced from the scene toward the ferry's waiting lines.

The first siren sounded behind them. "Here they come," Grace said, keeping pace with Matt.

"Hurry," Matt yelled. "They're already boarding."

"What's the plan exactly?" Grace asked, as the four raced between the lanes of remaining cars, trucks, and recreational vehicles.

"Working on it."

"Well, work faster."

"There!" Rebecca said, pointing to a woman exiting a fifth-wheel camper, seven cars ahead. The woman quickly made her way inside the cab of the truck as their lane was next to board. Matt grasped the camper door handle as the vehicle began to roll. The door swung open.

"In! Now!"

One by one, the four jumped in.

"I can't see," Logan said, as he stumbled forward.

"Your eyes will adjust," Grace said.

"What's that smell?" Logan asked. "Smells like rotten eggs and lavender."

"I think it's coming from in there," Rebecca said, pointing to a closed door a few steps away.

"Alright," Matt said, "as soon as we stop, we're out of here."

Rebecca leaned over the sink and peeked through the closed blinds. The camper slowly rolled onto the boat and alongside the ferry wall. The purr of individual engines now roared collectively inside the belly of the boat.

"Okay, get ready," Matt said, as he held the door's handle in anticipation. The camper came to a stop. "That's our cue." Matt opened the door. "Everyone out." Matt hopped down and held out his hand to help Grace and then Rebecca. As Rebecca's feet touched the floor, the truck's passenger side door opened. Matt quickly slammed the door closed on Logan's face.

"Can I help you?" the woman asked, facing the three.

"Just trying to get to the front of the ferry," Rebecca said. "We'll go around."

Logan stood, his face inches from the door. "Great."

A voice approached. Logan quickly locked the door just as the handle was tried.

"Yes, it is, Hank. See, I told you I locked it," the woman said. Logan let out a sigh of relief as he cautiously moved his hand away from the door. "Do you have the key though?"

Logan looked around for a place to hide. His eyes landed on an interior door and he quickly entered. Immediately, Logan was met with a more pungent smell of the odor.

"Aw, man," Logan said, as he swiped the air in front of his face. He closed the door and waited. He pressed his ear to the door.

The outside door was unlocked and opened. "Must've been something I ate," the woman said. "Round two."

Logan backed away quickly, bumping the back of his legs into a toilet. "Oh, no," Logan whispered to himself.

"You might as well head up to the passenger deck, honey. I may be a little while."

"You know there's no electricity, so no fan," the man said. "Can't be using up the battery either."

"I'll just pop the ceiling vent."

The knob turned and the bathroom door opened.

Logan quietly steadied himself inside the shower as the door closed. The only thing separating Logan from the woman's imminent assault was a little more than a foot's distance and a thin shower curtain. The door locked.

"Oh my goodness. Oh my sweet goodness," the woman said, sounding desperate to free herself from her khakis. Logan saw the woman's hand reach toward the vent through the space between the curtain rod and ceiling. She then stopped. "Oh, sweet mercy. Nope. No time." She quickly retracted her hand.

Logan slowly slid down the shower wall until resting in an upright fetal position. As the first shots fired, Logan clasped his ears and held his breath. He buried his head deep in his knees desperate to somehow separate himself from the escalating attack. A memory of a happier time came to Logan's mind (such thoughts often emerge in the midst of severe distress). It was summertime at their cousin's house on Lake Stevens. The cool water was a pleasant contrast to the warm sun as he and Rebecca pretended to be experienced free divers in search of lost treasure. Logan's grin faded as he was reminded of an inescapable truth: even the most experienced divers need to come up for air eventually.

Logan approached Rebecca, Matt, and Grace. The three sat at a window table near the rear of the boat. Blank faced, he sat down without saying a word.

"You alright?" Rebecca asked.

"I don't want to talk about it," Logan said, as he tossed his backpack onto the table.

A woman in khakis approached with her husband.

"That wasn't human," Logan muttered as the couple passed.

"Excuse me?" the woman asked.

"That. Wasn't. Human."

"You'll have to excuse my brother. Everyone else does too."

The woman smiled politely and the couple continued on.

"What's the matter with you?" Rebecca scolded.

"She knows what she did." Logan lowered his head. "She knows what she did." Logan took a breath. "Alright. So what have I missed?"

"Not much," Rebecca said.

"I've been engaged in biological warfare for the past twenty minutes, and you all have just been sitting up here staring at each other?" Logan retrieved a sketchpad from his pack. "What's the plan?"

"From the ferry dock, Esoteric is just one pier over," Matt said. "We go there. That's the plan. Pretty simple. What are you drawing?"

"A map."

"Of what?" Rebecca asked.

"This," Logan said making a circular motion with his hand. "Us. Where we're going. Where we've been."

"I don't think you'll need that much paper," Rebecca said.

"With any luck, we'll be back on Bainbridge by noon," Matt said, as he settled back in his seat and closed his eyes. "The sooner we figure this out, the sooner things can get back to normal."

Rebecca looked at Matt for a second before shoving Logan to let her out. "Logan, move."

"You okay?" Grace asked.

"Fine."

Rebecca stood against the wind, arms folded. The large vessel swayed from side to side under the power of the growing squall. Rebecca steadied herself through the icy blasts as tiny snowflakes swirled about. She looked straight ahead, her eyes fixed on a growing city. Low-hanging clouds draped over the tops of the skyscrapers like sheets too short for a bed. Sounds of downtown became faintly audible. The city was bleak yet alive.

Footsteps approached and stopped beside Rebecca. Logan tightened his scarf and looked toward the skyline. He took hold of the guardrail next to his sister. "Told ya. You don't ride a ferry and not stand on the deck. You alright?"

Rebecca nodded.

"What do you think the odds are of things actually going back to normal?"

"I wouldn't plan on it," Rebecca said. "Seems like everything's off."

"Right? Sorry, I mean . . . I agree with that sentiment. Whatever. Here, look at this." Logan held up his phone and scrolled through his pictures. "You know that girl I took to the eighth-grade dance? Bernadine?"

"You mean you actually went with someone?"

"Yes, I did. Look." Logan held the screen up to his sister.

"That is *not* her," Rebecca said, as she took the phone in her hands.

"I know."

"You know who that looks like, right?"

"I said, I know."

"That looks just like Mom. Not old Mom. Like," Rebecca pointed back into the passenger deck, "young Mom," Rebecca said, half laughing.

"Uh, I know."

"Ew. That's gross." Rebecca handed the phone back to Logan.

"Talk about things being off. I may need therapy."

"If by 'may' you mean definitely, then yes," Rebecca said with a smile. She looked at her brother. "When this is all over, I think we're going to have to redefine what normal is."

"There's no good outcome, is there?"

"What do you mean?" Rebecca asked.

"Well, either Mom and Dad stay the way they are, and we spend the rest of our lives with weird child-parents, or we find whatever it is we're searching for and Mom and Dad get divorced. Just seems like every step we take toward finding a solution will be one step closer to us not being a family anymore."

A voice over the ferry's public address system told passengers to return to their vehicles.

"City's coming up quick," Logan said.

"Unless we find the solution before they do."

"City's coming up really quick."

"Then we'd have control."

"Um." Logan took a step back. "Are we going to hit that?"

"They're the ones that need to grow up. You know, in more ways than one, I mean."

"Bec."

"We just need more time."

"Bec!"

"What?"

"Look!" Logan pointed toward the end of the pier.

Rebecca stepped away from the rail. The two turned and ran for the door. Before they could make it inside, the vessel made contact with the tall wooden structure, sending them both backward through the air as large splinters spread across the deck's floor. Logan's phone slid from his hand and overboard as the ferry's course was violently corrected. The vessel slowed in full reverse as it contacted the wing wall and ground forward. The metal-on-metal contact pierced the air like a thousand fingernails scratching a chalkboard until the vessel came to a swaying halt.

The doors flew open. Grace and Matt raced to their children. Ferry personnel were quickly on scene ensuring everyone's safety.

"We're fine," Rebecca said, as she brushed a few wood fragments from her coat. "We're fine." Grace and Matt brought Logan and Rebecca to their feet.

"Are you sure?" Grace asked.

"Yeah. Sure," Logan said.

"Yeah?" Matt asked, as he looked them both over. "Good." He looked back inside as ferry staff aided those in the cabin. "You're okay? You can walk?"

"Dad . . . I mean Matt. We're fine."

"Are you kids alright?" a uniformed man asked.

"We're fine," Rebecca said. "What was that?"

"Rogue wave. Sometimes happens in these storms. And what about you, young man?" the man asked. "Did you hit your face?"

"Did I . . . oh, this." Logan pointed to his black eye. "No, someone else did that for me."

"Really. We're fine," Rebecca said.

"Alright. Well, make your way to the front of the ferry to depart."

The four walked back inside where passengers were helped from the floor and minor injuries were treated. They walked down the stairs, which led them back to the cargo deck where they waited at the front of the vessel.

A man with a large beard and a reflective vest stood just beyond a yellow line painted across the floor. He looked down at the four. "Stay behind the line."

Logan slid the front of his shoe back behind the line.

"Boat leaves again in about thirty minutes," the man said. "Might be the last ride back to the island for a while."

"Thanks," Matt said.

Rebecca and Logan looked at Matt and Grace as if to gain confirmation to continue as planned. The sound of rotating gears filled the air as a metal drawbridge began lowering from the mainland to the vessel.

"Are we sure about this?" Grace asked.

"It's just around the corner," Matt said.

The four looked beyond the pier as the city slowly came into view. Window by window, floor by floor, the city's most prominent buildings slowly revealed themselves, as a frostbitten downtown welcomed the group to the journey that lay beyond. As the metal bridge secured into place, the four looked at the towering city and accepted its beckoning invitation.

11: Esoteric

The city was alive. Despite the cold, Seattleites filled the veins of downtown as a fresh pump of life poured from the ferry into the city's arteries. Horns honked, engines roared, and voices rang out as Rebecca, Matt, Grace, and Logan exited the terminal and made their way up the wooden pier.

"How far is the shop from here?" Logan asked.

"That building just ahead," Rebecca said, as she pointed to a large gray building.

"That's it? Guess I was expecting something a little more . . . unique. Like the bottle."

"If I remember right, there's plenty of weird to make up for it inside," Grace said.

The four walked along the pier as ocean spray cascaded over anyone brave enough to venture close to its edge. Grace wrapped her scarf over her nose and mouth as the temperature dropped with each gust of wind.

Matt was the first to reach the steps leading to the front door. The four peered through windows with cupped hands into the building's darkened interior. Matt rattled the door's handle.

"That's weird," Matt said. "The sign says 'open.'"

Just then a shadow appeared at the window and flipped the sign to "closed." The front door was unlocked and opened. The four stepped back. In the dull light of day, the shadow had a face.

"Sorry, kids. Closing up early today. I've seen storms like this one before. Trust me; it's not worth sticking around." The man stepped outside and locked the deadbolt.

"It's actually really important," Rebecca said. "Is there any way that we can speak to someone just for a moment about an item that was purchased here?"

The man ran his fingers through his gray hair as he directed his attention to the four. He looked at his watch. "Alright, what seems to be the problem? Your jumping beans not jumping?"

Matt retrieved the bottle from his backpack. "We were hoping that you knew something about this."

The man took the bottle in his hands. "Now where did you get that?"

"It was a gift given to my wife and . . ." Matt paused. "It was an early Christmas present."

The man inspected the bottle and looked at his watch again. "You're telling me that someone bought you kids this bottle for Christmas?"

"So you know what it is? Where it came from?" Grace asked.

"Yeah, I know what it is. I know where it came from." He nodded toward the building. "Alright. In."

"Thank you Mr . . ." Grace said.

"Jack. You can call me Jack."

The door unlocked and the four stepped inside. As they waited for their eyes to adjust, the bizarre surroundings came slowly into view.

"What is this place?" Logan asked.

"A place where answers are found," Jack said.

"Answers to what?"

"To questions you never knew you had."

"That's good," Logan said, as his eyes scanned the store. "Because we definitely have a few questions that could use some answering."

The four slowly split apart from one another, each taking a different aisle toward the back of the store. Rebecca ran her hand along a wooden shelf filled with small three-headed animals, strange skeletons, and other oddities. On the other side of the aisle, Logan walked, eyes fixed skyward. Strange creatures, mammoth tusks, and items only described as "otherworldly" hung precariously from exposed beams. Not watching his step, he suddenly came face to face with a man of only skin and bone. The horrible expression and protruding teeth gave Logan a scare as he jumped back.

Rebecca approached a cabinet with various shrunken heads. "Made in China?"

"Peru," Jack replied with a wink.

"And what about this?" Rebecca asked, pointing to the next case over. A full-grown petrified man stood behind dirty glass.

"As the story goes, Sebastian here was born with two hearts and during the Revolutionary War, he was shot through one of them. See?" Jack pointed to a visible hole in the man's chest. "Seeing that he had a backup, the shot didn't kill him."

"Quite the story," Rebecca said.

"Don't believe it?"

"Uh, no."

"Tell me"—Jack leaned against the glass casing—"when I say the word 'miracle,' what do you think?"

Rebecca pointed to the glass case. "That's not a miracle. That's . . . a tourist attraction."

"Perhaps. But what if?"

"You're telling me you actually believe that?"

"I'm simply saying, 'what if?'" Jack looked at Rebecca through a veil of floating dust. "Do you know what the definition of a miracle is?"

"Something good happening."

"The simple answer: an unlikely event that brings a welcomed consequence."

"So basically what I said."

"Like a gift?" Logan asked.

"That's right," Jack replied.

"And the complicated answer?" Rebecca asked.

"It's something that can't be explained by natural or scientific law. And that being the case, it's usually considered the work of the divine."

"You've seen one?" Logan asked. "A miracle, I mean."

"I've seen a few things that I can't explain."

"Like what?"

"Well, for instance, I've seen a person's missing limb grow back."

"Shut up. What, like a missing hand?" Logan asked.

"In this case, it was a foot."

"He's kidding," Rebecca said. "This is what he says to all his customers. This is how he makes a living."

"How did it happen? How'd the leg grow back?"

"That's one thing I've learned about miracles, or gifts as you put it: it's not so much *how* it happened, but *why*."

"What do you mean?" Logan asked.

Jack unlocked a glass case. "Take this arrowhead, for example. It's believed to have once belonged to William Clark of the Lewis and Clark Expedition." Jack handed the arrowhead to Logan. "I want you to have it."

"You're just giving this to me? Why?"

Jack smiled. "See?" He then looked at his watch. "This way please."

Jack unlocked a door at the rear of the store. The hinges groaned as the door opened to a tall staircase. The old wood creaked with each step as the five ascended. A large rustic office with a sweeping view of Elliott Bay met the group at the top. Leather bags and suitcases stretched across the tops of shelves packed with books and artifacts collected over a lifetime of travel and adventure.

"Wow," Logan said. "This is even better than downstairs."

"Looks like a lot of clutter," Matt said, as he spun a small antique globe.

"Some may call it that," Jack replied. "But each piece is a memory—each piece a story."

"What about this one?" Logan asked holding up an old sheathed blade. "What kind of a story does it have?"

"That I traded for when I traveled to Kenya for the . . . second time, I believe. After I finished my dissertation research in Nairobi, I visited a Maasai tribe with a couple of friends." Jack held the blade in his hands. "It was a good trade. Fair."

"You've been to Africa two times?" Rebecca asked.

"Many more times than that."

"So what about this?" Rebecca asked holding a smashed camera.

"I took that camera on every one of my trips. That is, until an Iranian officer didn't appreciate me having it. If a picture is worth a thousand words, that camera could fill libraries."

"And what about this?" Matt asked holding up a glass Coke bottle. "What's this from? Drinks with a warlord?"

"That's from yesterday's lunch." Jack set his leather briefcase next to a wooden desk. He sat down and retrieved a pair of black-framed reading glasses from his shirt pocket as he inspected the item brought to him. "Well, I have some good news and some bad news. But the bad news is more bad than the good news is good. Actually, most would probably consider it all just bad news."

"Let's hear it," Grace said.

"Well, the bottle came from this store—the good news."

"And the bad news?" Matt asked.

"For starters, it was from my personal collection. But perhaps the more unsettling fact is that the bottle was empty when it left the store."

"Empty," Matt said. "You sold an empty bottle? Then what was inside?"

"Gave an empty bottle. As for what was inside? I don't know."

"So where in the world did you get it?"

"An appropriate question." Jack turned the bottle on his desk. "Austria. The Klosterneuburg Monastery."

"A monastery? Like monks?" Rebecca asked.

Jack nodded.

"Monks make alcohol?" Logan asked. "That's pretty rad."

"Matt, what did we drink?"

Jack leaned back in his chair and removed his glasses. "So you drank it. And then what?"

"What do you mean?"

"Well, I'm guessing you didn't come here just to confess your underage drinking," Jack said, raising the bottle. A dark spot resting at the bottom of the bottle caught his attention. "And if you did come here to confess, I'm sorry, but I'm no priest . . ." Jack's sentence trailed off as he looked at the glass base. He tilted the bottle to the other side. An object slowly fell with gravity. "There's something inside."

Jack popped the cork and emptied the remaining liquid into his garbage can. He then looked through the opening. He opened his desk drawer and retrieved a pen. He poked the inside of the bottle as one would to get the last bit of peanut butter from a jar. A small vial dropped out of the bottle onto the desk. The four stepped closer looking at the container.

"What's inside?" Logan asked.

Jack held the item in his hand. "Suppose there's only one way to find out."

12: The Riddle

A tightly wound piece of parchment paper slid from the container and into Jack's hand.

"May I?" Rebecca asked. Jack handed over the rolled paper.

I come around, only once in a year
When the month turns twelve, you'll know that I'm near.
For some I bring stress, some debt and a bill
For some I bring toys, an excitement and thrill

Some don't acknowledge, some religions do ban
While others ignore me, because simply they can
Yet others remember, the truth that I bring
So 'It is finished,' be remembered in spring

You can see me through any lens, this is truth
But the lens most preferred, is found only in youth.
And this youth that you've found, there's no way to reverse
Except with the cure, for this pubescent curse

How you entered this maze, you'll not find your way out
For it's not what goes in, but what comes out of your mouth
The elixir you seek, is not food nor a drink
Rather three little words, will do more than you think.

One final thing, most important of all
The clock it counts down, so your window is small
Time's not your friend, it is not on your team
It races against you, it plots and it schemes

Downward it counts, soon sealing your fate:
To forever remain, in this childlike state.

"Cute," Matt said.

"What's it mean?" Grace asked.

Matt shook his head.

"Well, that answers the clock question," Logan said.

"What clock?" Jack asked.

Matt removed the stopwatch from around his neck.

Jack looked at the four. He scratched his trimmed gray beard. "So what's really going on here?"

The four looked at each other. Jack leaned back in his chair and tossed his glasses onto his desk.

"I don't think you'd believe us if we told you," Rebecca said.

Jack leaned forward. "Try me."

Jack was silent for a moment. He looked at Logan. "So you were in that camper bathroom the entire time?"

"Bruh, the entire time."

Jack looked at the others. "I believe you."

"You do?" Grace said. "May I ask why?"

"Because I'd be a hypocrite otherwise."

"So what about the poem?"

"Well, the first stanza is a little funny now."

"How so?" Rebecca asked.

Jack took the poem from his desk. "Christmas through the eyes of a child." Jack looked over the rest of the poem. "According to this, your condition is reversible."

"An antidote, right?" Rebecca asked.

"Seems to be. But it doesn't sound like you'll get out of your dilemma the same way you got into it. And it doesn't sound like you have much time."

"So how do we reverse it?"

Jack raised his eyebrows. "Three little words."

"What do you mean?" Matt asked.

"Not sure. But there, toward the bottom: 'Three little words will do more than you think.'"

Matt took the poem in his hands. "What are the three words?"

"I think you'd know better than me."

Matt shrugged his shoulders. "What else do you got?"

"That's all I got."

"Come on, that can't be it," Rebecca said.

"If you told me everything that happened and didn't spare any detail"—Jack looked at Logan—"which obviously you didn't no matter how unpleasant—then I know as much as you do."

"You said the bottle was from your personal collection," Rebecca said. "Why'd you give it away?"

"It was a favor."

"Great! For whom?"

"A stranger."

"Great."

"A woman came in the store a few days back looking for a Christmas present. Specifically some sort of antique bottle. She seemed desperate and pressed for time. I felt sorry, so I gave it to her."

Jack put on his reading glasses and typed at his computer. "But let me see if I can come up with something a little more helpful." After a few moments, Jack turned the monitor to the four. "This is a surveillance camera video of the woman."

Matt and Grace looked at the monitor. "I don't recognize her," Grace said. "Do you?"

"No," Matt replied.

"Look at what she's wearing," Rebecca said. "It's some sort of a uniform. Can you zoom in any?" Jack focused the footage on the company name embroidered on the uniform. The picture was pixilated but clear enough to read.

"West Queen Manor," Rebecca said. "What's that?"

"Looks like some sort of nurse's uniform," Logan said.

"Can you look it up?" Grace asked.

Jack returned to the keyboard and typed the name into a search engine. "Well, it looks like it's a few miles north of here on the corner of 3rd and Blaine. And it looks like it's a . . ."

A loud boom stopped Jack short of finishing his sentence as the room suddenly went dark. Jack peered out over his glasses. "Hmm. Looks like you may have to find out the old-fashioned way," Jack said, as he placed his glasses back into his shirt pocket.

"That's it?" Rebecca said.

Jack looked at his watch. "That's it. I need to make it to SeaTac." Jack offered the bottle to Matt.

"Keep it," Matt said.

"You can't just leave us like this," Rebecca said.

"'We glory in our sufferings, because we know that suffering produces perseverance; perseverance, character; and character, hope.'"

"Who said that?" Matt asked. "A Tibetan Sherpa?"

"God, actually. In a manner of speaking."

Jack stood from his desk and took his briefcase in hand. "Of course the writer was speaking about something else. But I think it applies to your situation." He then looked at Rebecca. "This isn't my story; it's yours." He looked at the other three. "All of yours. And from what I can tell, it's quite an unbelievable one."

"And you're a part of it now," Rebecca said.

"A supporting role, maybe." Jack picked his bag up off the floor. "Please forgive me, but I really must get going. Come on, I'll walk you out."

The five exited the building down a wooden fire escape and walked north toward the Great Ferris Wheel where Jack's Jeep was parked. "The number-four bus should take you to where you need to go," Jack said, as he unlocked his door. "You can catch it on 3rd Street, right up there. The bus system is still running; for now, anyway. Do you have enough money?"

"Yeah," Matt replied. "We'll be fine."

"I hope you find what you're looking for." Jack closed his door. The engine roared to life and the window lowered. A large wave crashed onto the pier spraying mist close to where the four stood. Jack handed the stopwatch back to Matt. "And I hope you find it soon." Jack rolled up his window. The Jeep moved away from the four toward Alaskan Way, where it entered the flow of traffic and drove out of sight.

"Can you believe that guy?" Matt said. "Magic monk wine? Really?"

"I think 'blessed' is what he alluded to," Grace said.

"Same thing."

"Well, either way, we have an address now," Rebecca said. "We find the woman from the security footage, we find out what's going on."

Matt shook his head. "No."

"What do you mean, no?" Rebecca asked.

"I mean, we go back and catch the ferry before it's too late." Matt looked out over the water. "There's one coming in."

"Why go back now?"

"You heard him. It's a wild goose chase. Who knows where that address will take us and what we'll find when we get there. I was right when I said that you and Logan should stay at home. I'm taking you both back."

The three stood.

"Back to what?" Rebecca asked.

"Back home. Your mom and I will figure it out on our own."

"Because you two are so great at that sort of thing." Rebecca shook her head. "No."

"What did you say?"

"I said, no. I'm not going back."

"The city is slowly freezing to death. First the ferry system will shut down; then the bus system. And once the snow really hits, unless Uber has a Snowcat, we'll be stuck walking."

"I'm not going back. And neither is Logan."

Logan looked up. "Huh?"

"I'm not asking," Matt said.

Rebecca cinched up her backpack. "Neither am I. And that's the difference between you and me: when things get difficult, I don't run. Neither does Logan."

"Not to be contradictory, but I think I may actually take after Dad—"

"Logan!"

"Yep, on my way. Danger. Risk. Sign me up."

"It's a bus ride."

"That's what I meant."

Rebecca and Logan walked from the pier toward the city. Matt shook his head. The four walked a short distance and were soon standing at the intersection of Alaskan Way and University waiting for the signal to turn.

"One block ahead are the Harbor Steps," Matt said. "They lead to First Street, and then it's just two blocks to the nearest bus stop." The adjacent light turned red and the "walk" signal shone brightly.

Matt and Grace walked a few steps behind Rebecca and Logan. "I saw your reaction when you saw the woman from the security footage," Grace said through her scarf. "You recognized her."

"I didn't react. This just seems like a waste of time."

"No one's making you come with us," Rebecca said.

The four approached the bottom of the steps.

"Up there?" Logan asked. "I can't even see the top."

"It's not that bad," Rebecca said, as the four began the ascent.

Buildings on both sides towered overhead. The once-tiny snowflakes increased in size as they fell indiscriminately past the light-wrapped trees.

"Largest staircase ever," Logan said, now panting.

"Maybe if you exercised every once in a while," Rebecca said.

"Have we met? I weigh like a buck twenty. I can't afford to exercise."

"I don't think you understand how exercise works."

"I think I'm dying."

"Stop it."

"Seriously, my body's shutting down." Logan checked his pulse. "I think . . ." Logan stopped and looked toward the top of the staircase.

Rebecca looked back. "What's the matter?"

"You've got to be kidding me," Logan said to himself.

Logan looked to his left and saw a sign to Pike Place Market. "I think I need something to eat. We haven't eaten all morning and I'm starving. All this running around, you know?" Logan took a step toward the alleyway. "Maybe we could just cut over and grab something really quick along the way."

"I could actually eat something too," Grace said. "Matt?"

"Trust me, we'll all be better off," Logan said, as he led the group off the steps and into the alley. The smooth concrete of the Harbor Stairs was now old cobblestone as the four walked behind aged buildings. Like the ugly backside of a Christmas tree, fire escapes, drainage pipes, and meters stretched from street to roof—unsightly necessities accompanied by battered dumpsters and thick steam escaping from manhole covers. Logan looked back toward the Harbor Steps.

"What's with you?" Rebecca asked.

"Thought I saw someone. It's nothing."

"What. Is. That?" Rebecca asked, as the alley turned from open sky to enclosed tunnel—the buildings on both sides of the alley connecting overhead. She stopped and stared at the mouth of the enclosure. "Gross." Rebecca looked around. "What exactly am I looking at?"

"It's the Gum Wall," Matt said. "You've never heard of it?"

"Heard of it? You mean it's a thing? Like something people know about?"

"People actually come from all over the world to see it."

"People come here to see this?"

"Well, they probably come to the city for other reasons." Matt looked at both sides of the alley. "It's expanded quite a bit."

Under the soft glow of the overhead canned lights, like an enormous sheet of saliva wallpaper, small wads of gum plastered the brick walls from the street to the exposed pipes above—a germophobe's Technicolor nightmare.

Rebecca looked around. "Disgusting."

"Rad," Logan said.

Matt reached into his pocket and pulled out a pack of gum. He offered it to the other three. Logan was the only one to take him up on his offer.

"Shouldn't we be in more of a hurry?" Rebecca asked.

"Here, give me a few more," Logan said. He shoved three more sticks into his mouth.

Matt took his gum and made a contribution.

"Really?" Grace said.

Logan secured half of his chewed gum between his front teeth. He took the other half and stretched it as far as he could reach. He attached both ends to the wall creating a rubbery green hammock. He stepped back to admire his work.

"Can we get going now?" Rebecca asked.

"The Market's just around the corner," Matt said.

The four were soon back under the falling snow as Matt led the three around the alley corner and onto the steep incline of Pike Street.

"Up here," Matt said, pointing to a set of narrow concrete stairs connecting the alley to the market above. Cheers and hollers grew louder as the four maneuvered their way up the crowded steps.

A young boy descending the stairs grabbed Logan by the arm and turned to walk with him. He shoved a piece of paper into Logan's coat pocket. "Don't return to Undertown," the boy said. He then quickly bumped past Rebecca and Grace out of sight.

Matt looked back at Logan. "What was that?"

"Yeah, who was that?" Rebecca asked.

"I don't know," Logan said, as he dug a flyer from his pocket. He flashed the paper for the others to see before dropping it to the ground.

Rebecca picked it up and stuffed it into Logan's pocket. "Find a trashcan."

Logan redirected his attention to the commotion above. "Why are they cheering?"

"Fishmongers."

"Fish what?"

"You'll see."

Atop the stairs, a mass of people filled the covered market. Dozens of shoppers gathered in front of the Pike Place Fish Company, while others stood near a street performer who was playing a cello.

"I can't see anything," Logan said, facing a wall of people.

"None of us can," Rebecca said. "Hey, why don't you stand on that big brass pig over there?" Rebecca turned to Matt. "Why is there a big brass pig over there?"

"That's Rachel, the market's mascot. It's actually a piggy bank to help support the market's low-income neighbors. Word has it, if you rub the pig's snout and make a donation, you'll have good luck."

"I don't know about that," Logan said, as he pulled himself onto the swine and slowly straightened his back. His view became unobstructed as he arose a full head above the rest of the tightly packed crowd.

"Those guys throwing the fish. They're the fishmongers," Matt said. Grace and Rebecca had almost less interest in men throwing large fish than they had in gum stuck to a wall. And that being the case, they were easily pulled toward the smooth sound of the nearby cellist.

Logan watched as a bearded man wearing bright orange waders and a beanie held a king salmon in both hands. He stood in front of a seafood ice display as numerous spectators waited in anticipation, cameras ready. On the other side of the display, another man with an even larger beard and a Seahawks hat stood ready. The man with the salmon then said something—half grunt, half undecipherable spoken word—and sent the fish airborne. The man behind the display caught the king salmon with ease. Logan cheered along with the rest of the crowd as the man then threw it back to the man in waders who worked the fish's mouth with his index finger for a woman recording the scene on her cell phone. The men threw the fish a few more times before the fish was finally wrapped.

A strong hand suddenly rested upon Logan's right shoulder. Logan's smile quickly faded as he looked at the scabbed knuckles.

"You're a dead man."

Logan's good eye widened knowing that the same fist that punched his face now clenched tightly onto his jacket.

13: Pike Place

"Hey, Chet." Logan carefully disembarked the pig. He subtly rubbed the pig's snout with his shirtsleeve.

"Stop that," Chet said, as he yanked Logan away from the statue. Logan reached toward the pig for one more rub. "What are you doing? I said stop that." Chet then pulled Logan into a headlock. "I saw you walking up the stairs back there. Couldn't believe my luck. Neither could the guys."

"The guys?"

"A few of the offensive line." Chet's bicep tightened around Logan's neck as he flexed. "Just over there."

"Neanderthal, Troglodyte, Missing Link. Yep, all accounted for."

"Always with the jokes. We'll see if you're still laughing when I'm done with you." Chet spun Logan around.

"Who's your friend, Logan?" Matt asked.

"What is this, the Lollipop Guild? Beat it." Chet leaned in. "You think that black eye hurt?" He flicked Logan's swollen socket. Chet looked at Matt. "Are you deaf, Munchkin? Turn around and walk away."

"Don't let him take me," Logan said, struggling for air.

"I won't," Matt said.

Chet smiled. "And what do you think the odds are of stopping me?"

"I suppose about the same odds as finding an arrowhead here at Pike Place," Matt said, as he made eye contact with Logan. "Let him have it."

Chet laughed. "And what's that supposed to mean?"

Then Chet yelled as he released Logan and stumbled a few steps holding onto his shoulder. The top half of a long arrowhead stuck prominently out from his t-shirt. Chet grabbed the piece of stone and yanked it from his skin. Matt and Logan were quickly lost in the crowd.

"Don't just stand there," Chet barked. "Get 'em!"

Matt grabbed Grace and Rebecca by the arms. "Time to go!"

"What now?" Grace shouted as the four raced through the crowd, bumping and shoving as they went.

"Ask your son."

"Sorry . . . Excuse me . . . Sorry," Rebecca said with each unintended contact. "Why are we running?" The crowd thinned a little as the four continued their escape past vendors and other street performers.

"Why'd you stab him?" Matt yelled.

"You said, 'let him have it!'"

"I meant 'give it to him.' I figured it's probably worth something."

"There," Logan said, pointing to an overhead neon sign that read, "Lower Floor."

The four stopped. Logan looked back just in time to see Nate, one of Chet's linemen, point at him. "Come on. This way," Matt said, as the four raced down the plain, sloped hallway to the floor below.

"What'd you do?" Rebecca shouted as she shoved Logan in the back.

Logan looked back briefly. "He started it."

"Who are they?" Grace asked.

"Some of the football team."

"What did you do?" Rebecca repeated.

"Alright," Logan said, as he slowed to a stop at the lower floor.

"Why is Chet chasing you?" Rebecca said, as she grabbed him by the shirt.

"I said 'alright.' Geez." Logan broke his sister's grip. He tried unsuccessfully to hold back a smile. "I put a laxative in Chet's Gatorade before last night's game."

"Before last night's game?" Rebecca asked.

"This way," Matt said, as he took the lead down the small hallway of storefronts.

"What was yesterday's game?" Grace asked.

"Parent appreciation night," Rebecca said.

"Since when are you into football?" Logan asked.

"Since . . . it's not weird to know about your school's football team."

"It sort of is for you."

"Which way?" Grace asked, as the four stopped at the intersection of three paths.

"I don't know." Hallways led this way and that, none of them leading to an exit. The shouts of Chet and the others were now on the lower floor—the interconnectedness of the hallways made it impossible to tell from which direction the voices came.

"So what exactly did you do?" Rebecca whispered as she shoved Logan into a small antique store.

"Alright," Logan said, as he straightened his coat. "After Chet beat me up—I think we can all agree on who is the real bad guy here."

"Keep talking," Rebecca said.

"Fine. *After he beat me up*, I cashed in a favor with the team's equipment manager's younger brother. It wasn't difficult to get ahold of Chet's water bottle. The rest is history. Coaches like to tell their players to 'leave it all on the field.' Well, I guarantee Chet did just that."

"Ohh, Looogan?" Chet called out from what seemed like every direction.

"I've heard of people doing some dumb things, but that may be one of the dumbest. He's literally twice the size of you." Matt peered down the hall. "And me."

"Alright, I get it."

"How could you be so careless?"

"I said I get it."

"No, Logan. I don't think you do. I can't protect you from him. Not like this."

"Like that really makes a difference. Even less so after you and Mom split."

Matt looked at Rebecca.

"Logan? Logan? Logan?" Chet called.

"We can't stay here," Matt said. "Come on." Slowly, the four reentered the hallway. Matt approached a corner; he turned and put a finger to his mouth signaling to the others to keep quiet. He peered around the shop's edge. The hall was filled with shoppers, none of whom posed a threat.

"This way."

The four walked to the opening at the end of the corridor. Storefronts lined both sides of the expanse. A large neon sign with a red, downward-pointing finger hung above a descending staircase in the middle of the room.

"We'll make for the first floor," Matt said, as the four emerged from the hallway.

Beyond the stairs, Chet and his gang entered the opening from the opposite hallway. Both parties stopped not more than twenty yards from each other—shoppers filled the space between. Logan looked back. Ryan and Luke, Chet's other linemen, approached from behind.

Both groups looked at each other knowing that it would be a race to the stairs.

"We're running again, aren't we?" Grace said.

"Uh-huh," Matt said.

Logan leaped out in front of everyone toward the stairs. Grace and Rebecca were close behind.

Both groups sprinted toward each other. Like a raging river to a boulder, Chet and his linemen split around the stairs' safety wall. Rebecca and Logan were the first to descend—Grace was close behind. Chet reached out his hand over the wall eager to grab a jacket collar or a fistful of hair. Matt jumped to the floor, sliding just under Chet's reach. He sailed over the top of the first set of stairs down to the midway landing.

Chet's momentum sent him past the mouth of the stairs crashing into Luke. Matt fell down the remaining steps.

"Are you alright?" Grace asked.

"Fine," Matt said, as he limped.

Once again, the four were in a subterranean maze of wooden floors and storefronts. Every turn was neither right nor wrong as they ran through the narrow corridors.

The sounds of the mob now echoed through the halls of the third level.

Rebecca looked around. "There," she said, pointing to an abandoned store. Rebecca ran to the old wooden door and kicked it open. The four entered the room and retreated into the shadows as Chet and two others raced by yelling

obscenities into the air. Rebecca pushed an old desk in front
of the door.

The four took a moment to catch their breath.

Logan walked to a window just in time to see Chet run by
in the opposite direction and stop. "Anything?" Chet yelled.

"Nothing," a voice replied.

"They're down here somewhere. Find them."

Logan moved away from the window toward the others. "I
think we're going to be stuck in here for a while."

"Thanks to you," Rebecca said.

"Thanks to me?"

"Your sister's right," Matt said, as he lowered himself to the
floor to inspect his ankle. "What were you thinking pulling a
stunt like that?"

"I stood up for myself. I thought you'd be . . . I don't
know."

"Proud? How could anyone be proud of that?"

"Matt," Grace said.

"No. He needs to hear this. You think what you did was
right? That your actions were somehow justified?"

"Well . . ."

"They weren't. Your actions have consequences. The only
thing is that this time it affects more than just you."

"I may actually become sick if I hear you give a lecture on
actions and consequence," Rebecca said.

"Tell me I'm wrong." Matt looked at his watch. "Because
that"—Matt pointed toward the hallway—"is not something we
need to be dealing with right now. I thought I raised you better
than that."

"Ha," Rebecca scoffed.

"What?" Matt asked.

"You couldn't raise a toilet seat."

"Watch what you say to me, young lady. I'm still your father. You need to show me respect."

"Show me a father and I'll show you respect."

"Alright, that's enough," Grace said.

Rebecca shook her head. "Forget it."

"Watch what you say to me," Logan said to himself. "Watch what you say to me . . . That's it!"

"What are you talking about?" Rebecca asked.

"Three little words. We won't need to keep running if Mom and Dad are back to normal. Here, give me the poem."

The elixir you seek, is not food nor a drink
Rather three little words, will do more than you think.

"So, what are the three little words?" Rebecca asked.

"I love you," Logan said.

"Excuse me?" Rebecca responded.

"Those are the words: I love you," Logan said.

The four waited for a moment.

"See," Rebecca said. "He can't even bring himself to say it."

"Now hold on. Just because I don't always say it doesn't mean I stopped loving you."

"So just Mom then."

A pound on the door startled the four. "They in there?" Chet yelled from down the hall.

"Thought I heard something," Luke said.

"We need to find a way out of here," Logan said, as he walked past the others toward the back of the room. "Bec, you still have your phone?"

Rebecca opened her flashlight app and illuminated the shadows. She walked toward Logan. "Come on, let's see if there's a back door to this place."

The two navigated around old boxes and furniture toward the back of the store.

"What's that smell?" Logan asked.

"Musty," Rebecca replied. "Probably rot."

Seeing only what her phone illuminated, Rebecca cautiously led the way. The floor creaked unnervingly beneath her feet. Rebecca soon approached an open door. Even the cobwebs looked old as they moved ever so gently by some unknown source of moving air. Rebecca looked back just to make sure the others were still near. Then she turned and ducked below the low-hanging webs and stepped across the threshold.

Rebecca swept the room with her light. Three small rectangular windows stretched atop the far wall. She stood well below their frame, too short to see out. She spotted an old desk and stood on it. With the extra height, she was just able to peer outside. The window was "street level" in every sense of the word; only the shoes of those walking by could be seen.

"Any luck?" Logan asked.

Rebecca slid her hand over the window trying to find a way to open it. "No." Rebecca hopped down. "We need to find another way out." Rebecca scanned the room with her light.

"Can I see your phone for a second?" Logan asked. He approached the windowed wall.

"I told you: those windows don't open."

Logan pointed the light along the lower half of the wall. "It's brick."

"Yeah, so what?"

"Why would there be brick on the bottom half of the bottom floor of a building? And underground no less?" Logan shined the light toward the ceiling. "Unless . . ." Logan stepped away from the wall widening the reach of the light. Matt and Grace did the same with their phone lights. The brick wall ended at the base of the window. "Unless it wasn't the bottom. But the top."

Rebecca stepped back to where the other three stood. The light from the three phones shone upon the brick outline. "The top of what?"

"Remember how I told you that part of downtown was built on top of the old city?" The wooden floor groaned eerily beneath the weight of the group's feet. Rebecca looked down and then at her brother. Logan's crooked smile was the last thing she saw before the floor gave way and the four plummeted into the darkness below.

14: Undertown

Bing Crosby's *White Christmas* played on an antique turntable. The needle glided along the wavy record producing a slightly distorted sound accompanied by the expected clicks and pops of an imperfect vinyl. Rebecca slowly opened her eyes. A single lamp atop a tall dresser illuminated the bedroom in a soft glow. Rebecca tenderly touched her bandaged head. She sat up trying to decide if what she saw was unusual to her or not. All the hallmarks of a typical bedroom were in place—bed, dresser, nightstand—but something seemed off.

Rebecca removed her blanket and stepped to the wooden floor. The needle on the turntable caught causing the record to repeat. Rebecca steadied herself and made for a large antique oval mirror next to a vintage lamp. She looked at her head. She then looked at a framed picture beside the mirror. The men in the picture wore suits and fedoras while the women wore vintage dresses, feathered scarves, and odd-looking face masks.

A man entered the room. "She's awake," he spoke into a walkie-talkie.

"Where am I?" Rebecca asked, as she stumbled away from the door. "Who are you?"

"William. But that's not important. What is important"—the man pointed to Rebecca with an unlit cigarette between his fingers—"is who *you* are."

"Me? I'm nobody."

"Bring her," a voice said through the radio.

William sat on the edge of the dresser. "How many more of you are there?"

"It's just me."

William pulled a pocket watch from his vest and checked the time. "Let's go."

"Where's my backpack?"

"I said, let's go."

Rebecca stepped into the hallway. William flipped his pocket watch closed and slid it back into his vest pocket as he closed the door behind them. The occasional working light bulb showed cracked plaster and torn wallpaper. Rebecca felt the floorboards bow beneath the disintegrating carpet with every step. The two stopped in front of an elevator door. William pushed the "down" button and the doors parted.

"Are you kidding? That looks like a deathtrap. When was the last time this thing was serviced?"

"In."

Rebecca entered. William stepped in and pressed a button with no number. The doors closed. The light dimmed as the elevator lowered. William lit his cigarette with a Zippo lighter.

"You can't smoke in elevators."

William glanced at Rebecca and grinned. "Says who?"

"Uh, everyone," Rebecca said, as she waved the air and stepped away from the growing cloud. "You must live under a rock."

"More than you know, kid." William took a long drag, leaned coolly against the elevator wall and slid his thumb into his pants pocket. Rebecca noticed for the first time that

William was missing most of his right middle finger. Then she saw a holstered gun hanging under William's arm.

William opened his coat with his four-fingered hand exposing the gun more clearly. "You want to hold it?"

Rebecca looked away.

The elevator doors opened to an empty lobby. The marble floors and detailed architecture revealed that the building was once a valued place of business. Now, however, deterioration was its hallmark. At the far end of the lobby, a man wearing a tattered bellhop uniform waited in front of a glass door.

"Sir," the young bellhop said, as he handed William and Rebecca face masks.

"What's this for?" Rebecca asked.

William took another long drag from his cigarette and then placed the mask over his face.

"Really?"

"Up to you," William said, as he ushered Rebecca into an enclosed space between the building and the outside world. William looked back to ensure that the bellhop securely closed the inner door. The bellhop gave a thumbs-up. Rebecca looked through the outer glass door. A thick yellow fog waited outside. Rebecca quickly placed the mask over her face and tightened the straps.

William opened the door and the two exited the building. Rebecca looked back and saw the yellow smoke sucked from the room. Outside, young people occupied the smoggy street; some wore masks, most simply wore scarves and goggles. Rebecca looked back to the building they had just exited—half laid in ruins, the other half in disrepair. She scanned the block only to find much of the same. Decay and ruin lined both sides of the street as a dilapidated city faded into a thick haze.

William and Rebecca walked to a 1937 Buick Limited parked curbside. A teenager awaiting their arrival opened the rear door. Inside, William held up a finger telling Rebecca to wait before removing her mask. The teenager got in and started the engine. William then pushed a silver button on the ceiling. Within moments, the air inside the car cleared. William removed his mask. Rebecca did the same.

"What is this place? Why is everything so . . . postapocalyptic?" Rebecca asked, as she looked out the window.

"Have you ever been told that it's dangerous to run a car in a closed garage?"

"Of course."

William pointed to the glass sunroof. Through the haze, Rebecca saw that this city had a ceiling.

"Down here, clean air is a luxury."

"Down here?"

William smiled as he lit another cigarette. "You ask a lot of questions." He took a drag and blew it into the ceiling vent. "If I were you, I'd focus on coming up with a few answers."

The Buick snaked its way through what resembled a downtown district. Like a song on replay, the scene changed yet remained the same with each turn: a handful of people wearing face masks and deteriorating buildings that faded into a dirty fog. The car passed a dilapidated sign that read, "Welcome to Beautiful Downtown Seattle." The words "Downtown Seattle" were scratched out and replaced with "Undertown."

"This is way more than thirty blocks," Rebecca said to herself as the car summited a small hill and started down toward a large building positioned at the bottom of a massive wall.

"What is that?" Rebecca asked.

"The seawall."

The wall disappeared into the haze in both directions leaving only what appeared to be a barrier that continued without end.

The vehicle pulled up to a crowd gathered outside the three-story structure—a structure reminiscent of Petra, protruding directly from the wall. Through the haze, Rebecca saw an empty balcony and what appeared to be a king's throne made of twisted metal and other junkyard materials. A dead, twenty-foot Christmas tree stood in front of the building.

"What are they all waiting for?"

"The tree lighting," William said with a smile. He looked at his watch. "Come on. The Orator will be out soon."

"The who?"

William placed his mask over his face. Rebecca did the same. The door was opened and the two exited behind the gathering. Scarves and handkerchiefs were wrapped and held to the noses and mouths of those listening. Rebecca looked at the backs of young people and the seawall as she followed behind William to a better vantage point.

Whistling overtook the chatter of the congregation. The mass quieted as the strange tune continued over the loudspeaker. An eruption of cheers echoed through the streets as a masked man emerged onto the balcony. Arms stretched through the sleeves of a trench coat, the Orator raised his ringed fingers past a worn top hat and waved to the mass below. He threw carbon filter masks from the balcony like candy. Those below fought over the gifts like dogs fighting over dinner scraps.

The Orator sat. The cheers quieted. Below, on street level, a young man stood handcuffed atop one of two circular platforms placed at the center of a roundabout. Beside each of the makeshift stages, remains of semitrucks sat. And from each of the truck's exhaust stacks, hoses ran beneath each of the platforms.

When Rebecca stopped moving, the man's words became clear as they overpowered the rhythmic sounds of her masked breath.

"My children," the Orator said. The crowd erupted in cheers again. "My children. How I love to hear your voices." The Orator quieted the crowd. "Being that we are so close to Christmas, it is with pleasure that I have the opportunity to give you a most valuable gift—the gift of discipline. Discipline is nothing more than an extension of love. And with the display of discipline that you witness today, I'm confident that there will be no question as to the depths of my love for you all." The crowd cheered.

"Even though the work may be difficult and the rules seemingly harsh, it's important—no, vital—to remember that life in Undertown is much better than a life above. They gave you rejection; I give you acceptance. They gave you chaos; I give you order. They gave you fear; I give you hope. They gave you a city of strangers; I give you a community of family. At times it may be difficult in Undertown. Believe me, I understand. But never forget that it is far better down here than the oppressive life you lived above!"

The crowd of young people cheered through their scarves and masks. When the assembly settled down, the Orator continued: "Family. That's all we have, isn't it? When it all comes down to it, who else do we have in this world besides family? Family is sacred. Family doesn't turn its back on each other. We expect that kind of treatment from them"—the Orator pointed skyward—"up there. But down here, we expect more from each other. We *need* to expect more from each other. We *deserve* more from each other. Otherwise, how are we any different from the takers above? They take. And they take. And they take.

"They brought you into this world, and instead of helping you succeed, they gave you away—offered you a broken system. They took from you the life you should've had. They take the gift of responsibility for granted. I do not. They take the gift of trust for granted. I do not. They take the gift of family for granted. I certainly do not."

The Orator took a moment as if deep in thought. "So when one of our own . . . a member of the family, behaves as those above, my hand is forced. It hurts like absolutely nothing else this cruel world can muster—to be betrayed by family. But I assure you, it hurts me far worse to dispense the ugly side of love. Which brings us, in part, to why we're gathered here today."

The Orator now addressed the young man in handcuffs. "Please state your name."

The young man stood proudly. "Simon."

"Simon. You have been charged with theft, rebellion, insubordination, and betrayal of order. How do you plead?"

"Free."

"Free. Of course you do. Which is ironic, really. You've been sneaking up and working, haven't you? How quickly you run back to the bonds that imprison you. I don't understand. Why work for them when you can . . ."

"Steal from them? Like all of you?"

"You can't steal what you're owed."

"And who says anyone up there owes me anything?"

"They do." The Orator looked to the crowd. "They owe us all. They have made you weak. They have made you poor. You are broken because of them and there's nothing you can do about it except live every day of your life righting their wrongs."

The Orator began to walk the balcony as if teaching a classroom full of students. "Undertown works when we take back what's ours, and then support the family. We all need to give our fair share. To be quite honest, I could've almost shown mercy had you not decided to take from your family. Tell me, what did you hope to do with the little you were saving? Better yourself? Improve your situation? Live the dream?" The crowd laughed. "Listen to me when I say—all of you, listen to me when I say—the best this life has to offer you is through me." The Orator looked at Simon. "You shouldn't have taken from me. You shouldn't have taken from your family."

"I recognize the provisions provided by Undertown. And as such, I gave accordingly."

"You took what's ours. Expanded territory, the new air filtration system, and one and a half meals a day—these luxuries aren't free."

"Is that why you wear that mask? Because the air is so clean?" Simon turned to the crowd. "How many more will you bury before your eyes are opened to his lies?" Simon looked back to the Orator and pointed to the building. "You live in there, where food is plenty and the air is clean while we starve and suffocate. How do you justify that?"

"A very good question—one that I will answer honestly. When an airplane loses cabin pressure and the oxygen masks are released from the ceiling, passengers are instructed to place the mask over their own face before helping even a child seated in the next seat over. 'Wait,' you may be saying, 'Isn't that selfish? Shouldn't you make sure that the child has a mask first?' At first glance, it may appear to be selfish, but I assure you that it isn't. And here's why: should you fail to place the mask over your own face in a timely manner, you and the child will be rendered unconscious, and then you both are in trouble. However, if you secure your mask first, you can then save the child."

"Your mask has been securely fastened for years and yet you still deny help to the child in the seat next to you."

A subtle commotion among the crowd began to rise.

"Not true. That is simply not true. The filtration system is working. But you know what? Let's be real for a second. Let's get into it. Family meeting. Right now. I've heard that there has been some talk among you regarding pollution: that it's worsening; that my staff and I should reduce our use of vehicles. I assure you, if we could, we certainly would. But we simply can't."

The Orator sat. "As a leader, it's important for my team and me to have access to transportation. Imagine if, up there, the police and fire department had to respond to calls without vehicles. They are a necessity up there and a necessity here as well. But the rumors of increased pollution, they're just that: rumors. There is no indication of the air worsening down here. Period."

The Orator stood. "But 'talk is cheap,' you might say. And you know what? Talk *is* cheap. You know what isn't cheap? Facts. And at no extra expense to you, facts are exactly what I give to you. Because your Orator cares about the things you care about, I, along with my development and research team, looked into this very matter after the filtration system was put in place. After extensive analysis, I have seen the data results; pollution levels have not risen. In fact, pollution is on the decline."

The crowd cheered again. Above the shouts, claps, and whistles, the Orator shouted, "That's not me. That's science!"

Simon shook his head.

The Orator quieted the group. "Is the air perfect? Well, even those above can't boast of zero pollution. But is it becoming more breathable every day?" The Orator removed the mask from his face to the gasps of those below. "You tell me."

The crowd roared. The Orator threw the mask to the side and waved with both hands. "You tell me!"

The mass quieted and the Orator sat on his throne. "Now back to the matter at hand. Simon, I ask you again: how do you plead?"

"I don't plead to you for anything anymore. You say to blame those above, but I refuse. I'm not a product of my past." Simon turned to the crowd. "And neither are you! My past is a part of my story, and your past is a part of yours. But it ends there! I own my story; my story doesn't own me." Simon looked to the balcony. "My past doesn't dictate my future."

"It does today." The Orator waved his hand and a guard pulled a lever causing Simon to drop inside the platform through a trapdoor. The guard then walked to the cab of the semitruck.

"You have been found guilty as charged. Your sentence: an hour in the box." The pounding of Simon's fists echoed among the crowd. "Too much pollution you say? You ain't seen anything yet." The Orator's coat fanned out as he turned and raised his arms. "Now who's ready to get this tree lighting underway?" The crowd yelled and cheered.

With another wave of the Orator's hand, the guard started the engine. Simon made for the small window placed opposite the exhaust; his face squeezed as far outside the box as the barred window allowed. Rebecca watched as a thick black smoke enveloped Simon's face and the opening.

The guard revved the engine. The bottom half of the dying tree suddenly lit with Christmas lights. The crowd cheered. The Orator presented the half-illuminated tree like a model on *The Price is Right*. "Merry Christmas!" The crowd cheered louder. "Merry Christmas!"

The Orator quieted the crowd. "Poor Simon. He looks exhausted." The crowd laughed. "Bring the next defendant." A young man was brought to the middle platform. "Please state your name."

Rebecca looked past the sea of hats and masks as best she could. She moved forward for a better view.

"Come on now, don't be shy," the Orator said, as he resumed his place on the throne of junk and metal. "State your name."

The young man stood timidly. "L–Logan. Logan's my name."

15: Change of Plans

Matt woke suddenly. Attached to his face was a kind of breathing apparatus. He wiped a thin layer of grime from the goggles placed over his eyes. A tube connected his mask to a small glass jar atop a nearby table. Inside the jar, a small tree seedling grew. He sat upright on a rickety cot. A single hanging bulb gently swayed from side to side illuminating the room just enough for Matt to see Grace lying unconscious on a cot beside him, her mask connected to her own glass encasement.

"Good, you're awake. We don't have much time."

Startled, Matt turned and saw a girl, no older than fifteen, standing in the doorway. Between the low light and the scarf wrapped around her face, the voice came from a mostly hidden source.

"Who are you?"

"Emily. And like I said, we don't have much time."

"What is this? What am I attached to?"

"Your lungs aren't used to the pollution, so I hooked you up with some clean air. Literally." Emily pulled a book from a sparse shelf and threw it into a leather messenger bag. "Can't believe I almost forgot Orwell."

Matt removed the mask from his face. Emily tossed him an old scarf, which he used to cover his face. A small pile of papers in the corner of the room caught Matt's attention. "Those flyers." Matt pointed. "Where have I seen those before?"

"Everywhere, hopefully. We've spent a great deal of time getting the word out."

Matt picked one up from the pile. "Getting the word out for what?"

"The end of Undertown."

"What?"

"Like I said, there's not much time. We have to leave."

"I'm not leaving without Grace." Matt looked at Grace and then around the room. "Where are the others? There were two others with us."

"So many questions. Look, when I found you, I thought you were dead. You and her—"

"Grace."

"Yeah. Grace. Whatever. You two were on the third floor of what used to be an old hotel. The other two fell farther; down through to the second and first floors. Everything's falling apart down here. I'm sorry, but your friends were found and taken by William."

"William?"

"The Orator's right-hand man."

"Who's the Orator?"

"Look, there's like an entire backstory down here—years and years of it—and unfortunately I don't have time to explain all the important names and dates. The only thing that you need to know is that in less than twenty minutes there's going to be an event."

"Event? What kind of an event?"

Emily took a breath. "In less than twenty minutes, a vessel will strike the seawall and flood the city."

"No way."

"Don't believe me? Stick around and find out for yourself."
Emily found another item worth keeping. She stuffed it, too, in
her messenger bag and slung it over her shoulder.

"Well, call it off."

"You fell into a revolution, my friend. Certain things
were set into motion long ago—things that can't simply be
'called off.'"

"There are still people down there."

"Trust me, at this point it's by choice."

"Not for my children."

"You must've hit your head harder than I thought. Look, I
wasn't going to bother with any of you—too much of a risk—
but I know that's not what my brother would've done. So,
despite my better judgment, I brought you here. But you're
awake now, so my job is done."

"Brother? Where's he?"

"Topside. Waiting for me." Emily was overtaken by a fit of
coughing. "He's been working a real job. Saving money. Sort
of frowned upon down here." Emily composed herself. "Gotta
get out of here for good, you know? Before it kills me. And you
need to leave too."

Matt didn't move.

Emily sighed. "You're not leaving, are you?"

"Not without everyone I came with."

"Fine. Your watch."

"What about it?"

Emily looked at her own watch. "You have exactly eigh-
teen minutes and nine seconds before this place is underwater."
Matt synchronized his watch with Emily's. Emily looked at
Matt and pointed to Grace. "Wake her. Get topside."

Matt went to Grace and gently nudged her shoulder.
"Grace, you need to wake up."

"Good luck to you," Emily said, as she made for the door. Just then, her phone buzzed, stopping her cold in the doorway. Emily sighed. "Well, this changes things."

"What does?"

"Simon's been arrested."

"Who's Simon?"

Emily went to Grace and slapped her in the face. Grace suddenly woke—eyes wide. She grabbed at her mask and tore it from her face. She coughed and choked. "Where are the kids?"

16: Logan on Trial

The Orator stood. "I don't know you, Logan." The Orator turned to one of his aides. "Why don't I know him?" He turned again to Logan. "Why don't I know you?"

Logan didn't respond.

"My apologies. I try to make it a point to meet all the new residents of Undertown—especially during these trying and mutinous times. Please forgive the setting for our introduction. It really is no way to get to know one another." The Orator crossed his legs. "How long has Undertown been your home?"

Logan looked around.

"Come now, don't be shy."

"This . . ." Logan coughed and cleared his throat. "This isn't my home."

"And where is your home?"

Logan thought for a moment.

"Or to put it another way: in six months, where will home be?"

"I'm not entirely sure, I guess."

"And where are your parents?"

"At this moment?"

"That's all we have."

"I'm not sure."

"I see. It's all becoming clear to me now. Up there can be confusing. They've obviously done a number on you already."

The Orator addressed the crowd. "When did 'stability' become so foreign? They move you from house to house, apartment to apartment, duplex to duplex. Somewhere along the way, you became the ragdoll in their selfish game of pass the offspring. But you can relax. Take a deep breath because you're home now."

The crowd cheered.

"That being said, like most homes, this one has rules. Without rules, there is chaos; and without punishment, there's no reason for rules. It gives me no pleasure to do this—especially since we just met. Awkward." The Orator stood. "Logan. You have been charged with distribution of propaganda against Undertown. How do you plead?"

"How do I plead?"

"Yes, yes. This is the part where you say 'guilty' or 'not guilty.'"

"And if I say 'guilty'?"

"Then you'll be punished for your crime."

Logan looked to the black smoke still spewing from Simon's box. "Not guilty," Logan said quickly. "Definitely not guilty."

"I want to believe you. I really do. It's just that . . . well, it's just that you *are* guilty." The Orator held a flyer in his hand. "You were in possession of this."

"That? Some kid shoved it in my pocket back at Pike Place."

"Kid? What kid? Speak up now; who was it?"

"I don't know."

"You're trying to protect someone. I'd consider your own well-being at the moment if I were you."

"I don't know."

"Tell me then, what does the flyer mean?"

"How do you know it's propaganda if you don't know what it means?"

"Don't"—the Orator composed himself—"Don't get smart with me. Obviously it is and you're clearly covering for someone, so to that I say 'very well.' You have been found guilty as charged. Your sentence: an hour in the box." The Orator waved his hand and a guard pulled a lever causing Logan to drop down inside the platform. The guard then walked to the other side of the enclosure where another truck sat. The Orator looked to the crowd. "Who's ready to light the rest of the tree?"

The crowd cheered.

The Orator waved his hand signaling the guard to start the engine.

"Wait!" a voice yelled out. "I gave it to him. The flyer is mine."

The crowd parted. Rebecca stood, mask in hand.

The Orator stopped the sentencing and pointed to Rebecca. "Bring her to me."

17: Rescuers Down Undertown

Emily peered around the corner of a brick building. "Come on." Matt and Grace followed close behind. The Orator's voice echoed through the empty streets as speakers transmitted the tree lighting ceremony to all of Undertown. "Now that we're out in the open, just act natural and keep your face covered."

"Where are we going?" Grace asked.

"The Orator's building. That's where they most likely took Logan and Rebecca. That's where they have my brother. Each will be tried and convicted."

Matt looked around. "Where is everyone? It's like a ghost town down here."

"Same place."

"Why?"

"To watch my brother suffer."

"And Rebecca and Logan?"

"They're a bonus." They'll put them in a box and fill it with exhaust."

"But that'll kill them."

"Sort of the point."

"How long can someone last in there?"

"Not long. But they could give them each a year in the box and it wouldn't much matter because"—Emily looked at her watch—"in just under fourteen minutes, this'll all be underwater."

"So what's the plan?" Grace asked, as the three passed an old fence bordering a dirt field.

Emily stopped. The three looked out across the lot. Dozens of headstones marked the burial site of Undertown's dead— some made of stone, most made of wood or metal. Emily walked to the middle of the cemetery and knelt before a small metal cross; the word "Joey" was scratched in the rusted cruci- fix. Matt and Grace noticed that the date of death was just over a month ago. Emily unwrapped an infinity bracelet from her wrist and twisted it around the crossbeam.

"Joey was like a little brother to us. He was alone down here when he arrived, so we looked after him. He made us all get these bracelets. Simon doesn't wear any kind of jewelry, a little too macho for that, but he wore the bracelet. I don't think Joey ever took his off." Emily's smile turned cold. "His lungs were just too young, too weak, you know? A child like him deserves better than this. They all do." Emily kissed the cross. "No more death." She then pulled a pipe from a neighboring makeshift cross. "Come on."

The three exited the field and were soon back on broken asphalt. Emily stopped in the middle of the smoggy road. She looked up and down the street. *Come on,* she said to herself. *I know you must be around here somewhere.* She grabbed a flare from her messenger bag and fired it up.

Matt looked at his watch. "What are you doing?"

"There," Emily said, as a pair of headlights rounded the corner a block away. "One of the Orator's Mind Guards." A pickup truck approached and stopped. A young, masked patrol officer stepped out and approached.

"Everything alright? Why aren't you at the ceremony?"

"Oh, we were on our way. Is it true? Did they really catch Simon?"

"Yeah, the idiot got himself another audience with the Orator. It's not going to end well this time."

"Finally. It's about time he gets what he has coming to him."

"What's with the flare?"

"Wanted to get your attention." Emily walked close to the officer. "We were busy removing those propaganda flyers from sector L." Emily held up a fistful of crumpled papers. "Doubt we'll be finding many more after Simon's sentencing."

"Suppose not."

"Do you think that you could give us a ride to the rally? We really don't want to miss it."

"I'm sure you don't. But I'm not covering that sector."

"Figured as much; seeing that we're talking way out here." Emily put her hands on the officer's shoulders and straightened his coat. "Are you sure you can't just give us a quick lift there?"

"And what's in it for me?"

"Well, you know, May Day is just around the corner. Maybe we could spend the day rioting through the streets together."

"May Day's like my Christmas. I've already started planning for it."

"Me too!" The two moved a little closer. "I'll bring the rocks."

"I'll bring the Molotov cocktails." The officer looked behind him toward the ceremony and then back at Emily. "Alright, I'll give you a lift." The officer looked at Matt and Grace again. "Do they need to come too?"

"Yes. But maybe after your shift, we could meet up and talk about the evils of capitalism and hygiene."

"Alright, I'll drop you a block away. After the rally, meet me back here. I've been working on a new protest chant if you'd like to hear."

"I'll bet it rhymes and everything."

"It does. Sort of."

"I think this may be the start of something special."

The officer looked at Grace and Matt. "You two in the back."

The officer got in and turned the ignition. The engine chugged a little but failed to start. The patrol officer let out a nervous laugh and tried again.

"Everything alright?" Matt asked through the bed window.

"It's fine. Shut up. Sit down." The officer said something like a prayer under his breath before attempting again. He turned the key and the engine fired. The truck rumbled and shook as it idled. The young man turned to Emily. "Shall we, m'lady?"

The uneven pavement felt like train tracks as the truck rumbled its way through the city toward the trial. The conversation between the Orator and Simon boomed through each district as every street corner was outfitted with a large speaker.

The officer looked over at Emily. "Wanna shift?"

"I'm alright, thanks."

"Suit yourself." The officer shifted into fourth gear never looking away from Emily.

"How about you just keep your eyes on the street, slick."

"I grew up on these streets. I could drive them with my eyes closed."

"Well, you may want to open them then."

"Whoa!" The officer slammed on the brakes causing the truck to skid to a stop just behind the last row of spectators.

About one hundred yards away, the bottom half of the Christmas tree was suddenly lit.

"Looks like you're too late."

Emily opened her door. The cheers from the crowd drowned out the noise of the distant generator. Emily stepped onto the truck seat and then onto the roof of the cab.

"Hey! What the . . . ?" the officer said.

Emily stood looking over the mass of people in the square. She took a small pair of binoculars from her bag and panned the crowd. She first spotted the box with exhaust spewing from it. She looked to the right and saw Logan. She then panned the crowd until she spotted William holding a girl not far from the roundabout.

Emily hopped down onto the truck's bed. "They're all there. This is going to work." She took the pipe from her satchel. "Get ready."

"What are you going to do?"

Emily didn't respond. She jumped to the ground and began walking alongside the truck toward the driver's side door. She gripped the pipe tightly in her hand and raised it up.

"Wait!" a voice called out from somewhere in the crowd.

Emily stopped just shy of the window.

"I gave it to him. The flyer is mine," Rebecca said.

The next voice came over the loudspeaker.

"Bring her to me."

Emily lowered the pipe. "Crap." She looked at her watch. "This is going to be close." She stepped back toward Grace and Matt. "If I don't make it out with Rebecca, promise me that you'll save Simon."

"We can't leave without Rebecca."

"Look, if I can't save her . . . just promise me you'll get Simon out of here. Now go and hide."

Before Matt could answer again, Emily was already back at the driver's side window. She lowered her scarf and goggles.

The officer struggled to get out of the truck. "Hold it right there! Don't move!"

"Yeah, yeah. Simon's sister. Mutineer. Conspirator. Revolutionist. Writer of unapproved literature. Blah, blah, blah. Here, let me get that for you." Emily opened the truck door. "Take me to your leader. I'm ready to answer for my transgressions against Undertown."

The officer grabbed Emily. He kicked the back of her knee forcing her to the ground. Emily fell into the officer on her way down. "Get off me. Hands behind your head." The officer promptly zip-tied Emily's wrists. He then stood Emily to her feet and proceeded through the crowd.

"Does this mean I won't get to hear that chant of yours?"

"You're going to get me clean air for a month. Move."

Matt and Grace emerged from behind a nearby dumpster as Emily and the officer made their way toward the Orator. Once the mass of people had fully engulfed the two, Matt returned to the truck. Near the driver's side door, on the ground by the front wheel, lay a set of keys.

Matt took the keys in his hands. "She's good."

18: Prisoners

The sea of people parted as William forced Rebecca toward the Orator's building.

The Orator turned and entered the building. As soon as the door closed, he doubled over and let out a string of violent coughs and dry heaves. The Orator's aides assisted him to his office where a large oxygen tank sat ready for use. The Orator twisted the valve open and breathed through the connected plastic mask.

"The things I do for this town."

William shoved Rebecca into a revolving door. Within seconds, Rebecca's long hair reached for the ceiling as the yellow fog was quickly sucked from the enclosure. William held his fedora as the same purification process was enacted upon his entry. He removed his mask and promptly placed an unlit cigarette in his mouth.

"Wow," Rebecca said, as she stepped out of the rotating door and into the lobby.

Half foyer, half wooded park, trees and other vegetation filled the three-story vaulted ceiling. Two weeping willows positioned on opposite sides of the room lightly swayed in the shadows of numerous towering pines and oaks. Crawling vines stretched across what remained of the lobby's front counter and the wall behind it. A group of butterflies fluttered past Rebecca's face; she tracked their movement until they led her eyes toward a large room at the back of the building.

"Watch your step," William said, as he traversed the twisted root system that snaked throughout the marble floor like a school of tangled leviathans. The two navigated their way to the oversized office located on the opposite side of a massive glass wall. Inside, the Orator stood, hands clasped behind his back, looking out to the lobby.

"From each according to his abilities, to each according to his needs." The Orator turned to face Rebecca. "Tell me. What did you see?"

Rebecca stammered, intimidated by the moment and a little confused by the question. "What . . . what did I see?" Rebecca looked around.

"Out there," the Orator replied pointing across the lobby, toward the yellow haze.

Rebecca thought for a moment.

"Good heavens, girl. The question was a means to an end, and quite frankly I don't see one in sight. So allow me to ask the more important question: do you know what I see?"

Rebecca shook her head.

"I see need. I also see ability. And when those two become out of sync, I see a problem. The young man in that box has ability, but he has yet to grasp the concept of need."

"And the box?"

"His education." The Orator smiled at Rebecca and walked to a desk on the opposite side of the room. Behind the desk, toward the top of a vaulted ceiling, a large window gave a view of an angry sea. Rebecca's eye caught a small wooden horse— one of few items on the desk.

"The Trojan Horse." The Orator touched the small statue and a spring-loaded blade shot out from its base. "A reminder of societal fragility and the importance of vigilance." The blade retracted.

The Orator reached over and turned a knob, which released a gas into the air. "Don't worry; it's just oxygen. Pure." The Orator took a deep breath. He then set a small bottle of water on the table and twisted the cap open. "Thirsty?"

Rebecca shook her head.

The Orator took a drink and set it back on the table. "We exist down here because everyone is committed to the cause, and they're willing to give up everything for it." The Orator leaned back in his chair. "Either you've come here to escape trouble, or you've come here to bring it."

The Orator placed the flyer on the table. A slight breeze from the oxygen lifted an edge of the paper. The Orator weighted the flyer with the wooden horse. "What does it mean?"

"Let Logan and me go and I'll tell you."

William let out a laugh as he retrieved his lighter from his pocket.

"Don't even think about lighting that in here," the Orator said. "Everything in here is saturated with oxygen. One spark and you'd light up like a Christmas tree."

"Just habit."

The Orator turned the oxygen valve closed and looked at Rebecca. "No. That won't be possible. Punishment is demanded for your crime. Besides, speaking of Christmas trees, ours is only half-illuminated. I can't disappoint the children. Tell me what the flyer means and I'll consider reducing your punishment."

Rebecca looked at the flyer. It made absolutely no sense to her; she couldn't imagine how it could make sense to anyone. The hieroglyphic-like characters were childlike—similar only to that of a nursery wall vandalized by a toddler.

"Either that, or we can light the tree right now."

Rebecca thought, trying to come up with an answer.

"Nothing?" The Orator approached Rebecca and stood close enough for her to smell his words. "You will be punished. You both will." The Orator looked at William. "Make the call. Light the tree."

Just then, a young person was ushered into the lobby at gunpoint. The Orator stood and walked to the window. William followed.

The Orator spoke into his walkie-talkie. "Remove the scarf, hood, and goggles."

Rebecca quietly made her way unnoticed to the oxygen valves.

The guard removed the hood and scarf from his captive.

Rebecca opened every valve. The odorless, tasteless gas began filling the room.

"It was just a matter of time," the Orator said. He turned to William. "Bring her in here."

William walked to a nearby cabinet. He opened one of the small doors and set his lighter down in place of a bottle of liquid and a rag. He then made one for Emily.

"How's your hand?" Emily asked, as William approached. William dumped the contents of the bottle into the rag as he approached. "Wait, what's that?"

"Not taking any chances this time."

"Wait. Hold on just a second." Emily struggled to free herself. The rag in William's four-fingered hand drew closer to her face. "No. Hold on. Wait, wait, wait. You're not supposed to knock me out."

The guard grabbed Emily by the hair and held her head still. William put the rag to Emily's face. "Breathe."

～☙～

Logan sat in the encasement. He stared up toward the barred window—the cell's only source of light. A small rock hit him on the head. Logan rubbed his forehead. He took the object in his hand and studied it for a moment. He stood, walked toward the small window, took the metal bars in his hands, and pulled his face toward the opening.

"You there, kid?"

"Yeah. Yeah, I'm here."

"That was charcoal."

"Charcoal?"

Simon gave a weary smile as his hands lay lifelessly between the bars. Exhaust from the semi still ran thick, though no longer in a blinding black smoke. "First time to Undertown?"

"Yeah."

"Are you enjoying your stay?"

"No, not really."

Simon laughed and coughed. "The charcoal. It's a natural filter. Most down here carry it. You put it between a scarf or piece of cloth."

Logan tore a piece of his shirt and made a makeshift face scarf; he secured the chunk of charcoal between the two layers of cloth by his mouth. "What is this place?"

"Have you ever heard the phrase, 'out of sight, out of mind'?"

"Sure."

"If you could locate that phrase on a map, it'd be Undertown."

"Where are all the adults?"

"One of the few adults down here just dropped you in that box. There's a handful more; they work for the Orator. They enforce his laws in exchange to live in that building over there. All other adults, well, they're above—up there—living their busy lives, secretly grateful a place like this exists; even if they don't know that it does."

"Is it true what you said? Do kids down here really die?"

Simon was quiet for a moment. "Yeah."

"From what?"

"You feel that burning sensation in your throat? The constant need to cough? You've been down here, what, a few hours?"

"I think so."

"Pollution. It's already wreaking havoc on your system. You can't burn fuel in an enclosed environment and not expect there to be some sort of negative consequence."

"Why doesn't anyone leave?"

"That, kid, is a complicated answer."

"What do you mean?"

"Well, on the first level, there are those who don't want to leave. Undertown gives them some resemblance of security. They want someone to tell them what to do and how to live their lives. Also, they've bought into the lie that they're owed something—that negative life circumstances somehow justify a life of taking what's not theirs. It's bad enough that they steal, but then they give it all to the Orator believing that he'll take care of them—that he has their best interests in mind. They trust him more than they trust themselves."

"On the second level, are those who want to leave but feel they can't. They've helped create and sustain a flawed system that now controls them."

"Controls them how?"

"Fear, mostly. Some are just simply lazy—happy to let someone else do all the work for them—but for the most part they're afraid."

"Afraid of what?"

"Afraid of taking a chance. They've relied on the Orator for so long that they've lost sight of their own abilities." Simon began coughing.

"You alright?"

"Never better, kid. You've heard of elderly couples—couples who are married for sixty or seventy years—that die within a few minutes of each other?"

"No."

"Well, it's a thing. It happens. An otherwise healthy individual passes away shortly after the loss of a loved one."

"Why?"

"Why do you think?"

"I don't know. Loneliness?"

"That's part of it. But loneliness, in and of itself, isn't lethal. They choose to die. They decide they don't want to live life on earth without the one they love. It's ultimately a choice. The same is true with the will to live. Some people have it. Like Aaron Rolston. The guy survived by cutting his arm off to free himself after being pinned by a rock in that Utah canyon. And then there's Beck Weathers who survived a night exposed on Mt. Everest. They both looked death in the face and said, 'not today.' So if people can will themselves to live and die, they can certainly will themselves to believe they are somehow flawed, or less than capable."

"So why doesn't someone do something about it?"

"They did."

"And?"

"Some listened. Most were unable to hear past the lies and propaganda spoken by the Orator. Many chose to stay." Simon leaned his forehead against the bars. "You know something's wrong when people stop questioning death." Simon sighed. "The views of these young people. But perhaps I expect too much from them; they are children after all."

"So what happens next?"

"What happens next is that a large boat is going to crash through that big wall over there and flood Undertown."

"Could you just run that last part by me again?"

"When the system is killing people, when the system kills your little brother, it's time to remove the system."

"So what, now you're going to make everyone pay?"

"You don't punish people for being afraid. But if you could remove the source of that fear, would you?"

"At this moment? No."

"You're just saying that because you're stuck in a box that's directly in the flood path."

"Uh, yeah. Pretty much. Aren't you just replacing one fear for another? Sending them out to a world where they may not be prepared to live?"

"Think of it like the mother eagle pushing her young out of the nest. Those who have decided to stay down here, in this, don't realize they have wings. They don't know that they're more than capable. But they will."

"And what about us?"

"Well, the good news is that the event should take place in three stages, so that buys us a little time."

"Stages?"

"First, the vessel will impact outside the Orator's office filling it with water. Then the water will break through to the building's foyer. The glass walls of the building are reinforced, but will eventually give way. An alarm will sound and those out in the street will have enough time to make it topside before the third and final stage."

"And the bad news?"

"Well, we're not exactly out in the street, are we?"

"How much time do we have?"

19: Flooded

Emily slowly returned to consciousness, awakened by the alarm on her watch.

"Turn that off," the Orator said.

William went to Emily's tied hands and silenced the alarm. Emily sat captive on a wooden chair opposite the Orator facing the seawall. She looked at the window. A crack of lightning outlined thrashing waves as the winter storm raged.

"You and your brother have been a thorn in my side for some time now. Why do you insist on spreading your lies to these young ones? Filling their heads with false hopes and expectations when they know, first hand, how unforgiving the world up there really is?"

Emily turned to Rebecca who stood just to her right. "This is important. How long was my watch alarm going off?"

"Do not disrespect me in my own office. I asked you a question."

Emily kept her eyes on Rebecca.

"It just started before you woke."

Emily twisted her bound wrists.

"Whatever it was that you were waiting for, you missed it," the Orator said, as he turned Emily's satchel upside-down. Dozens of papers fluttered to the floor. "I told you what would happen if you were ever caught again. You will not influence these young minds anymore." The Orator held his hands behind his back. "You have been found guilty as charged."

"And what's my charge?"

"Oh, does it really matter? And since the two boxes are currently occupied, we'll just execute your punishment right here and now."

William wheeled a small gas-powered generator beside Emily. Connected to the exhaust was a five-foot rubber tube with an attached mask.

William secured the mask to Emily's face. "And what of the tree outside, sir?"

"What about it?"

"The kids are all gathered, but half the tree is still dark."

The Orator snapped his fingers. "I almost forgot. Well, go on and light the rest. It is Christmas after all."

William retrieved his walkie-talkie from his desk and gave the approval.

Rebecca begged him to stop until the faint sound of an engine and cheers could be heard from outside.

William walked to the generator beside Rebecca and gripped the pull cord in his hand. "Now for the star."

"I will not be rebelled against," the Orator said. He nodded at William. William pulled the cord. Nothing. William pulled the cord again. Still nothing. Emily twisted her wrists all the more knowing that the generator would eventually fire.

William adjusted a small knob and a lever on the machine. "There, that should do it." He gripped the pull cord once more.

"Don't do it," Rebecca said, holding out a flame burning from William's lighter.

"And what exactly do you think you're going to do with that?" William looked at the Orator and then at Rebecca. He smiled as he took hold of the cord.

The Orator looked at the open oxygen tanks and then at William. He yelled for William to stop but it was too late. William had already called Rebecca's bluff and pulled the cord with everything he had. Rebecca let the lighter fly. The engine roared to life as the growing flame hit William's pant leg. Immediately, William's pants caught fire. His scream could be heard from the street as he jumped around trying to extinguish the flame.

Rebecca ran to Emily and ripped the mask from her face. William rushed to the desk where he grabbed the water bottle. He doused the flame with little success.

"More water!" William yelled.

Just then, a shadow grew in the room. A massive, fast-moving object eclipsed the window. William stared at the wall as the shadow moved across his face. The empty bottle dropped from his hand.

The building shook as a vessel's hull tore into the wall. Water poured through the seawall and crashed to the floor. William raised his hands, welcoming the wave. The impact sent everyone in the room sliding across the floor toward the glass wall.

The lobby guards looked in awe as the room filled like a human-sized fish tank. The air raid siren sounded, giving the guards their cue to run for their lives.

The eerie blare of the siren scattered the mass of young people in the square. The lobby guards expedited the crowd's departure by their screams: "Breach! Breach!"

Amid the chaos, Matt quickly put the truck in gear and turned the ignition.

Nothing.

"Come on!" Matt said, as he pumped the gas pedal.

"Matt, the way is almost cleared," Grace said, as the mass of people scattered and thinned before their eyes.

"I know." Matt turned the key again. "Come on." The engine fired.

"What are you waiting for?"

"Pedal."

"Oh." Grace reached for the gas and pressed it to the floor. The bald tires spun. Matt steered the truck, avoiding those left running across the square.

"When I say so, slam the brakes."

"Alright."

The truck rapidly approached the two boxes.

"Now!"

Grace transferred all of her weight to the brake pedal. As she did, Matt turned the steering wheel causing the truck to skid 180 degrees. Grace ran from the cab and kicked out the exhaust tube from the two boxes.

Grace yelled Logan's name as she ran around the perimeter of the box. A suffocated cough came from the small window. "You're alright," Grace said, as she took Logan by the hand. "You're alright."

"Never better."

"We're going to get you out," Matt said, as he grabbed the rope from the bed of the truck.

Logan nodded.

"Matt, look."

Matt looked around the box toward the Orator's building. Through the building's massive front window, the Orator's office filled quickly with seawater.

"Rebecca and Emily are in there," Grace said.

"Emily?" Simon asked. "She's here?"

"Go," Matt said. "I'll get them out."

Grace gave Logan's hand a squeeze and then raced past a few remaining loyalists toward the seawall.

Rebecca surfaced and gasped for air. The shock of the freezing water was almost more than she could take as she shivered through short, restricted breaths. She pounded the glass as the water rose. Rebecca looked for something to break the window when she saw Emily lying sideways on the floor still tied to the chair. Rebecca took a breath and dove under. Her head ached from the frigid water as she swam to the floor. Rebecca lifted the chair. Emily coughed as her head broke through the water's surface. Rebecca then slowly lowered the chair back underwater so she could find something to cut the restraints.

Rebecca resurfaced to find Grace yelling her name and pounding on the glass. The water inside the office was now well above Grace's head and quickly rising. Rebecca looked down at her mother for a brief moment before she made for the Orator's desk, which was floating above the surface. She grabbed the Trojan Horse and dove to Emily.

Emily's restraints floated to the floor as the last zip tie was severed. The two swam to the top. Both gasped what was left of desperately needed oxygen.

Emily gave a weary smile. "Thanks."

"Uh-huh," Rebecca said.

Suddenly, Emily was pulled under. Rebecca screamed as the Orator took hold of her from behind.

"I can't swim," the Orator yelled as he pulled Rebecca down as a means to support himself above water.

Outside, Grace pounded on the glass. She frantically searched the lobby for anything that she could use to break the window. A familiar backpack caught her eye—one with a baseball bat strapped to its side.

Rebecca fought with all her strength, but the Orator's weight was too much for her to sustain. Rebecca began to sink as space between the water's surface and the ceiling was now only a matter of inches. The Orator tilted his head back and took in the last available air.

Everyone was submerged. The Orator kicked Rebecca away and struggled toward his oxygen mask. He tore the hose from the mask and placed it in his mouth.

Emily and William twisted and turned as they sank to the floor. Their arms and legs flailed about as both tried to gain the upper hand. As Emily struggled to free herself, William's hand swiped across her face and she took full advantage. A red cloud suddenly spread around William's hand as Emily's teeth sunk deep into William's index finger. A mass of air bubbles escaped from William's mouth as he yelled in pain.

William cradled his bleeding hand, swam to the Orator, and pointed to his mouth for some air. The Orator shook his head. William reached for the hose, but the Orator refused. William grabbed for the hose again, this time ripping it from the Orator's mouth. Air streamed skyward as the two fought for control of the hose.

William was pulled from the Orator. Looking past his charred legs, a determined Emily yanked what was left of his burned shoe. The number of those fighting for the hose was now three. William pulled his gun from his holster and fired. The bullet whizzed past Emily's head and soon lost its velocity and sank to the floor.

Emily looked at the wall and then at William. He fumbled with his weapon as blood clouded his line of sight. Emily grabbed William by the hand and yanked it back toward herself.

She slipped herself under his reach, her stomach and face now beneath and parallel to his outstretched hand. Emily arched her back to see the wall as she aimed from an upside-down position. She fired the gun from William's hand. Emily watched in anticipation as the bullet raced toward the glass. The bullet made contact but failed to break the glass. Emily pulled the trigger again, but the gun no longer fired. She looked back at Rebecca who was losing consciousness. She looked at the glass. A figure ran toward the wall.

Grace threw the baseball bat with all of her strength at the glass wall. The bat's contact sent an explosion of water into the lobby, throwing Grace across the room's expanse as thousands of gallons of seawater dumped into the rest of the building. Emily and Rebecca were pushed to the front of the building and slammed against the outer wall.

Water dripped from Rebecca's bangs as she lifted herself off the floor. Her head jerked back as William grabbed her by the hair.

"Gotcha."

A sudden blow to the head rendered William unconscious. Grace dropped the baseball bat and went to Rebecca's side.

Emily sloshed through knee-high water hugging herself for warmth. "C-c-come on. This w-way."

Grace put her arm around Rebecca trying to warm her as they raced to the front door. Rebecca retrieved her pack and Logan's as they exited the building. The three pushed themselves through the revolving door. Emily jammed the bat into the entrance locking it from the outside.

"Where's Logan?" Rebecca asked.

"Working on it," Emily said, as the three raced away from the building.

"Simon!" Emily shouted.

"Emily." The two embraced.

"What happened?"

"Pulled the hitch off," Matt said from under the truck.

"Logan," Rebecca said. "Are you alright?"

"So good."

"We're going to get you out of there."

"We gotta go," Emily said, as sounds of falling metal and concrete echoed through the empty streets.

"Give me a minute," Matt said, as he tied the rope. A stream of water rushed past the group.

"I don't think we have a minute," Emily said, as she followed the trail of water back to the building.

Grace leaned against Logan's cell. "I just need to . . . sit down for a minute."

"Don't go to sleep," Emily said, as she took Grace by the shoulders. "Stand up. Come on."

"Put her in the truck!" Matt yelled. "We're only going to get one shot at this." Matt looped the rope through itself. "Al . . . most . . . got it."

Two bullets suddenly hit the truck next to Matt. He quickly rolled away. "Get down," Matt yelled.

Rebecca and Emily dove behind the truck—the sudden shot of adrenaline momentarily overpowered the hypothermia. The Orator yelled a string of undecipherable obscenities and accusations as he fired indiscriminately from the balcony.

"That's going to have to do," Simon yelled as he raced to the truck; he jumped in and gave the key a turn. The engine cranked, but didn't start. "Come on," he said, as he gave it another crank while pumping the gas pedal. "Come on. Come on!" He continued pumping the accelerator and cranking the engine. Simon slammed his hand on the steering wheel.

"Truck won't start! I think the engine's flooded." Simon jumped out of the truck and raced toward the hood.

"In a few seconds, this'll all be flooded," Matt said.

"Emily," Simon yelled, "get out of here."

"I can't just leave you here."

"No time. We agreed, remember?" Two bullets struck near Emily's head. "Emily, go! While you still have time." Emily looked at her brother; he put his hands on her shoulders and smiled. "Come on, Em. Simon says." Emily gave her brother a worried smile. "Don't worry. I'm right behind you. Promise. Now go." Emily hesitated for only a moment longer. Then she ran.

Simon popped the truck's hood and began working on the engine. Matt dropped back under the truck to finish securing the knot. He took the rope in his hands only to find that one of the Orator's bullets had severed it. Matt tried to connect to the two ends.

"The rope's shot. Literally. Doesn't reach." Matt raced back to Simon's side.

"Won't really matter if we can't get the truck started."

A few additional bullets struck just above Simon's hand. Then the gunfire stopped. An ominous sound rumbled through the street. Simon and Matt exchanged looks, knowing a greater danger was on its way. The two looked around their respective sides of the hood; both were met with a rush of wind. Behind the wind, a massive ocean wall poured from the building.

Simon's hands began to tremble. He looked Matt in the eyes. "I . . . I'm sorry." Simon backed away from the truck. "I'm sorry." He stumbled once, gained his balance, and was soon in full sprint away from the truck.

"Rebecca! Get into the driver's seat."

"I can't drive this," Rebecca said, as she entered the truck.

"You have to." Matt reached over Rebecca. "Okay, look. The truck's in drive." Matt shifted the gear handle down. "Now it's in reverse. 'R' and 'D.'" He then looked behind him and turned the steering wheel to position the truck in line with Logan's cell.

"Isn't the engine flooded?"

"You have to clear the fuel. Press the accelerator to the floor for as long as possible. When I tell you, start the engine. We'll only get one shot." Matt shut the truck door. "You can do this."

Rebecca pressed the pedal to the floor. She looked in the side mirror to see the fast-approaching flood.

"Dad?"

"Logan, move back."

"Dad?"

"Not yet."

"Dad!"

"Now!"

Rebecca cranked the engine. An enormous backfire sent a black cloud billowing from the exhaust pipe. Rebecca screamed with excitement.

"Push the gas! Push the gas!"

Rebecca slammed the gas sending the truck violently into the box. Matt grabbed Logan and the two jumped into the truck bed.

"Drive," Matt shouted. "Drive, drive, drive!"

Rebecca threw the gear shifter up and stomped on the accelerator. The truck sped forward as the wave crashed onto what remained of the two cells. Matt and Logan backed themselves up against the back of the cab as the waters gained.

"Hold on," Rebecca yelled as she made a hard right. The truck slid onto a cross street as the wall of water raged past.

Grace fell sideways on the seat. "Mom, get up! Mom!" Rebecca shook Grace's shoulder.

"Here it comes," Matt said, as the floodwater continued its pursuit.

"Mom's out!" Rebecca yelled. She shook her head fighting off her own fatigue. She reached over and buckled Grace in as best she could.

Matt looked through the cab's window and into the rear-view mirror. "Faster, Bec," Matt said, as the waters gained.

"Dad? We're running out of city."

Less than a mile ahead, Undertown's south wall stood.

"Don't stop," Logan said, as he looked above the cab.

"There is a *house* at the end of the street."

"I know."

"You know what?"

"Logan's right. We must be running along First Avenue."

"The underground extends well south of here," Logan said, as he looked ahead. "The road should continue."

"Should?"

"We're out of options," Matt said.

"Look on the bright side," Logan said. "This time you're supposed to hit a stationary object."

Rebecca added pressure to the gas pedal. Matt and Logan ducked behind the cab and covered their heads. Floodwater now shot through the windows of the side buildings, adding to its assault from the rear. Rebecca buckled her seatbelt.

"Hold on!" Rebecca yelled.

20: Three Little Words

The impact was quick and harsh. The truck tore through the house like a wrecking ball. Barely slowing, the vehicle blew through the dining room, kitchen, and bedroom before exploding through the house's back wall. Sailing over a small drop, the truck landed on another road. The impact threw Rebecca's foot from the accelerator. The truck slowed as it swiped the walls of the sewer-like street. Sparks created by the repetitive impacts were the only light in an otherwise dark tunnel.

Not far ahead, a second wall stood—a wall marking Undertown's true and final end. The second impact was sudden. The rear wheels lifted off the ground as the hood crunched and folded into itself.

Ringing: that's all Rebecca heard. What happened next would only be remembered in fragments. Flashes of consciousness played tricks on Rebecca's mind as time and space became relative. Rising waters. Canned voices yelling. A poorly lit tunnel. Stairs ascending. Only after Rebecca felt the warmth of an unknown source did she finally give in to the pull of unconsciousness.

Rebecca opened her eyes. Her face was the only part of her not enveloped by a sub-zero sleeping bag. She looked around the room—it became clear that she was inside a tent. She felt like an overheated mummy as she shifted her arms and legs. She ran her hand along the inside of the bag until she found the zipper. Dozens of hand warmers spilled out to the floor as the bag opened. Rebecca sat up and wiped the sweat from her forehead.

She ran the tent zipper down to the floor and peeked her head out the canvas flap. Short pine trees surrounded the campsite. A sizable, snow-covered rock face was to her right. Everything was still, including two deer that stood just beyond the tents. She waited a moment for any sign of life—any sign of movement.

Weird, Rebecca thought to herself as she crawled outside. She stood and turned only to find herself face to face with a tall, shadowy figure. Rebecca let out a short scream and pushed the person away. His head rolled off his shoulders and into her arms. Rebecca quickly dropped the head, stepped backward, and tripped over a small pile of logs. She stumbled in the dark until a sweater display finally brought her to the floor.

"You're okay," Matt said.

"Who was that?" Rebecca asked, out of breath.

"Just a mannequin."

"Where are we?"

Matt helped Rebecca to her feet. "REI."

Rebecca looked at the nearby tents, trees, and wildlife again—the context made it clear that it was all merely a large camping display inside a retail store.

"Come on, you should try to get a little more sleep. It won't be long before we need to leave."

The adrenaline quickly faded from Rebecca's body and she felt exhausted.

"Where's Logan?" Rebecca asked, consciousness once again fading.

"He's fine," Matt said, as he brought Rebecca back to her sleeping bag.

"What about Mom?"

"Right over there."

Rebecca laid back down. "What happens now?"

"We need to get you and Logan somewhere safe. It was a bad idea to bring you two along."

"Now you care what happens to us," Rebecca said, half asleep.

"Bec, I would never want anything bad to happen to any of you."

"Words may break my bones, but sticks and stones will never hurt me." Rebecca smiled. "Or something like that." Rebecca mumbled a few words until a steady deep breathing replaced her undecipherable talk.

Matt returned to his folding chair and to Grace. A small plastic campfire separated the two. Matt picked up a piece of paper and continued drawing on it.

"What are you working on?"

"Oh, the map that Logan started. Thought I'd help fill it out a little."

Grace sat for a moment looking at the fake dancing flames. "Do you remember the first time we went camping?"

Matt looked up from his pen and paper. "Yellowstone, wasn't it? The kids were still pretty young."

"No, before the kids. Right after we were married."

Matt thought for a moment. "Mt. Pilchuck." Matt smiled. "How could I forget about that?"

"Because people tend to repress traumatic memories."

"Good point."

"How that skunk ever got into the tent . . ."

"He was looking for a fight; I'm tellin' ya."

"Skunks don't look for fights."

"That one was."

"Well, I think it's safe to say that he won."

"It was like a little, hairy, spray tan machine."

"A very full spray tan machine." Grace pulled her sleeping bag snug over her shoulders. "What I wouldn't give to see that view again."

"The skunk's butt?"

"The mountaintop, Matt. The mountaintop. I'd take the view from a *hilltop* if my legs could get me there."

A silence settled around the campfire.

Grace sighed. "So what about the poem? Anything new there?"

"Three little words." Matt slid the stopwatch out from around his neck. "And the clock keeps ticking." Matt held it up for Grace to see.

Grace noticed Matt's attention focused on the back of the watch. "What is it?"

"That's strange. Never noticed that before."

"Never noticed what?"

"Initials. Engraved on the back. B.S. That's appropriate." Matt put the stopwatch back around his neck.

"What do you think?"

"I think we should try to stick to one ridiculous clue at a time," Matt said, as he focused his attention on the poem.

"So three little words."

"Yeah."

"Do you think Logan was right?"

"About the words being 'I love you'?"

"Yes."

Matt looked up from the paper.

"You don't have to mean it. The poem doesn't say you have to mean it."

"Right, they're just words." Matt looked at the poem. "Alright, we both say it then. You changed too, so the answer may lie with you as much as me."

"Makes sense."

Grace sat up a little in her chair.

Matt subtly cleared his throat.

"Ready?" Grace asked.

"Sure. No big deal."

"Right. No big deal."

The two looked at each other. A few moments passed.

"I thought you were going to go first," Grace said.

"I thought you were."

"This is silly. It's not like we haven't said it before."

"Right? We've said it before."

"Lots of times."

"So many times."

"So here we go."

"Here we go."

A moment passed.

"I love you," Grace said.

"I love you too."

The two watched each other.

"You look the same," Grace said.

"So do you."

"Do you feel any different?" Grace asked.

"I mean . . . do you?"

"I don't think it works until we go to sleep. Remember, we woke up this way."

"Right. Okay then." Matt stood. "I'm just going to . . . head back to my tent. Goodnight."

Grace was soon alone with the glow of the fake fire. "Good talk."

21: Aftermath

"Would ya look at this mess?" a man said to his partner, as an unmarked car approached the perimeter of what appeared to be every emergency vehicle in the city. Swirling snow and flashing lights dominated the scene as detectives Roberts and Sanders stepped out of the vehicle and under a band of yellow caution tape.

"What do you got?" Sanders asked as she and Roberts approached a uniformed officer.

"A large boat crashed into the seawall sometime around three-thirty in the morning. A small portion of the old city is still underwater."

"Well, is it safe to be up here?" Roberts asked.

"Engineers have been down there all morning. They say everything is still structurally sound. Just a little wet."

"Whose boat is it?" Sanders asked.

"Over there," the officer said, pointing to a man talking expressively in front of a police car. "But where he was last night is another story."

"And where was he last night?"

"Visiting family in Issaquah. Looks like the boat was stolen. But that's not the worst of it."

"You don't say."

"It seems that the old city was . . . operational."

"What do you mean, 'operational'?" Roberts asked.

"Yeah, and by whom?" Sanders added.

"Tough to say exactly, but some of the items found down there are a bit strange."

The three walked over to a table to view some of the evidence that had been collected.

"Is that a teddy bear?" Sanders asked.

"Yes, along with quite a few toys and small clothing."

"There were kids down there?"

"By the looks of it, lots of them."

A little way down the pier, a white sheet was placed over someone lying on a stretcher.

"How many made it out?" Roberts asked.

"From what I understand, everyone did."

"Then how do you explain that," Sanders said, pointing to the stretcher.

"Like I said, the old city was operational. They had everything you might expect: housing, school, . . . a cemetery."

"I wouldn't expect any of that," Sanders said. Just then, a commotion erupted not far away.

"Looks like they got another live one."

"What do you mean?"

"We've been picking kids up all morning," the officer said, as the three walked toward a young man in handcuffs. "A lot of breaking and entering. Theft."

"Let me go!" the young man shouted. "I didn't do anything!"

"Found him hiding on the boat."

"It's okay," Roberts said. "What's your name?"

"Simon."

"Alright, Simon. Tell me what you were doing on that boat."

"Like I told him, I was looking to see if everyone was alright. I need to find my sister."

"Were you two down there when it happened?"

"Down where?"

"You're telling me that you don't know anything about the old city?"

"I mean, I've heard rumors. Who hasn't? Figured they were just that though. Rumors. Look, I really need to find my sister."

"We'll find her. There are a lot of officers on the streets tonight. Would she know to get to a shelter or a police station?"

Simon looked past Roberts and Sanders to a nearby building. A figure moved into the shadows. He took a breath. "Yeah. She knows to go to the police station."

"Good. Now, what were you really doing on that boat?"

"I didn't do it, if that's what you mean. Like I said, I heard a loud crash and I went to see if everyone was alright."

"So you heard the crash and rushed right over?"

"Yeah."

"And what did you see when you boarded?"

"Nothing."

"No one was on the boat?"

"No one."

"But you just said that you raced right over there."

"I did."

"So you're saying that whoever crashed the boat left before you got there?"

"That's what I'm saying."

A stretcher was pushed along the dock and into Simon's view. An arm slipped out from under the white sheet—an arm with an infinity bracelet wrapped around it.

Simon closed his eyes; he cleared his throat. "Freezing out here. Maybe we can finish this conversation somewhere else?"

"Alright, take him to the station," Roberts said. "And get him a blanket, will ya?"

Roberts and Sanders walked toward the point of impact. Emergency workers, all wearing carbon filter masks, entered and exited the old city.

"Is it safe to go down there?"

"Carbon monoxide levels are off the charts. Other than that, like I said, it's structurally sound."

"Where can we get a couple of those masks?"

Dozens of flashlights swiped back and forth in what remained of Undertown—the two lights belonging to Roberts and Sanders were near the roundabout. Sparks from welders illuminated the seawall as the large vessel still protruded out from the Orator's building.

Though large pumps extracted seawater from Undertown's streets, the water level where the detectives stood was still ankle deep.

"What do you think?"

Roberts shined his light toward what remained of the Orator's building and then in the opposite direction. "I just bought these shoes." Roberts stopped someone walking by. "Hey, is there any way to get some light down here?"

"We're working on it."

Just then, a portion of Undertown illuminated. Roberts and Sanders looked around in amazement.

"Can you believe what you're seeing?" Sanders asked.

"I see it. But I don't believe it." Roberts trudged through the water away from the seawall. Soon the two were on dry land. Roberts stopped at the first side street.

"What do you see?"

"Probably nothing."

"Are those tire marks?"

"Looks like it. Like someone was in a hurry to leave."

"Could've been there a long time."

"Probably." Roberts shined his flashlight down the darkened street. "Let's find out." He walked away from the construction lights and toward the south wall. The two shined their flashlights onto the side buildings revealing every broken window.

"Do you see that?" Roberts asked.

"What."

"Up ahead."

In the distance, faint yellow lights quietly flashed on and off. Roberts and Sanders made their way to a house with a large hole through the front door.

"Watch your step," Roberts said, as he illuminated the street.

Besides the two flashlights, the truck's hazards were the only light in the narrow street.

"Anyone in there?" Sanders asked, as she approached the open driver's side door. Roberts shined his light into the passenger's side window.

"Anything?"

"No." Roberts focused his flashlight on the floor. "Wait a minute. Thought I saw something move."

A rat screamed and leapt out the window. Roberts jumped back.

"You alright?"

Roberts shined his light back on the truck floor, then on the retreating rat as it scurried down the corridor. "Think he knows something we don't?"

"Look." A scarf and goggles floated atop the water farther
away down the tunnel.

The door to Grace's tent unzipped; Rebecca crouched down
just outside. "Time to go."

"What time is it?"

Rebecca was already gone. Grace reached for her necklace
and found her wedding band. She put the ring on; it fell loosely
to the base of her finger. Grace removed the ring. "It didn't
work."

Two flashlights scanned the camping display. Hands on their hol-
sters, Sanders and Roberts approached the four tents. Roberts
entered one of the tents and tapped the side of a sleeping bag
with the tip of his shoe. He then stepped on the sleeping bag.

"They're not here," Roberts said.

Sanders shined her light across the floor.

"Anything?"

"A hat. Scarf. Wait a minute." Sanders pulled out a picture; it
was the same one that Grace used to prove her identity to Rebecca
and Logan the previous day. Sanders passed the photo to Roberts.

"Where have I seen her before?"

"I was thinking the same thing. Is she the one caught on
surveillance at the Bainbridge police station?"

"That's it; she was there."

"Busy little bee." Roberts walked to the front door. "Snow's
covered their tracks. We'll head back to the car and send this
picture around. They couldn't have gotten far, not on foot."

Snow dropped from the sky at an overwhelming rate as the four trudged up the sidewalk.

"I can't believe we stole all this stuff," Rebecca said through her covered face.

"Stole is a strong word," Matt said.

"Can we take these masks off yet?" Logan asked through his skull-face bandana. "My nose is sweating. Either that or it's running. I'll be honest, I can't really tell at this point."

Matt looked around. "Yeah, it's probably alright."

"The sooner you take that hideous thing off your face, the better," Rebecca said.

Logan pulled the bandana down around his neck.

"I was wrong. That's much worse."

"Keep it up and a yellow snowball's in your future."

"Gross. Stop that, you two," Grace said.

"Just sayin'. I haven't drunk much water since we started out."

"Logan."

"So it's probably really concentrated."

"Logan!"

Grace and Matt walked together. "Well, it obviously didn't work."

"Yeah," Matt replied.

"What now?"

"I don't know. We need money. Pretty sure Emily took everything I had while we were still unconscious. We're not going to get very far on foot in this weather."

"Is that?" Logan said. "Great. It is."

"What?" Rebecca asked.

Through the falling snow and low-hanging clouds, a pointed skyscraper came into view. "Smith Tower."

"Yeah? So?"

"So Smith Tower is south of the ferry terminal."

"You mean we're farther away than when we started?"

"Not much farther, but yes," Matt replied. "Excuse me," Matt said to a man walking in the opposite direction. "Could you spare a few dollars? The four of us are trying to get home and need bus . . ." The man stepped into the street and passed. Matt stopped and watched as the man pretended that they didn't exist. "The Seattle freeze is alive and well. This may be a little more difficult than I thought." Matt looked at his watch.

"Well, we're not giving up that easily," Rebecca said. "You're more than welcome to though, Matt. Come on, Logan; we'll have better luck at Pike Place."

"Pike Place? I don't know if that's such a good idea."

"What are the odds Chet will be there again? Besides, all we need is a few dollars for a bus or a cab. We'll be out of there in no time."

⁊᷉⁊

Like the day before, Pike Place Market was packed with holiday shoppers despite the frigid temperatures and falling snow. Though the pier crash was a popular topic among tenants and customers, the event hardly generated enough care or concern to trump the need to make and spend money so close to Christmas.

"Any luck?" Rebecca asked, as she emerged from the crowd.

"No," Logan replied. "Where've you been?"

"Just over there."

Matt approached the two. "You'd think that we could pull together a few bucks between the four of us. I got a dollar," Matt said, retrieving the crumpled bill from his pocket. "You two get anything?"

"Yeah," Logan replied, "pneumonia. My hand warmers are all used up."

"This is ridiculous," Grace said. "At this rate, we'll age back naturally."

"And what do you propose?"

"Be right back." Grace walked toward the sound of a cellist. The cellist stopped his playing as Grace approached. The two spoke for a moment before the young man nodded. Grace walked up to Matt with her jacket in hand. "Hold this a minute."

"What's she doing?" Rebecca asked.

"I don't know."

Grace returned to the young man as she tied her hair in a bun. She then stood in a pose as if waiting for a theater curtain to open—for the show to begin.

The young man began to play. A familiar prelude penetrated the morning air. Grace began to dance. As the impromptu performance began, it seemed to be the result of hours of carefully choreographed rehearsals. Music and dance entwined in a moment of perfect harmony. The three watched. They went from being amused to being amazed; from being amazed to being mesmerized; all in a matter of seconds. One by one, those too busy to spare a moment suddenly found the time to watch. A few onlookers soon became a growing crowd. With their phones raised, these passersby vied for position as video was captured and pictures snapped. Even the fishmongers were distracted by the performance as evidenced by a sudden fish to face contact.

Grace closed her eyes and moved with an eloquence once lost but never forgotten. Now fully engaged with the perfectly played strings, Grace's movements were poetry in motion. Those in the crowd whispered through smiling lips words of amazement as the young girl danced with the confidence and skill of a seasoned professional. No one wanted the performance to end—most of all, Grace.

The last note hung heavy in the winter air. Grace bowed her head. A moment of silence proceeded. When Grace looked up, an eruption of applause and whistles broke the quiet. Grace covered her mouth as she smiled. Rebecca and Logan rushed over to her. Hugs were exchanged among the three as Matt approached.

"That was amazing," Rebecca said.

Grace wiped a rolling tear from her face.

The quick patter of heels fast approached. "Y'all, that was fire," Tiffany said.

"Right?" Logan said.

"Literally fire."

"Oh my gosh," Rebecca said.

"Y'all just made my Christmas Eve. Here, you earned it." Tiffany dropped a fifty-dollar bill in the cello case. "Just added the live video as a highlight. It's already getting some real attention." Tiffany showed the phone. "See? You know, I was just talking to the ballet dancer Grace Stevens the other night. Do you know her?"

"Yeah, I've heard of her," Grace said.

"Well, I think she would've been really impressed. I should get the two of you connected. See where it goes. Here, give me your contact information."

"Uh, I can't."

"Why?"

Grace looked at Matt. "Why can't I?"

"I'll take care of this," Logan chimed in. "Hi. How you doing? Name's Logan. Logan Ste . . . You know what, let's just forget the last name. What she's trying to say is she doesn't have any contact information. Never has." Logan smiled, proud of himself for his quick thinking.

"Well, in that case," Tiffany said, as she pulled out her phone.

"Whatchya doin'?" Logan asked.

"Calling Grace. I'd kick myself if I didn't try to get y'all connected."

The four looked at each other as Tiffany called the number. Grace's backpack started buzzing.

"Is she not there?" Grace asked, as the cellist divvied the proceeds.

"Guess not." Tiffany then noticed the mesh side pocket on Grace's backpack—the screen of the phone tucked inside went dark when the call ended. "Think I'll try her again though."

Tiffany called Grace's number once more. The screen inside the mesh pocket illuminated.

The cellist handed Grace her share of the money. "Thank you."

"Thank *you*," the young man said. "I made more in those couple of minutes than I have all morning. I was actually about to pack it up before you came along."

Tiffany tried to read the phone's caller ID. She was just about to make out the name on the screen when Grace quickly turned.

"Thank you so much for your generous gift and for trying to connect me with Mrs. Stevens. That would've really been something."

"Well, with all the views your performance is getting, I wouldn't be surprised if the two of you end up having the introduction regardless."

"What do you mean?"

"It's just one of those things that tends to happen with people who become instafamous." Tiffany showed Grace her phone—views of the performance continued to quickly increase.

"Get ready for your fifteen minutes of fame."

22: Closing In

The detectives approached their snow-covered car. Roberts turned on the engine and cranked the heat. The wipers struggled to remove the snow from the windshield. "We need to find these kids soon," he said, as he pulled up the Bainbridge police station video footage on the dashboard screen. "Look familiar?"

"That's her," Sanders said. "Along with three others." Sanders pointed to the screen. "Look there. You can only see two of their faces."

Roberts held up a printout from the REI surveillance footage. "Same here." Only the faces of Grace and Matt were clearly captured on the security camera.

"Definitely the same two."

"The footage puts them heading north. Any thoughts?"

Sanders didn't immediately reply. Her attention was on her phone.

"Any thoughts at all."

Sanders remained focused on her phone.

"You millennials. I'm curious, would you be able to survive without that thing?"

"No. Probably not."

Sanders brought the phone closer to her face.

"Not to play the role of homeroom teacher, but unless it's helping in our investigation—"

"I know where they are. Or, *were* at least. This dance performance is trending."

"Trending?"

"Spreading across the internet really, really fast." Look. Sanders showed Roberts the phone.

"@therealtiffanycartnight?"

"She's someone I follow."

"She a suspect in a case?"

"No."

"I don't know what that means then." Roberts watched a portion of the dance. "That's the girl. Where?"

"Pike Place Market."

"When?"

"Less than an hour ago."

"Let's go."

❧

"I don't think the bus is coming," Rebecca said.

Matt looked at the posted schedule. "It'll be here any minute."

"That's what you said at the last bus stop."

Matt looked down the road for any sign of life. Then he sat down on the bench with the other three.

"What do you think, Matt?" Grace asked.

"I'm not sure. Maybe there's too much snow now. But I think we should stick around a little while longer. If a bus does come around, it'll be a lot faster than walking." Matt stretched his back. "It is nice to sit for a minute though."

The four sat in a row under the small shelter and watched as large snowflakes continued to fall.

"So," Logan finally said. "There was this pirate ship out in the middle of the ocean."

Rebecca rolled her eyes.

"The pirate manning the crow's nest yells down to the captain that a Royal Navy ship is approaching on the horizon. The captain hears this and yells to his men, 'Prepare for battle, ye scurvy dogs, for today we fight!' While the men are running to their battle stations, the captain turns to his first mate and says, 'Mr. Ward.'

"'Yes, cap'n.'

"'Get me my red shirt.'

"'Aye,' replied Mr. Ward and got for the captain his red shirt.

"The Royal Navy ship approached and great battle raged. At the end of it all, the pirates were victorious. They defeated the British ship. As the pirates were assessing damage and tending to the wounded, Mr. Ward asked the captain, 'Ye mind telling me somethin', cap'n: why'd ye ask for your red shirt before the fight?'

"The captain smiled as he cleaned the blade of his sword. 'Ya have much to learn, Mr. Ward, if ye someday want to captain your own ship. The reason I asked for the red shirt is so that neither my men nor the enemy would see me bleed should I be wounded in battle.'

"'Aye, that makes sense, sir. Smart.'

"A week later, the pirate ship is still at sea. The pirate in the crow's nest is surveying the waters with his telescope when he spots something on the horizon. He double-checks just to make sure that his eyes aren't playing tricks on him. The man leans over the rails of the crow's nest and yells down to the captain that there are *ten* British Royal Navy ships approaching on the horizon.

"Upon hearing this, the captain turned to his first mate. 'Mr. Ward.'

"'Yes, cap'n.'

"'Get me my brown pants.'"

Rebecca chuckled. Then Matt and Grace did the same. Like children in church, the continued laughter soon became funnier than the joke itself. Logan, too, was soon close to tears. A loud snort then came from Grace. She covered her nose and mouth as she and the others laughed all the harder.

"Stop it," Rebecca said, trying to catch her breath. "My tears are going to freeze to my face."

"Well, my 'tears' are about to freeze to my legs," Grace said.

Those passing by on the sidewalks looked with curious eyes as the uncontrolled laughter reached its peak.

Grace pointed to the backpack. "Are there any tissues in there?"

"And the tissue is for . . . ?" Matt asked.

"My nose, thank you very much," Grace said with a smile.

"I don't see any, but here." Matt tucked his arm into the sleeve of his shirt. He then offered the sleeve to Grace. Grace looked at Matt. "It's fine. It's technically not even mine." Grace took the sleeve and blew.

"Instantly regret that decision," Matt said. "Kidding."

Logan blew his nose into a pile of snow that he scooped into his hands.

"Seriously, what's wrong with you?" Rebecca asked.

Matt and Grace sat for a moment looking at the falling snow.

"That really was quite amazing," Matt said.

"Yeah, I needed a good laugh."

"No, I mean back there at the market. Really . . . beautiful."

Grace looked down. "Beautiful, huh?" She dug a small hole in the snow with her boot. "Can I ask you something?"

"Sure."

"When did you think that we were in trouble?"

"Honestly, as soon as we stepped off the ferry."

"No, I mean us."

"Oh." Matt sighed. "It's difficult to pinpoint an exact time."

"Not for me."

Matt looked down the corridor of buildings toward the water. A small stretch of highway passed between the two walls of skyscrapers. "Then I think I know."

"No, you don't. You don't."

Matt looked at the highway again. "I'm pretty sure—"

"Last spring, we were invited to the Lewis' house for a dinner party. Do you remember?"

"Sure. That was the night we all walked down to the marina to watch the sunset."

"That's right." Grace nodded her head. "That's exactly right."

"I'm a little lost. Did I do something that night?"

"It's not something you did. It's something you didn't do."

"What didn't I do?"

"It's going to sound stupid. It's starting to sound stupid in my head."

"Try me."

"You didn't hold my hand."

Matt waited for more of the story.

"That's it," Grace said.

"That's when you thought we were in trouble? When I didn't hold your hand?"

"See, told you. Sounds stupid."

"Have we ever been big hand-holders?"

"I don't think holding hands is all that unique or couples-specific. And yes, there was a time when we did."

"Well, if you were that bothered by it, why didn't you say something?"

"Because, Matt, it didn't bother you."

"I don't know, Grace. That just seems like a lot of weight to put on a single night."

"Well, like I said, that was the night I thought we *might* be in trouble. It was all the nights after that I knew we were."

Matt looked down as if trying to find his next words somewhere in the snow. He looked at Grace and then past her to an approaching vehicle. "Grace, I . . ."

"What. What is it?"

"I think we've stayed here long enough."

"There they are, up ahead," Sanders said, pointing through the steady movement of the windshield wipers.

"Come on," Matt said. "We need to start moving."

"Walk?" Rebecca asked. "There's no way we'll get there before night."

"Westlake Mall isn't far," Matt said, as he stood and slung his backpack over his shoulder. "We can catch the monorail and that'll take us to the Space Needle. I'm sure we'll be able to grab a bus or taxi there."

"That's them," Sanders said.

Roberts flipped on the flashing lights.

"Come on," Matt said, as he started to run.

Roberts' tires spun a little as he maneuvered down the street. He turned the wipers to full speed as the snow fell harder against the windshield.

"They're running up Lenora Street," Sanders said.

"Got it." The turn onto Lenora made the car slide a little. Roberts shook his head as he straightened the vehicle.

The four quickly made their way to Fourth Street and turned south toward Westlake Mall. A snowplow passed by carving a path down the middle of the road.

"I'll never say this again," Grace said, "run in the middle of the street."

The four's pace increased as they ran behind the plow.

"Where are they?" Roberts said, as he turned onto Fourth.

"Ahead two cars."

"Can't pass with these snowbanks."

"Up there," Matt said, pointing past the Westlake Center Christmas tree to an outdoor staircase. "You can get to the monorail from inside the mall. It's just around the other side."

"What about you?" Rebecca asked.

"I'm right behind you," Matt said, as he handed Rebecca his backpack. "The money's in there. Get us some tickets." Matt then split from the group and continued down the street. He stopped for a moment and looked back as he reached Pine Street.

"There," Sanders said.

Matt took a right at the intersection and raced between traffic back toward the water.

"They're going in circles," Roberts said, as he pressed the accelerator a little farther to the floor. "Running scared."

Sanders looked at her partner and then back at the road. The vehicle made another fishtail as it turned onto Pine Street, now just a half-block behind Matt.

"You've been a naughty boy," Roberts said as he closed the gap.

Matt looked over his shoulder. His lungs began to burn as the neon Public Market sign came into view over the horizon.

"You can run." Roberts glanced at Sanders. "The guilty ones always run."

The car was now within a few feet of Matt.

"Alright, we're on him," Sanders said. "Slow down and I'll take him on foot." She gripped the door handle. "You can slow down any time now."

"Uh," Roberts said, with a slight amount of concern as he pressed the brake.

"Slow down."

"I'm trying," Roberts said, as the car slid freely on the snow and ice.

Matt slowed his run to a jog, and his jog to a walk as the car caught up with him and then continued past. Matt waved as the car continued its spin down the hill and out of sight.

~⁓~

Logan paced back and forth on the monorail's loading platform. "I'm barely in high school and I'm already a criminal," he said, hands cupped on his head and breathing heavily.

"Calm down," Rebecca said. "You're not exactly a big fish. You're more like a small Candiru parasite."

"If that was supposed to make me feel better, it didn't."

"Hey!" a woman called out.

Logan jumped.

"You're that girl from Pike Place. The dancer."

"Yeah, that was me," Grace said with a smile.

I just love those kinds of surprise performances. You were great. Can I get a picture?"

"Oh, uh, sure." The woman moved in close. "So . . . doing some last-minute shopping at Pike Place?"

"Pike Place? No. Just picked up a few things from here at the mall." The woman raised her phone. "One . . . two . . ." the woman looked at the picture.

"So how did you know about it if you weren't there?"

"Saw it on my feed. Wouldn't be surprised if it got you on Fallon." The monorail then approached from around the bend. "Well, Merry Christmas."

"Merry Christmas." Grace looked at Rebecca and Logan. "Who else do you think might've seen it?"

"Where is he?" Rebecca asked, as a mass of people disembarked the train.

Grace looked to the side doors hoping Matt would rush through. Those waiting on the platform now funneled into the train. The monorail doors slid closed and the three were left standing alone.

"We need to keep moving," Rebecca said. "I'm getting the tickets." Rebecca unzipped the side pocket to Matt's backpack and retrieved his wallet. "Four tickets please."

"That'll be sixteen dollars." Rebecca pulled the fifty-dollar bill from the wallet. A business card fell to the ground. Rebecca picked it up. "Here's your change."

"When does the next one leave?"

"Should be here in about seven minutes."

"Thanks." Rebecca took the tickets in one hand; the business card in the other.

"What's that?" Grace asked.

"It's a business card. Logan, what's Premiere Architecture?"

"The name pretty much sums it up. It's like the Microsoft of the architecture world . . . or Apple, depending on your persuasion. That guy Dad was talking with the other night at the party? He's Dad's boss. He owns it."

Rebecca flipped the card over. "So stupid," Rebecca said, as she closed her eyes.

Just then, the side door opened and Matt rushed onto the platform. "Good. You're still here," Matt said. "When does the next train leave?"

"What's the hurry?" Rebecca asked. "Afraid you'll miss your meeting?" She held up the business card with Nicolas' handwritten appointment. "You knew the whole time, didn't you? I can't believe it."

"Knew what?"

Rebecca's stomach started to turn. "I'm such an idiot."

"What are you talking about?" Grace asked.

Rebecca handed Grace the card. "He scheduled a meeting for Christmas morning." Rebecca turned to Matt. "Even when you knew that it'd be our last one together."

"Rebecca—"

"Is that why you didn't want us to come along? So you wouldn't have to explain yourself when you just 'happened' to not make it back?"

"Rebecca—"

"Stop it. Stop saying my name. I hate hearing you say it." Rebecca began to back away as the next train arrived. "I really do hate you." She turned and headed for the side door. She pushed the door open, began down the stairs, and abruptly stopped when she heard a familiar voice from below. Rebecca looked over the railing down through the space between the staircases. Two floors down, Chet and the rest of his loudmouthed friends made their way up toward the platform.

By the time Matt reached the door, Rebecca had already opened it. "Rebecca—"

"Shut up. Just . . . shut up and get on the train."

"I'm not taking another step without you," Logan said. "We all need to stick together."

"Chet's right behind me."

"Hold the door!" Logan said, as he rushed toward the train.

"Go," Rebecca said. Logan was the first to board, then Grace, then Matt. Rebecca took one step onto the train. She then stepped back onto the platform as the doors closed.

"Rebecca, what are you doing?" Matt said through the glass.

Just then, the group burst through the doors. "Where is he?" Chet demanded from no one in particular. He scanned the platform and then the monorail. "There!"

Rebecca raised her hood over her head and stepped away from the train as Chet and the others rushed past yelling obscenities and threats.

The monorail slowly pulled away from the platform. Chet kept pace. He pounded the window with his fist. "I'm coming for you, Logan." Chet stopped his pursuit as the train pulled away. "It only has one stop. Come on."

∿︎

Logan dropped onto a padded bench seat; he removed his beanie and anxiously ruffled his hair.

"How long does it take to get to the next stop?" Grace asked.

"A few minutes. Not long," Matt replied as he took a seat across from Logan. The three rode in silence for a moment as the train snaked its way between skyscrapers.

"I know what you're thinking," Matt finally said, feeling the burn of Grace's stare.

"Oh, I doubt that."

"It's not like I had that much of a choice."

"Of course you did."

"I need this next move."

"You mean you need to look out for yourself?"

"Ready or not, this part of our life—the *us* part—is quickly coming to an end. When it's over, I won't be upset; I won't be bitter. But I will be prepared."

"What is that, the Scout's guide to divorce?"

Matt zipped the pack closed. "I'm not starting the next chapter of my life with a blank page. And if you're smart, you wouldn't either."

"I just can't believe you'd trade your last family Christmas for a business meeting."

"I can't believe you still don't understand why."

Before Grace could respond, she saw something out the window. "They're back." On the street below, a black Land Rover wildly sped up from behind the train.

Logan twisted in his seat and then stood. He walked toward the rear of the train to see the approaching vehicle. The SUV swerved dangerously through traffic kicking up clouds of snow. Logan looked down and followed the SUV as it overtook the train.

"They're going to beat us there," Logan said. Logan turned to Grace and Matt. "They're going to beat us there, and then they're going to beat me there."

"They'll still need to park and then get there by foot," Matt said. "We'll just get off the train as soon as it stops."

"What about Bec?" Logan asked.

"One problem at a time," Matt said, as he slung his backpack over his shoulder. Logan did the same.

Passengers leaned forward in unison as the train's brakes were applied.

"Okay," Matt said, "when the doors open . . ."

"Yeah, yeah. Run," Logan said. "Story of my life."

Buildings passed by slower and slower as the train approached the end of its run. Inside the station, passengers lined the platform like spectators at a parade. Faces passed by in a blur, until one caught Logan's eye.

"Rebecca, she's here," Logan said, as he pressed his hands against the window. He then quickly stepped back.

Rebecca waved mechanically, her hand operated under Chet's control.

23: Arrested

The train and the crowd left. All that remained were two groups and an empty platform.

"What do you want?" Matt asked.

"Just him," Chet said, pointing to Logan.

"And if we say no?"

"Well—" Chet put both hands on Rebecca's shoulders and pulled her close. He smiled at Matt. "Do you really want to go down that road? 'Cause I'm good either way."

Chet's friends laughed.

"Shut up!"

His friends went silent.

"Let go of me!" Rebecca said, as she fought Chet's grip.

"Three days ago, being in my arms wasn't such a bad place to be."

"You're a pig."

Chet snorted and rooted his nose into Rebecca's neck. He looked at Logan and Matt with a smile. He then looked at Grace. "How about you? Ever thought of being with a real man? I don't even mind the braces." Chet kissed the air toward Grace. "So what's it going to be? Either way, Christmas comes early."

Matt stepped toward Chet. The closer he got, the smaller Matt felt. "If you touch her . . ."

Chet looked at his friends and back at Matt with a smile. Then he delivered a sudden blow to Matt's head with his free hand. Matt stumbled backward but didn't lose his footing.

"Tough little dude. Tougher than your friend Logan there."

Chet's friends laughed.

"Shut up!"

His friends went silent. "Never seen anyone take a punch like Logan did. He looked like a newborn giraffe." Chet began shaking his legs and stumbling around, laughing. "At one point, I wasn't sure if he was trying to run away or if he just got lost on his way to the ground. He finally found it, but not before taking a swing at me. You paid for that, didn't you? One more pop sent him down. And just when I thought I'd seen the funniest thing in my life, he starts crawling around on all fours trying to find his glasses. Which, by the way, are fake. Dork. He didn't find them, but he did find that huge pile of dog crap. I have never, in my life, seen a dog at the school. Ever." Chet turned to his friends. "You ever seen a dog on campus before?"

"Nope."

"Anyway, his hand was firmly planted in the wet pile and it slides out from under him. I swear, for anyone else that would've been the end of it. But somehow, he manages to slip head-first into it. At this point, everyone's laughing. To the point of tears. Dying. A girl sees that his nose is bleeding and hands him two tampons. Tells him she volunteers in the nurse's office and that it's a special kind of high school cotton ball. And the idiot believed her."

"So he stands up, face covered in crap, tampons sticking out of each nostril, and we all. Just. Lose it." Chet looked over at Logan's bowed head; he then shoved Rebecca away. "And that's why you're a nobody. That's why you'll always be a nobody. Because you're weak. Pathetic."

"I won't let you take him," Matt said.

"You don't have a choice." Chet's friends quickly grabbed Matt by the shoulders and dragged him over to the opening in the concrete left by the departed train. Just when they were about to throw Matt to the concrete below, a voice called out.

"Let him go," Roberts said.

"Piss off."

"I don't piss."

Sanders glanced at her partner. Roberts shook his head knowing what he said didn't sound quite right.

"Let him go! Now!" Sanders said, showing her badge.

Nate and Luke brought Matt away from the opening.

"We were just messing around," Nate said, as he straightened Matt's collar.

Two groups naturally formed. Chet and his friends on one side; Matt, Grace, Rebecca, and Logan on the other. Roberts and Sanders stood in between.

"Get lost," Roberts said to Chet.

Chet didn't budge.

Roberts gave Chet a second look. "Get lost or I'll arrest you."

Chet smiled at Logan. "This isn't over."

"It's over," Roberts said.

Chet winked at Sanders; he then looked at Logan once more before motioning to his friends to leave.

"Oh, tough guy tells you to leave, so you leave." Roberts shook his head. "Some people's kids."

Roberts approached the four. "Sit." The four sat on a nearby bench. Roberts sniffed his runny nose. He grabbed a handkerchief from his pocket, blew his nose, and shoved the piece of cloth back into his pocket.

Gross, Logan said to himself.

Roberts paced a couple of times in front of the bench. "You must be Rebecca." The other three looked down to the end of the bench where Rebecca sat. "We received a tip about ten minutes ago. Said you caught the monorail."

"You called the police?" Matt said. "Because of the business card?"

"That made it easier," Rebecca answered.

"Time is running out," Matt said.

"I know it is."

"And how exactly do you two fit into all of this?" Sanders asked Rebecca and Logan.

"They don't have any part of this," Grace said. "We don't even know them that well."

"I didn't ask you."

"That's actually true," Logan said. "They seriously don't. Ask them what my favorite color is."

"Quiet."

"And we don't know them," Rebecca said, as she looked at Matt.

"You and you," Roberts said, looking at Matt and Grace. "You two are in real trouble. You've really done a number between here and Bainbridge. You're an airplane theft away from being a couple of Barefoot Bandits. We have surveillance footage of the two of you virtually every misstep of the way. But as for you two"—Roberts looked at Rebecca and Logan— "I believe that you've been with them."

"But you don't have proof, do you?" Matt said.

Roberts looked at Matt, clearly growing annoyed. Roberts then looked at Rebecca and Logan. "Where are your parents?"

Rebecca and Logan exchanged glances not knowing exactly how to respond.

"Hello? Do they know where you are?"

"Yes," Logan said immediately. "They most def know where we are." Rebecca nudged Logan's shoulder. "Sorry, they most definitely know where we are."

"Are they somewhere nearby?"

"Pretty close."

Roberts looked at his partner for reassurance that his question made sense. He then directed his attention back to Rebecca. "And what do you think they would say if they were to find out that you were running around with these two?"

Rebecca looked at her parents. "Probably that the four of us have been together long enough."

"And how about you?" Roberts asked Logan.

"That we should think about the future and start looking out for ourselves."

"Alright," Roberts said to Rebecca and Logan, "you two, go home. Whatever game you thought you were playing with these two, it's over."

"Wait," Grace said. "Please. Don't split us up."

Roberts looked at Matt and Grace. "Look. I don't know what your relationship is with those two, how long you've known each other, or what part they've played up to this point. Do you really want them to be punished for your mistakes?"

"But we're their . . . friends," Grace said.

"Good friends don't just look out for their own best interests. They don't drag others through the mud of their own poor decisions." Roberts looked at Rebecca and Logan. He pointed to Matt and Grace. "These two think it's fun to destroy things, and they don't care that others have to clean up the mess. People like these, they take friendship for granted. But if it's all the same to you," Roberts said, as he pulled out his handcuffs, "I'm more than happy to take you all in."

"There you are," a voice called out from beyond the ticket booth.

"Jack?" Rebecca said.

"Do you know these two?" Roberts asked.

"How's it going? Uh, yeah. I'm a friend of the family."

Roberts looked at Rebecca and Logan.

"I thought you said that your *parents* were nearby?" Sanders said.

"Oh, they are," Jack replied. "Actually, if they were any closer, you'd probably trip over them. These two aren't in any trouble, are they?"

"These two?" Roberts motioned to Rebecca and Logan. "Not yet."

"Well, why don't we keep it that way. Besides, I heard that the incident at the pier is keeping you all pretty busy. I'm sure you wouldn't mind a little less paperwork on Christmas Eve. Here." Jack handed the detectives a business card. "It's good for twenty-five percent off anything in the store."

"Esoteric?" Sanders said. "You haven't heard?"

"Heard what?"

"Sorry to say, but there's a large boat illegally parked in your store."

"I hadn't heard that," Jack said, as he glanced down at Rebecca and Logan. "Well, the coupon doesn't expire."

"Alright, you're free to go," Roberts said.

Rebecca and Logan looked at Matt and Grace. Then they made their way past the ticket booth and down the long ramp leading toward the base of the Space Needle. Rebecca looked back to see Matt and Grace handcuffed and led away.

24: Mind Your Manor

"**H**ow'd you know where to find us?" Rebecca asked, as the Jeep pulled out from the roundabout beneath the Space Needle.

"Someone posted the video of your mom's dance at the Market."

"Wait, I thought you said that you had a plane to catch," Logan said.

"I did until it was cancelled because of the storm. I'm still on standby. But there I was in my hotel room. I woke up to find a dozen messages on my phone telling me about the crash at the pier. No one had anything specific, not even the news outlets. So I made my way down there to see for myself. No one could tell me much, so I walked over to Pike Place for some coffee. Got warmed up a bit. I had just walked out of Starbucks when I heard all this commotion a ways down the street. I walked toward this crowd of people, and there in the middle of it all, a car crunched up against the concrete barrier posts. Apparently, it slid out of control down the hill."

Jack continued. "Two detectives got out. They seemed alright. The vendor on the other side of the posts was a little shaken up, but otherwise fine. About the same time that the ambulance arrived, I heard the detective's radio say that the same girl from the Pike Place video was taking the monorail

201

from Westlake." Jack looked over at Rebecca. "What exactly have you gotten yourself into?"

"They think our parents had something to do with the pier crash."

"And why do they think that?"

"They found something of mine: a picture of Mom. An old picture back when she was young."

"Let me guess," Logan said, "you 'accidentally' left that behind."

Rebecca didn't respond.

"Oh, my gosh. You did leave it behind on purpose."

"And obviously, you haven't made it to the manor yet," Jack said.

"No," Rebecca replied.

Jack tapped his thumb against the steering wheel.

"What?"

"I'm thinking."

"About what?"

Logan looked out the rear window of the Jeep. "Is it just me, or is that SUV following us?"

"I'm thinking about what to do with you two." Jack looked at his watch.

"Just drop us off at the manor."

"Don't you have any family nearby? I'd feel a lot better if I knew you were somewhere safe."

"How about this. You drive us to the manor and if it's a dead end, we'll call our Aunt Beth. She lives nearby."

Jack tapped his thumb.

"Come on. You can even walk with us inside."

"Alright. But you go to your aunt's house if you need to."

"Promise."

Logan looked out the rear window again. The vehicle was gone. He let out a sigh of relief as he turned to Rebecca. "What do you think is going to happen to Mom and Dad?"

"Well, they were arrested. Usually, that's not a good thing. But they're together for a while longer, so that's good."

"I mean, what happens at midnight when they're still in jail? What happens if they're stuck that way?"

"I don't know."

"Then why'd you turn them in?"

Rebecca looked out the front window for a second. "Your snow boots."

"You're blaming this on my snow boots."

"Yes, this whole thing is your snow boots' fault."

"Really?"

"No. I'm trying to make a point." Rebecca sighed. "Walking around in the snow. Would you rather have only one boot, or both boots without any laces?"

"Both boots without laces."

"Me too."

"Awesome. That's great. I don't get it."

"You walk around with only one boot, you're going to get frostbite. Two are better than one, even if they aren't perfect."

"Yeah, but both of our boots are sitting in jail."

"And as long as they are, we have time to figure out the riddle before they do."

"And if we do? Then what?"

"Then we can decide what happens. If we find the antidote, then we hold the power. It's time we had a say whether or not our family stays together."

A uniformed officer lowered the tripod, bringing Grace into the camera's frame. The picture was taken.

"Turn to the right," the officer said. Matt turned, giving the officer the needed profile.

Grace wiped her fingers though it was impossible to remove all of the ink.

Each of Matt's fingers were inked and rolled onto paper.

"Busy night," one officer said to another.

"Tell me about it."

"Which holding cell are we putting the minors?"

"Uh, holding cells two and three. Girls in two, boys in three. Any more though and we're transporting them all to juvy."

"Alright, this way." The officer led Matt and Grace down a sterile hallway illuminated by fluorescent lights. The door to holding cell two opened. "Okay, in ya go." Matt and Grace looked at each other. "He's not going off to war, kid. Move it."

Grace entered the cell. A bench lined the perimeter of the room's three inner walls. The uneasiness of suddenly being the room's focus prompted Grace to quickly find a seat.

Jack's Jeep tires crunched to a stop outside a four-story brick building. He shut the engine off. "Well, here we are. Come on, I'll walk you in."

The front door of the manor swung open under the power of the wind. The side window curtains danced in place as snow swirled about inside the building. Rebecca and Logan stepped inside and closed the door. The sizable lobby was modestly decorated with aging furniture and secondhand Christmas decorations.

"See," Rebecca said to Jack. "It's a retirement home. Doesn't get much safer than this."

"You obviously haven't seen *The Visit.*" Jack looked around and then at his watch. "Alright, but if you don't find anything, you be sure to call your aunt."

"Of course."

Jack sighed. "Stay out of trouble. The both of you."

A gust of wind blew Rebecca's hair as Jack left. The door closed and everything was calm.

Logan sniffed the air. "Smells funny in here. Not like 'ha ha' funny, but you know. Funny."

"Where is everyone?" Rebecca said, as she quietly walked past a shabbily decorated Christmas tree and reception desk. "Look," Rebecca said, pointing to a white coat draped over a chair. "Looks like the same kind of coat that was on the surveillance camera."

Outside, Jack retrieved his keys from his pocket as he walked down the sidewalk toward his Jeep. "Excuse me," Jack said, as he passed a group of young men.

"Excuse us," Chet replied.

Rebecca looked around to make sure no one was watching, then hopped up onto the countertop and dropped to the other side.

"What are you looking for?" Logan asked. "And as a follow-up question, what are we doing at a retirement center?"

Rebecca pulled a binder labeled *Staff Directory* from below the countertop. Logan walked toward the door and gently pulled one of the window drapes to the side. The wind-whipped powder made it virtually impossible to see past the manor's walkway. After a moment, Rebecca held the opened binder up to Logan. "Look familiar?"

Logan took a step toward his sister. "Is that the woman from the store?"

"She's a nurse here. Mystery woman has a name: Cynthia."

"Why would a nurse send a Christmas gift to our house?" Logan asked, as he stepped back to the window. "And a bottle of wine no less? For being in the medical field, she really doesn't understand the danger of sending alcohol to someone with a drinking problem." Logan again pulled the drape to the side. This time four figures approached through the snow.

Rebecca ran her finger along a posted weekly schedule. "Maybe we can ask her. She's working tonight."

"Holy crap, they're here!" Logan ran and jumped up onto the counter. He tripped over the counter's edge and plummeted to Rebecca's feet. Logan pulled Rebecca to the floor as four silhouettes appeared at the door's frosted glass.

25: Silent "U"

Matt stared at a crack in the floor. Halfway down the bench, a young man leaned forward from the line of seated cellmates. The movement in Matt's peripheral prompted him to look over. "You've got to be kidding me," Matt muttered to himself as he returned to studying the floor's imperfections.

"I had a feeling our paths would cross again," Simon said, as he approached Matt.

"I find that hard to believe."

"Sorry about running out on you back there." Simon sat next to Matt. "Looks like you fared alright though. And the others?"

"Not sure how that concerns you."

"What can I say, in high-stress situations you either fight, flight, or freeze. I'm a flight guy. Guilty. We all have our survival instincts."

"Fight, flight, or freeze, huh?"

"It's gotten me this far."

"You do realize that you're sitting in jail, right?"

"Alive. Doesn't really matter where."

Matt sighed. "Grace is in the next cell over. I'm not sure about Rebecca and Logan. We lost them near the Space Needle."

"I'm sure they'll be fine. They seem to fend for themselves well enough."

"Yeah. What about Emily?"

"She made it out too. We got separated at the pier, but she's fine. So what did they get you for?"

"We had a narc on our team." Matt looked around the cell. "What about the rest of them?"

"Mostly breaking and entering. Minor theft."

"Don't you feel responsible?"

"Of course. Proudly."

"You sent them all out into the cold."

"That's one thing about a revolt: there's just never a perfect time." Simon looked around the room. "They're free. And that's all that matters."

"Again, you do realize you're sitting in jail, right?"

"The air is clean. No one's dying tonight. That's a start."

"So what's your plan? How're you going to get out of this one?"

"Maybe you're not too familiar with how jail works, but they lock the doors from the outside. No one's leaving tonight. Besides that, there's a massive investigation going on about what happened at the pier last night. You make it out, you'll be back here faster than you can say Dunkin's Toy Chest."

"Why would I say Dunkin's Toy Chest?"

"Why wouldn't you? The point is you might as well get comfortable."

"No. There has to be some way out of here."

"This isn't a movie." Simon leaned back and closed his eyes. "No one's tying up the guard with ribbon and cutting the lock with magic tinsel. The only way you leave this cell is if they say so."

An officer opened the cell door. "Matthew Stevens. Come with me."

Simon opened one eye. "Doesn't mean I'm wrong."

∾⁊ᵒᵉ

"Smells funny in here," Chet said. The four stood in the entryway.

Logan and Rebecca remained perfectly still under the countertop. Chet walked up to the reception desk where he noticed an open binder.

"What is it?" Nate asked.

"Dunno." Chet leaned over and took the binder. "Just a directory."

"Is that important?"

"Dude! Dunno!" Chet flung the binder back behind the desk. It landed on the floor next to Logan.

Chet walked to the far end of the lobby. He checked himself out in the large hanging mirror. To his left and right, hallways stretched long distances. "Split up. You find them, you bring them to me."

After a few moments, Logan crawled out from under the desk. "We need to get out of here."

"And go where?"

"As far away as possible."

"But we haven't gotten any answers yet."

"And maybe that's okay. I'm actually starting to warm to the idea of having child parents. Oh sure, going through puberty at the same time as your mom and dad will be a little weird—"

"Shh." Rebecca retrieved the directory from the floor and flipped the page back to the nurse. "She's here somewhere." Rebecca put the binder back in place and pulled out another. The cover read, *Building Code and Compliance*. Rebecca flipped through the book, stopping on one particular page.

"What do you see?"

"It's a map of the building." Rebecca ripped the page from the binder. "Here," she pointed to a small box. "Employee break room. Let's start there."

Rebecca and Logan jumped back over the counter and proceeded toward the large mirror.

"Which way?"

Rebecca rotated the map upside down, and pointed to the right. "That way."

The steps of Logan and Rebecca were cautious as they walked down the poorly lit hallway toward what sounded like Christmas music.

"What are you doing?" Rebecca asked.

"Walking backward. Don't need Chet and the three dumb men sneaking up on us." Logan tripped and fell to the floor.

Rebecca helped him up. "Why don't you leave the multi-tasking to me?"

"Watch your step. I think this old carpet is starting to come up a little."

"Come on, sounds like there's some kind of a party going on up ahead."

The Christmas music became louder as Rebecca and Logan approached a double door. The two were about to enter the banquet hall when a familiar voice spoke over the sound system.

"Can I have your attention, please?" Chet said, holding a microphone in one hand and a turkey leg in the other. "First things first: Merry Christmas, old people. Now, I won't take up too much of your time, as most of you don't have a lot to spare. Especially you, old timer," Chet said, pointing to a man with an oxygen tank. "I'm looking for two young people. Obviously, they'll stand out. Like new slats on an old fence. But I haven't spotted them yet. So Logan and Rebecca, wherever you are, it's time to end this."

"Boo," a woman said from a table near the front.

"Hey, Life Alert, I ran into Santa on the way here; he wanted me to tell you that he's bringing you a casket for Christmas. Okay? Now, as I was saying . . ."

Rebecca looked at the paper. "Come on. The break room is in the basement. The stairs are just down the hall."

The door to the break room swung open. Rebecca closed and locked the door behind her. The two then approached a wall of lockers.

"She's not here," Logan said, as he walked into a small kitchenette. He opened the refrigerator.

"What are you doing?"

"I'm hungry. Just seeing if there's a string cheese or Go-Gurt or something."

The sound of the doorknob turning caught both their attention. Rebecca ran behind the kitchenette wall as a key was inserted and the door opened.

Rebecca peered around the corner. She leaned back toward Logan and whispered, "It's her."

"Who?"

"Seriously? Cynthia. What are you eating?"

"Gusher. Want one?"

"Yeah."

"You can't be in here," the woman said. "You need to leave."

Rebecca was just about to step out and explain the situation when another spoke before her.

"We were just looking for our friends," Chet said. "We thought we saw them come in here."

"No, I'm the only one here," Cynthia said, as she grabbed her coat and closed her locker. "I'm going to have to ask you to leave. Like right now. I'm in a hurry." Chet looked over the woman's shoulder as he and his friends were ushered back into the hallway.

Rebecca ran to the door as it closed. "No, no, no, no." She clenched her fists and gently put them to the door.

Logan walked to Cynthia's locker. He shook the door handle. "Locked."

The small lock was then suddenly smashed—pieces of it fell to the floor. Logan jumped. Rebecca stood holding a fire extinguisher. "Geez, a little warning next time?" Logan said, as he opened the small metal door.

"What's inside?"

"Pictures taped to the door. Uh . . . some clothes, perfume." Logan sprayed the perfume. "Woof."

"Anybody in those pictures look familiar?"

Logan scanned the photos. "Nah. Looks like most were taken with people here."

Rebecca looked at the few items on the small metal shelf. "What's that?"

"What?"

"Up there."

Logan retrieved a thin black book. "Looks like some sort of planner."

"Here, let me see." Rebecca took the book and flipped through its pages. "Look." She retrieved a loose piece of paper.

Logan tilted his head to see the end of Rebecca's pointing finger. "It's a list of all the residents that are under her care."

Rebecca looked at a page stapled to the back of the list. The stapled page was titled *Presents to Buy*. "Cynthia must buy and send presents for residents who can't do it themselves."

Beside each of her patients, an item to purchase was listed alongside a mailing address. Rebecca ran her finger down the list. She stopped at an entry. "Logan."

"That's our address." Logan looked at the corresponding patient. "So the bottle was sent by someone in this building?" Logan looked at his sister. "Who?"

"Looks like a Ms. Brinkman. Room 206."

"What about Chet?" Logan asked, as Rebecca closed the locker.

"He was kicked out of the building."

"And you believe that?"

"Well, we can't stay down here." Rebecca looked at a nearby clock. "Time's running out." She slowly opened the break room door. "Come on." The two stepped out into the hallway. "At the very least, he's not down here anymore."

"There he is!" Chet yelled from the opposite end of the hallway. "I knew they were down here."

"I mean, did you actually look to make sure the coast was clear?" Logan said.

"Logan?"

"Yeah, yeah."

"Run!"

Chet ran full speed from the opposite end of the hallway. Not far behind, Luke, Ryan, and Nate rounded the corner like a stampede of buffalo charging through a ravine.

Logan panted as he reached the top step of the basement staircase. "There's no way I can outrun them."

Rebecca stopped to look at the map. "This way!" The two sprinted down the hallway back toward the sounds of the banquet room: Christmas music, collective chatter, clanging dishware. Not far behind, Chet spewed threats and profanity. Logan began narrating the chase in an Australian accent:

"The beast gains on its prey. Helpless and feeble, the young male prepares himself for the inevitable."

"Shut up," Rebecca said, as the two raced up a large winding staircase.

Chet rounded the corner at the top of the stairs and tripped over a cane.

"What's the matter? Fallen and you can't get up?" an elderly woman said, as she slid her cane back to her side. "Tell Santa to keep the casket."

"Room 206. Right over there. We're only going to get one shot at this." Rebecca pounded on the door.

Logan bent forward out of breath. "I think I'm going to throw up."

Rebecca anxiously bobbed in place as she looked back and forth between the hall and the door. "Come on. Come on. Come on."

The door opened.

"Can I help you?" a gray-haired man asked.

"Sorry to bother you," Rebecca said. She looked down the hall and back. "But would it be okay if we step inside for a moment?"

"You want to come in?"

"Yes, I think we can spare a few minutes. Thanks for asking," Logan said, as he and Rebecca brushed past the man.

"Would you mind closing that?" Rebecca asked.

The man shut the door and looked through the peephole as Chet and the others rushed past. "Why are you running from those boys?"

"Because walking wouldn't be fast enough," Logan said, as he caught his breath.

"You'll have to excuse my brother. It's a long story. I'm Rebecca, by the way. The enervated one over there is Logan."

"How dare you call me that."

"It means tired."

"Oh, well add it to the list anyway."

"The name's Benjamin."

"How you doin', Benji?" Logan asked still wheezing.

"Well, come in then. Might as well make yourselves comfortable."

Rebecca and Logan entered the living room. A few neatly wrapped presents sat beneath a small Christmas tree. Framed photos hung on the wall. "Are these pictures of your family?" Rebecca asked.

"They are," Benjamin said, as he heated a teakettle.

"Sorry to barge in on you like this. Especially with it being Christmas Eve and all. You must be expecting them soon," Rebecca said, motioning to the pictures.

"No. I'm afraid not."

"Never seen a storm like this," Logan said, as he looked out the window. He quickly retracted his head at the sight of Chet's vehicle. "It's messing a lot of things up for everyone. I'm sure they'll make it though."

Benjamin smiled politely. "No, I don't think they will."

"Come on. No storm is that bad," Logan said.

"I'm afraid some are."

Rebecca noticed a small stack of letters on the coffee table. "Will your wife be home soon?"

"My wife? No. It's just me now."

"I'm so sorry."

"What does this mean?" Logan whispered to Rebecca.

"I think we're too late."

"Too late for what?" Benjamin asked.

"It's nothing." Rebecca tried to gather her thoughts. "I think we were looking for your wife. I'm sorry. We shouldn't have come here. We didn't mean to bother you, Mr. Brinkman."

"Well, first, my wife didn't die. We've been divorced for a long time. And second, my last name's not Brinkman. It's A'houle."

"That is tragic," Logan said.

"It sounds worse than it is."

"Uh, how it sounds is all that it is. So, a-h-o-l-e?"

"Not that it matters, but it's spelled a-h-o-u-l-e. The 'u' is silent."

"Why on earth is the 'u' silent? If ever a letter should speak up—"

"Logan. Shut up."

"Fine, but I gotta know something; how bad was it?"

"How bad was what?"

"The bullying. With a last name like that, it must've been bad."

"Is there a reason you're here? Or is it just to dig up a bunch of painful memories the night Christ was born?"

"Again, sorry for my brother."

"Because so far we've covered my estranged family, my ex-wife, and the fact that I was bullied because my name sounds like a butt. All in under a minute."

"Got this a couple days back," Logan said, pointing to his eye. "I think you and me are a bit alike."

"And that's supposed to make me feel better?"

"Well, you don't have to be mean about it."

"Again, why are you actually here?"

"Mrs. Brinkman. Do you know who she is?"

"Yeah, I know her. The name anyway. She's the woman who lived here before me. She moved out a little while back. I keep getting her mail though." Benjamin pointed to a stack of envelopes near the kitchen. "Haven't gotten around to sending them along yet."

Rebecca took a few envelopes in her hands; she flipped through them front to back. Rebecca looked at one more closely and then showed Logan. "Written to Dad with this room's return address. And look who it's from."

"Cynthia."

"You don't think that Dad and her were—"

"No way."

"Then why is she sending him letters and gifts?"

"I don't know."

"Matthew Stevens is your father?" Benjamin asked.

"Yeah," Rebecca said.

"Wait here a minute." Benjamin left for a moment and returned with a small shoebox of unopened letters. "Found these the other day in my closet. She must've left them behind by mistake. They're all written to your father too."

"I wonder why he never got them," Logan said.

"He did. See here," Benjamin pointed to the corner of one of the envelopes. "Return to sender. Just like the one in your hand."

The teakettle whistled.

Logan took one of the letters. "So two different women were writing Dad from this room."

"Seems to be that way."

Logan took an envelope. "What if we were to open one of them?"

"Do you really want to know what some strange woman is writing to Dad?"

Logan put the letter down. "Good point."

The apartment phone rang.

"Wait a minute." Rebecca reached for her backpack. "Remember the letter I told you about in Dad's office?"

"Yeah."

"Well, Dad took the letter from me, but I still have the envelope."

"Why are you carrying garbage around? Is that why you carry disinfectant wipes?"

"Look."

"Yeah, it's another letter from Cynthia. So what?"

"It has a different return address. This one came from Green Lake."

Logan looked at the letter.

"It was the last one written, so that must be where we need to go next."

"You won't read a letter written by a strange woman, but you want to go to her house?"

"Good point. But at least we know Aunt Beth lives somewhere around that area too. We can always make for her house if things get weird."

"Honestly, how much weirder could things get?"

Benjamin walked into the living room, with a puzzled look on his face. He held the phone out to Rebecca. "It's for you."

26: One Phone Call

"Sit," the officer told Matt. Matt sat down and looked around the room—a large space filled with desks and police officers. He spotted Grace speaking to Sanders.

"Hey, look who it is," Matt said. Roberts took a seat on the opposite side of the desk.

Roberts leaned back in his chair and folded his arms. "So why don't you tell me what's going on here? You steal over a thousand dollars in clothing and equipment, you were involved in one of the biggest Seattle waterfront disasters in recent memory, and you crash a vehicle into the Bainbridge police department. But that's not the first time you've crashed your car, is it?"

"Excuse me?"

Roberts turned his monitor toward Matt. "Let's add 'stolen identity' to your growing list of criminal activity, shall we?"

Grace looked at the monitor Sanders had just turned. "Does she look familiar?"

A news article illuminated Grace's face.

Of course she does, Grace thought to herself. She read the headline: Famed Ballet Dancer Injured in Horrific Viaduct Crash. Three pictures accompanied the article: headshots of Matt and Grace, and one of a mangled car on the side of the highway. Grace began to read the article. ". . . husband, acclaimed architect Matthew Stevens, fell asleep at the wheel causing the accident just before midnight. He was charged with a DWI . . ."

"Does she?" Sanders repeated.

"Does she what?"

"Look familiar?"

"No."

"Well, she's the one you've been impersonating these past few days." Sanders turned the monitor back toward herself. "We know that you and your boyfriend over there stole their identity, their SUV"—Grace fidgeted in her seat—"and that ring and necklace." Grace instinctively touched it. "Hand it over."

"It's my—"

"It's your what? Your wedding ring? Your necklace? I'm sure the real Grace Stevens will be happy to see that again." Grace unhooked her necklace and handed the items over.

"It's not what you think."

"What isn't?"

"Any of it."

Sanders leaned back in her chair. "Now would be a good time clear the air."

Grace leaned forward as if wanting to tell a secret. "Something happened two nights ago."

Humoring Grace, Sanders leaned forward and whispered, "What happened two nights ago?"

"Something I can't explain."

"I suggest you try."

"I know this will sound crazy, but that woman in the picture *is* me. I went to sleep two nights ago and woke up this way. We've spent the past two days trying to figure out how to get back to normal."

"We?"

"My husband and I," Grace said, pointing to Matt.

"So you're telling me that you two are actually Grace and Matthew Stevens?"

"That's what I'm telling you, yes."

"And how do you suppose this happened?"

Grace leaned back in her chair. "We drank some old monastery wine."

"Holy wine did this to you?"

"No. I don't think so anyway."

"So it didn't?"

"No. I mean, I don't know if it was 'holy' wine. Not really sure what the criteria is for that."

"So maybe just your typical run of the mill, miracle monk wine."

Grace sighed. "I guess."

"You see all the young people in here tonight? They all have some kind of story—all crazy, none of them true. But I have to hand it to you; your story is by far the most unbelievable."

"Thanks."

"That wasn't a compliment."

Matt looked down from the monitor—the same article Grace read shone brightly on the screen. "What happens next?"

Roberts placed a phone in front of Matt. "You get your one call. Better hope someone answers." Roberts stood and stretched. "You and all your little friends have made a lot of work for us. Not like I had anything better to do tonight. I need coffee." Roberts cuffed Matt to the chair. "Don't go anywhere."

Matt looked at the phone; his finger tapped the desk. He looked over at Grace as she handed her necklace over to Sanders.

Grace looked over; their eyes met for a moment. Matt lifted the receiver and dialed. He waited as the phone rang.

"Hello?" a man answered.

"Is this . . . room 206?"

"It is."

"This may be a strange question, but are there by chance two children there with you?"

"Why, are you after them too?"

"After them too?"

"Here, let me get the girl. I'm guessing you'll have better luck with whatever it is you need with her."

Rebecca placed the phone to her ear. "Hello?"

"Rebecca?"

"Matt? How'd you know we were here?"

"Lucky guess."

"Wait, where are you calling from?"

"This is my one call."

"This is your one phone call from jail?"

"It is."

"Sorry, but Cynthia isn't here."

"Cynthia?

"Yeah, we know all about it."

"No, Rebecca, you don't."

"Well, we're on our way to find out. We have a new address: Green Lake."

"Rebecca, listen very closely to me. Don't go there."

"Why? Afraid we'll find out about your secret?"

"There are some things that you don't need to know. This little adventure we've been on, it's over."

Rebecca walked over to the door and looked out the peephole. Chet raced by again. "What about your meeting tomorrow? Pretty sure Mr. Cartnight won't let a kid run his company."

"It's much more complicated than that."

"And I'm sure you can't tell me why."

Matt was silent.

"Well, you've never been one to finish what you start. Except of course for when it comes to something stupid like a building. Luckily, it's not up to you this time. Better ask for another phone call."

"Rebecca, don't go—"

Rebecca slammed the phone onto the cradle. She closed her eyes.

"What'd he say?" Logan asked.

"He said not to go to the address. He actually sounded scared."

"So what are we going to do?"

Rebecca plopped onto the couch. "I'm not sure."

Benjamin carefully poured steaming water into one of the ceramic mugs. "Well, tea always helps me think." He filled the other two mugs and placed small covers on each. "Maybe taking a moment to rest isn't such a bad thing either."

Benjamin returned to the living room with the beverages. "Now, what really brings you to my doorstep on Christmas Eve? And in the middle of a snowstorm no less?"

Benjamin quietly set the tray on to the coffee table in front of Rebecca and Logan. Both were fast asleep.

27: Bully

Rebecca opened her eyes. Logan and Benjamin were talking about something. She propped herself up and rubbed the sleep from her eyes. She then took her mug from the table and sipped.

Cold.

She put the mug back on the coffee table and took her journal from her backpack.

Benjamin leaned back in his rocking chair. "So three little words. What do you think they are?"

"Got me, Benihana. I'm just along for the ride."

"I love you," Rebecca said. "The three little words are 'I love you.' The only problem is that they have to be meant."

"And the laxative. During parent appreciation night?"

"Yeah," Logan said.

"Right in his water bottle, huh?"

"Yep."

"Well, that makes sense why those boys want to beat you up. And what about your parents?"

"Nah, they don't want to beat me up."

"No, I mean where are they?"

"Oh, in jail."

"In jail? I'm sorry to hear that." Benjamin set his empty mug on the table. "The thing about facing bullies is that you can't always meet them on their level. Sometimes you need to use your own God-given skills."

"I think God made me a smartass, so I've got that going for me."

"I can vouch for that," Rebecca said, as she finished writing and put the journal back in her pack.

"Then he made you clever and quick-witted. Use your words, not your fists. Bullies oftentimes intimidate with their size and strength. You can defend yourself with your brain. But be smart about it."

"And therein lies the problem," Rebecca said.

"How about you go back to sleep for a little bit?" Logan replied. "Go ahead and shut your eyes and shut your mouth."

"Words, not fists," Benjamin repeated. "Trust me."

"Because that's what you did when you were bullied?"

"Because I was the bully."

"Whoa, Shyamalan twist," Logan said.

"I may have started out as the victim, but it didn't take long for me to turn the tables. If they wouldn't respect me, then they would fear me. But respect through fear is not respect at all. It's compliance by intimidation and threat. It worked: the name-calling eventually stopped. But it came at a high cost."

"You were just standing up for yourself."

"At first. But then I let my anger get the better of me. I soon became the thing I hated; and I didn't even realize it. I was particularly cruel to new students and for no good reason. I just wanted them to know, day one, not to mess with me. I demanded respect when I should've earned it."

"And how do you earn it?"

"Building character, showing kindness." Benjamin looked at one of his family pictures. "Respect by intimidation isn't respect at all. It's just fear. Took me a long time to realize it."

Rebecca looked out the window. It was night. She then looked at her watch. "We should really get going."

Logan looked out the window. "Chet's car is gone."

"Can I call someone to come pick you up?"

"Appreciate the offer," Rebecca said. "But it's okay. We really need to do this on our own."

Benjamin stood and the two shook hands.

"Thanks again for letting us into your home."

"Take care, Benji," Logan said, as the two shook hands. "You're the nicest A'houle I've ever met."

"Remember what I said, young man. Don't stoop any further than you already have. Leave the mud for the pigs."

"I'll try."

"Are you sure you two will be okay?"

"Always moving forward," Rebecca said with a smile.

"Even during a storm? Looks like it started snowing pretty good again."

"Especially during the storm. Someone once said that suffering produces perseverance; perseverance, character; and character, hope.'"

"The apostle Paul," Benjamin replied.

"No, it was some guy at the pier," Logan said.

"We'll be fine, but we're running out of time."

"And where again are you going?"

"From what I can figure, the one place that's ever scared my father."

28: Struggling in a Winter Wonderland

An officer escorted Matt and Grace back down the hallway to their respective holding cells. The doors closed.

"Any luck?" Matt asked through the bars to the next room over.

"Literally, couldn't think of one number. Who actually remembers anyone's phone number anymore? You?"

"I actually talked to Rebecca."

"You did?"

"The kids are safe. They made it to the manor."

"Well, that's a relief. At least they'll be alright until we figure this mess out."

Matt didn't reply.

"What?"

"Chet's there too. I don't think they're staying."

"What do you mean they're not staying?"

Matt didn't respond.

"I swear, Matt. If anything happens to my children, I'll never forgive you."

"Our."

"What?"

"They're *our* children. Don't think that I don't care about them or that I wouldn't do anything to keep them safe."

Grace sighed. "Where are they going?"

"Somewhere I promised myself that I'd never go back."

Rebecca and Logan stepped outside the manor into the storm—the sudden drop in temperature surprised them both.

"Where to?" Logan asked through his face mask.

"This way," Rebecca said, pointing north.

Winds blew the powder from the street skyward; it swirled wildly in the yellow glow of the streetlights as Rebecca and Logan shuffled their way through the shin-high snow.

"Are we seriously going to walk all the way to Green Lake in this?"

"Unless you have a better idea."

"Green Lake's like, miles away."

"Complaining won't get us there any faster."

"I'm just statin' facts."

"So am I."

"Bruh."

"Put it on the list."

Streets and sidewalks were no longer distinguishable from one another in the rising snow. Rebecca and Logan trudged down the deserted street where parked cars and trucks were slowly buried under a blanket of white.

"Do you hear that?" Logan asked.

"The silence? Yes, and it's fantastic."

"No. Stop a second."

The two waited for a moment.

"I don't hear anything. Come on."

"Wait, there it is again. You don't hear that?"

"Hear what?"

Just then, headlights shined from behind the two of them, casting their shadows onto the powder. Logan and Rebecca looked at each other and then turned shielding their eyes. "Oh, Looogan," a voice called out from behind the headlights.

"Rebecca?"

"Yeah?"

"Get me my brown pants."

29: Ghosts of Past

Matt stared at the ceiling. The cold cell wall made for a sufficient prop to rest his head as he sat on the equally cold bench.

Simon strolled up to Matt, hands in pockets. "Were you able to get through to anyone?"

Matt moved his eyes from the ceiling to Simon. "Do you believe what you said, that our past doesn't dictate our future?"

"What do you mean?"

"Yesterday in Undertown, before the flood, I heard you over the speaker. You said that your past doesn't dictate your future. Do you really believe that?"

"Why? Because I've gone from foster care to Undertown to jail?"

"Yeah."

"The way I see it, you're either running toward your future or from your past."

"Either way, at least you're moving forward."

"You ever try driving a car by only looking through the rearview mirror? It won't take long before you crash. But I think the more important question is: how many people are in the car when you do? My focus isn't backward. It can't be. I need to keep my eyes on the road ahead—for myself and for Emily."

"What do you remember about your parents?"

Simon took a seat on the bench.

"My parents? Bits and pieces." Simon looked at the floor and smiled. "My dad used to play the piano and my mother would sing. They were good; at least to a six-year-old anyway. They would go on for what seemed like hours. I used to think that they were famous, ya know? My sister and I would hide under the dining room table and listen. I remember the table-cloth almost reached the floor, so we were out of sight. It was our secret place. We just sat and listened."

"Sounds nice."

"It was. Of course, my sister and I would also hide under the same table during the yelling, the threats, and the tears. Funny how they could love each other in the morning and hate each other at night."

"What happened?"

"I don't even really know. One day a woman I'd never met before came to the door and took my sister and me away. Then we moved around a lot—a condo here, a house there—families of all different kinds. Some nice; some not so nice. We played the game. We put on smiles and did what we were told until the day they tried to split us up. That's when we decided to ditch the system."

"How'd you know where to go?"

"We didn't. The first few nights on our own, we had enough money for a motel room. But money soon ran out and we were desperate. On the street, you hear things. Where to sleep. Where to eat. Didn't take long before we found out about Undertown. We were there for three years, four months, and seventeen days."

"I'm sorry about what happened to Joey."

Simon rubbed his wrist where his bracelet was.

"That must have been difficult to get through."

"Still is. So what about you? What do you remember about your parents?"

"BC or AD?" Matt grinned. "Before Crisis or After Divorce."

"Either. Both."

"Our parents divorced when I was thirteen, so my memory of them while they were together is pretty clear."

"Our?"

"I have a little sister too." Matt took a breath. "Mom and Dad were okay, I thought. We were happy. They never fought. No screaming or threats or anything like that. I don't know, maybe they just hid it well. We did the family vacation thing—Yellowstone, the Grand Canyon—we celebrated birthdays and Christmas. We were fine until we weren't, ya know? One night, Mom just left. I did everything I knew how to make her stay, but it wasn't enough."

"So she never tried to contact you?"

"I didn't say that. But a guy can only stomach a sob story and excuses for so long." Matt shook his head. "Whatever doesn't kill you makes you stronger, right?"

"Unless of course it's still killing you." Simon looked at Matt's clenched fists. "You looking to do something with those?"

Matt loosened his hands.

"I'm guessing your eyes are still on the rearview mirror."

"After they split, we didn't see much of our mom. My dad said that she needed to find herself, whatever that meant. I'm not sure she ever did. Dad remarried a couple of times. When I turned eighteen, I was so out of there. I hated that house so much. I felt a little bad leaving my sister behind, but I was done with family. I promised myself that when I was older, things would be different; that when I had a family, I'd always be there. I promised myself that I would never do what my mother did to us."

"Matt."

"Yeah?"

"When you were eighteen? What are you talking about? Man, if you start to lose it now, you're not going to do well in juvy."

Matt realized how odd his last words must have sounded. "Right." He took Mr. Cartnight's business card from his back pocket. He flipped it over and looked at the hand-written appointment. "I've got to get out of here."

"And go where?"

Matt tore the card in half. "Toward my future."

"Well, you're not going to Shawshank your way out of this one. Like I said, this isn't a movie. No one leaves unless they say so."

"Alright, everybody up," an officer said through the bars. "You're being moved."

Simon stood. "Doesn't mean I'm wrong."

30: Bruises and Bloody Noses

"**W**here are you taking us?" Rebecca asked.

"It's more about the journey than the destination," Chet said, as he stretched his arm over the backseat.

"What, are you going to beat me up again? Real original."

"You're right," Chet said. "Bruises and bloody noses heal"—Chet flicked Logan's eye—"eventually. Maybe it's time for something a little more long-lasting."

"What, are you going kill me?"

"All in good time."

31: Family Reunion

"Alright, let's go, let's go, let's go," the officer said.

"Where are you taking us?" Matt asked.

"Juvy."

"Now?"

"Trust me; no one wants to take you to a new facility in the middle of a snowstorm, but as of just now, we've officially reached capacity at this station and we now need the cell for newly arrested adult offenders." Then addressing the entire group the officer continued, "What's going to happen is we are going to restrain your hands in preparation for transport, then you will be ushered outside where vans will take you across the city to a juvenile facility.

"Alright, here we go. Everyone in a straight line. Once the restraint is applied, officers Franks and Smith will take you to the transport vehicles." The officer began to zip-tie the wrists of each of the young people in the cell.

Matt and Simon stood in line; each took their turn having their hands bound. The male and female cells emptied. Matt was side by side with Grace as the line of young people made their way down the hall and into the main room.

At the same time, two men were led toward the cells. The two groups slowly made their way toward the newly arrested pair. The men approaching had a strange yet familiar appearance.

"Is that . . ." Matt started.

"How are they alive?" Simon asked.

"This isn't going to be good," Grace said.

"My kids!" the Orator yelled. "Where are you taking my babies?"

The two men approached the middle of the line. The Orator and Simon made eye contact.

"You!"

32: Eh Tu, Bec?

"High school has not been good, has it, Logan?" Chet said. "You're by far one of the saddest freshmen I've ever met. No one likes you, and I swear that's not an exaggeration. Goths, preps, stoners, nerds, loners. Even that foreign exchange student doesn't like you. I don't even know how that's possible because she speaks like zero English.

"What I'm trying to say is that I didn't think there was a single person who would care if you never came back. But I was wrong." Chet reached over to Rebecca and pulled her coat collar down. "Aw, babe, it's fading. When I gave her that, I found out for the first time that she had a brother."

Logan looked at his sister. "Him? He's your boyfriend?"

"Surprised?" Chet asked.

"You mean besides the fact that you two like talking about me while making out."

"That's not what I . . . I didn't say that," Chet said.

"Well, that's what it sounded like, Chet, and that's messed up."

"I wasn't talking about you while—"

"You're right. That is worse than getting beat up. Worst. Journey. Ev—"

Chet reached over and slammed Logan's head into the side glass.

"Hey!" Rebecca reached for Logan.

Logan rubbed the back of his head.

"I see you at school. You eat alone. You walk alone. You have no friends. I'll bet the only conversation you have is with your sister on the ferry ride home. Tell me I'm wrong. Do it. Tell me I'm wrong."

Logan looked down.

"Seriously? That was a total guess. I didn't actually think . . . oh, that is sad. The only person you can count on. The only person that might actually care if you were dead."

Chet reached into his pocket and pulled out a phone. He threw it onto Logan's lap. "Press play." Logan took a breath. He looked at the phone and then at his sister. "Don't look at her. I said, 'press play.'"

Logan took the phone. A scene began to unfold—a scene all too familiar. The video started out shaky, but the audio was clear: laughing. It's been said that laughter is the best medicine; it made Logan sick the first time, and it turned his stomach now. The person filming the scene eventually gained composure and the video steadied. Logan watched himself get punched for the second time, crawl on all fours, and slip headfirst to the ground.

Logan pressed pause. "Thanks, but I already know how this one ends."

Chet smiled. "No you don't."

"Chet, stop it," Rebecca said.

"Keep watching."

"Don't do this," Rebecca said.

Logan looked at his sister. He then looked back to the screen and continued watching. A new depth of humiliation found its way into Logan as he saw himself the way others did. Logan paused the video. "I don't want to watch this anymore."

"I will put your head through that window."

"Chet, please," Rebecca said.

Logan pressed play. The worst of the scene played out just as Logan remembered, both in-person and online. Then the video continued—a segment that was never uploaded to social media.

The school crowd thinned and Chet walked up to the camera.

"Did you get all that?"

"Mm-hmm."

"Here, let me see," Chet said, as he took his phone back from the one who filmed the fight.

Logan's face went pale as Rebecca came into view.

"Thanks, babe," Chet said.

The screen went dark.

33: The Fight Before Christmas

"You! You did this!" the Orator shouted as he lunged at Simon. Grace and Matt were shoved away as the sudden attack sent the room into a brawl. The Orator tackled Simon into a line of water coolers sending the containers toppling from their bases. Water raced across the tile floor.

Simon head-butted the Orator and struck him in the face with his tied fists. He then freed himself with scissors found atop a nearby desk.

"Matt!" Simon shouted as he tossed the scissors to Matt through the crowd.

Matt caught the scissors and severed his and Grace's zip ties.

One of the officers grabbed the Orator and brought him down. Amidst the struggle, Simon removed a taser from the officer's belt.

Matt threw the scissors onto a desk. "Now's our chance," he said, seeing a clear path to the front door.

Grace left Matt's side and retrieved her necklace and ring from Sanders' desk. "Alright, ready."

A hand grabbed the back of Grace's coat and jerked her backward.

"I remember you," William said, as he slowly pulled Grace through the water.

Matt leaped onto William's back to choke him out. William threw Grace into the closet desk knocking her out; he then turned his focus on Matt. He reached back and flipped Matt onto the desk just above Grace. Matt quickly gained his composure and smashed William in the face with a closed laptop. William dropped to his knees, and then fell face-first into the shallow pool of water.

Matt rolled off the desk to Grace's side. He scooped her up off the floor and carried her to dry ground.

William's eyes opened, blood pooled around his nose. He pushed himself up off the floor and steadied himself against the desk.

Simon fought his way toward William, taser activated, until Roberts stepped in and blocked his path. The two stood a few feet apart.

The scissors that were once on the desk were now in William's hand. He moved toward Grace.

Roberts looked at Simon's taser. "Know how to use that? The 'on' switch is the little button on the side."

Simon looked past Roberts. Matt tried to wake Grace, unaware of William's approach. William tossed the scissors into the air and grabbed them like a dagger.

Simon looked at Roberts and smiled. Roberts looked at Simon's outstretched hand and then down at the pool of water surrounding his feet.

Robert's shoulders dropped. "Ah, come on."

Simon released the crackling taser. The weapon hit the floor sending an electric pulse through the brawl. In an instant, everyone standing in water fell.

Matt blocked the knife from striking Grace's face as William fell forward unconscious.

Matt's face slowly came into focus as Grace opened her eyes.

"You're okay," Matt said. "You're okay."

"What happened?"

"Come on. We won't have much of a head start." Matt helped Grace to her feet.

Grace looked back at all the unconscious people. "What'd you do?"

"Freeze," Sanders yelled from the other side of the room. Matt and Grace turned but continued moving toward the door. "Don't leave. Do not leave this building."

Matt took two wool hats and police jackets from a nearby desk as he and Grace continued to back away. "I'm sorry," Matt said, as he took his confiscated items from Roberts' desk. "We have to."

Sanders grabbed a radio. "Officers be advised. The pier suspects, one male, one female, ages fourteen, have escaped. Last seen traveling by foot north on Twelfth and Pine. They are fugitives. And they are dangerous."

34: Dad

Logan cradled the phone in his hands.

Rebecca tried to speak; all she could do was mouth, "I'm sorry."

Logan closed out the video clip; it minimized, nestled among other video thumbnails. He was about to hand the phone back when one title caught his eye—a thumbnail simply titled: Dad.

Logan tapped the small icon.

"Okay, give it back," Chet said.

Logan turned away as the video played. The scene showed like paparazzi trying to sneak a peek at a celebrity. The video was at the school football field. Spectators filled the school's grandstand bleachers. The camera stopped moving and focused on a specific section of fans. The camera then zoomed in on one lone man and a voice from off-screen called out.

"Chet."

The phone quickly lowered but kept filming.

"Hey, coach."

"What are you doing out here? Game's about to start."

"I was just . . . I just needed a minute."

"You alright, son?"

"Fine. I mean, my dad's here."

"He is? Show me."

"Right over there. Brown wool coat. Wearing a hat with the school logo."

"You've waited a long time for this. How are you feeling?"

"Why do you think he's here?"

"Just a guess, but probably because he was invited."

"Coach?"

"Parent appreciation night, remember?"

"Right."

"What is it? I need your head in the game, so if there's something bothering you."

"Do you think that if I have a good game, maybe he'll stick around?"

"You've led this team to a near-perfect season. You give us a win today, play like you've been playing, make him proud, he'll stick around."

"Yeah."

"Okay?"

"Yeah, okay."

"Alright, it's almost time. Lots riding on this one. You good?"

"Yeah, I'm good. Right behind you."

The coach slapped Chet on the shoulder. "Good man."

"Hey, coach?"

"Yeah, Chet?"

"Thanks."

"Show him what he's been missing all these years."

The camera then panned from the floor back to the stands. Once again, the man in the wool jacket and school hat came into view. The shot stayed on him for a moment before the clip ended.

"Stop the car," Chet said.

"Stop here?"

"Just stop the car!" The SUV pulled over on the Aurora Bridge.

Logan handed the phone back to Chet. "Chet, I didn't know."

Nate handed Chet back his keys. Chet pressed a button unlocking the back hatch. "Just go."

35: Run, Run . . .

Matt and Grace burst out the front door only to wind up face-to-face with the transport officer.

"Hold it right there!"

Matt took Grace by the hand and the two ran.

"In pursuit of the two fugitives!" the officer yelled into his radio. "Headed east on Pine!"

"We'll never be able to make it on foot."

Just then, a truck skidded to a halt in front of the two. "Get in!" Emily yelled through the lowered window. Matt and Grace didn't hesitate to jump into the bed of the truck. "Where's Simon?"

"Go! Go! Go!" Matt yelled.

"Not without my brother."

"He didn't make it out."

Emily stepped on the gas causing the wheels to slip. The officer was about to overtake the vehicle when a perfectly thrown snowball made direct contact with his face. The impact slowed the officer just enough for the truck to speed out of reach.

"Nice throw," Matt said.

"Thanks," Grace said with a smile.

"What happened to Simon?" Emily yelled through the rear window.

"He saved us," Grace said.

Matt looked at the cross street. "Where are we? What street are we on?"

"What do you mean, he saved you?" Emily asked.

"Fourteenth," Grace said. "Why?"

"We just passed Denny . . . and there goes John Street. Then it's . . ." Matt closed his eyes to think. "Thomas, Harrison, Republican . . ."

"So he's still locked up?" Emily yelled. "Why didn't you go back for him?"

"Like he did for us in Undertown?"

Matt opened his eyes. "Emily, we need to turn west before Mercer Street."

"I need to go back for him!"

"It's impossible," Grace said.

Two police cars turned onto the street in pursuit. "Here they come!" Grace yelled.

Two additional police cars approached from the left.

"Don't stop!" Matt yelled.

Emily rammed the front wheel of the flanking vehicle. Matt slammed his head against the truck's cab upon impact.

"You okay?" Grace asked.

"Fine," Matt said, as he sat down.

"No, you're bleeding."

A stream of blood trickled from Matt's forehead past his nose.

"Everyone alright back there?" Emily shouted.

"We're fine," Matt said.

"Where does this road take us?" Grace asked.

"Emily, get off this street. Doesn't matter where; just get off it."

"Why?"

"It'll take us right into . . . great." The truck passed a large brick column surrounded by large trees. "Volunteer Park."

"And that's bad because?"

"Because," Matt looked back at the entrance. Police cars slid to a stop, blocking the way. "We're trapped."

36: Best Served Cold

Logan and Rebecca exited the car onto the bridge. Chet made his way to the driver's side door.

"Chet," Logan said, "there's something I need to say—something I'll regret if I don't say it now."

Chet stopped, snow accumulating on his shoulders.

"I'm not sorry."

Chet's head turned slightly.

"You deserved what you got and I'm glad you were humiliated in front of your dad." Logan instantly realized that he might have overplayed his hand with that last bit. He swallowed as Chet walked back toward him.

"What did you say?"

"Uh, I don't remember."

"Say it again."

"It's been a long day. I'm not sure I can be completely responsible—"

Chet grabbed Logan by the shirt. "Say it!"

"You know what, fine. You want to hear it again? You deserved what you got. I embarrassed you once. Big deal. I think that makes the score like a thousand to one. And just to make sure we're all on the same page and there's no mis-understanding, if I could go back in time knowing that your father was going to be in the stands, I wouldn't have changed

257

a thing. In fact, I would've tripled the dose. Your father never stuck around after the game—you can only imagine the look on his face after seeing you at your lowest point. Guess what? I don't have to imagine the look on my father's face. I've seen it. You've brought me to my lowest point so many times I stopped keeping track. So please, do me a favor, save your tears and self-pity for someone who gives a shit."

Rebecca, Luke, Ryan, and Nate—none could believe what they heard and the expression on each of their faces proved it. They all waited for Chet's response.

Chet tightened his grip on Logan's coat.

"Take it back."

"Suck a fart."

Chet slowly walked Logan toward the edge of the bridge. Logan tried to dig in his feet, but they only slid through the snow.

"Dude, what are you doing?"

Logan's back hit the side rail and bent backward. Rebecca screamed at Chet. Logan's back slowly bent farther backward over the rail and toward darkness. His feet slipped out from under him. Rebecca pleaded with Chet to pull her brother back.

Logan tilted his head forward to look Chet in the eye. "Don't drop me, man."

"Why?" Chet inched Logan farther over the side.

"Because I'm not your dad. Plus I don't want your ugly face to be the last thing I see on this earth."

The next few moments felt like an eternity to Logan as he waited in the balance.

"You'd be lucky if my face was the last thing you saw." He pulled Logan back onto the bridge. Logan dropped to the street against the safety wall.

"You've got a massive amount of huevos, Logan. I'll give you that."

"Just the normal amount, I think. But thank you."

Chet leaned against his SUV. Logan caught his breath.

"Did you tell me to suck a fart?"

"I was having a bit of an out-of-body experience."

Chet shook his head. "The one person I hate the most and I can't stop caring what he thinks of me."

"He should've stuck around after the game."

"You're lucky; you know that?"

"Well, I'm still on the bridge and not under it, so I count that as a win."

"You know your old man."

"Lucky is putting it generously."

"What do you mean?"

"He's changed a lot over the past year or so." Logan picked some snow up off the ground and tossed it. "He and my mom are getting a divorce. I dunno, it's complicated."

"Divorce messes everything up." Chet held out his hand to Logan and helped him up.

"Does this, uh, mean we're okay?"

"I didn't throw you over, did I?"

"I guess I just assume that not murdering someone is more of a baseline for acceptable social interaction, not necessarily a sign of friendliness."

"Some would see it as me saving your life."

"Would they though?"

"So where are you two heading anyway?"

"Green Lake," Logan said.

"And what's there?"

"Answers, hopefully."

"To what?"

"Look, all I know is that our dad doesn't want us finding out whatever it is that he's hiding there."

"So you make it to Green Lake and you'll be able to stick it to your old man?"

"Something like that." Logan took a breath. "So it's still like three miles away. What would it cost to get a ride there?"

"Forget it," Rebecca said.

"Name your price," Logan said.

Chet thought for a moment. "Alright, on one condition. A thousand dollars and you do my homework for the rest of the school year."

"I take it you're most concerned about your math homework."

"No way," Rebecca said.

"Deal," Logan said.

"Logan, we are not making a deal with him."

"Who said anything about 'we'?"

"What?" Rebecca said.

"I'll get your thousand dollars and do your homework, but she stays behind."

"Done."

"Logan, what are you doing? You can't leave me here alone."

Logan walked toward the passenger side door. "It's a terrible feeling, isn't it? Being alone. Just be glad no one's filming it."

"Logan, I'm sorry. Logan!"

The SUV pulled away from Rebecca. Logan watched the side mirror as Rebecca faded into the night and snow.

37: St. Mark

The small pickup truck slid side to side as it rounded the curvy street inside the park.

"Alright," Matt said into the cab, "up ahead there's a round-about. Take a right. It's the only other way out of here."

"Any other ideas?" Emily shouted. "Look!" Across an open field, a half-dozen flashing lights rapidly approached from the exit. The truck and police cars were on a ninety-degree collision course.

"Hold onto something!" Emily shouted as she turned off the road and onto a semi-wooded portion of the park. The truck bounced like a Rally Car, tossing Matt and Grace side to side.

The flashing lights remained in pursuit as the truck climbed a steep bumpy hill. Grace slipped on the snowy truck bed toward the open tailgate.

"Matt!"

Matt reached for Grace's outstretched arm, taking hold of it, and pulling her back.

"Almost lost you."

The two stood as the truck overtook the hill's peak and began its rapid descent. Grace looked over the cab. She grabbed Matt by the coat and pulled him off the truck with all of her strength. The two landed on the ground and watched as the truck slid toward a tennis court that was built into the hill-side. The truck broke through the chain fence and dropped grill first over the six-foot cement wall. The snow muffled the impact as the truck stood perfectly on end and then fell upside down.

"Emily," Grace said.

"Get up," Matt yelled as two police cars overtook the hill. "They won't be able to stop either." The two ran toward the tennis court as two cars sped out of control toward them. "Don't look back!" Matt yelled as the vehicles gained on them.

Matt and Grace dropped over the wall and onto the tennis court; the two cars slid overhead, crashing right in front of them.

Matt looked Grace in the eye. "You okay?"

"Yeah, I think so."

"Come on. We need to keep moving."

"Emily!" Grace yelled.

Emily hung upside down. She opened her eyes as the sound of additional cars crashed over the wall. Emily tried to free herself, but the seatbelt was jammed.

"Get out of here," Emily said as she struggled to free herself. "I'm fine. Besides, I need to make sure Simon's alright."

"Hold it right there," a voice called out from one of the nearby cars. An officer struggled to exit his overturned vehicle.

"Go!" Emily said.

"Don't move!" the officer said.

"Emily . . ."

"Now, you idiots!"

Matt and Grace made for the far side of the court dodging outstretched hands of officers as they maneuvered their way through the wreckage.

"Where are we going?" Grace asked.

Matt quickly surveyed the area. "There," he said, pointing to a well-manicured hedge.

"The cemetery?"

"Come on."

The two ran toward the hedge, and then alongside it to an opening. They raced along headstones as the sounds of their pursuers closed in around them.

"Get down!" Grace said. The two ducked behind a large slate of marble. Three officers ran by.

Matt sat down in the snow and leaned against one half of a companion headstone. Puffs of breath lingered in the air. Grace sat beside Matt.

"What are we going to do?" Grace asked.

Matt shook his head. "We need to be on the other side of Lake Union." Matt looked at the stopwatch. "There just isn't enough time to get there on foot." Matt rubbed his hands together for warmth. "Even if we could fly, I don't know if we'd make it in time."

"We can. Tell me you have the seaplane keys on you."

Matt shoved his hand into his coat pocket. A set of keys hung from his index finger. "We need to move. This place is swarming with officers."

"Look over there," Grace said, pointing to lights in the distance.

Past the cemetery's tree line, an unusual structure stood. Its general shape was square, but its walls were layered, like massive vertical stairs. The center of the building came to a peak, not dissimilar to that of a pyramid.

"What is that?" Matt asked.

"St. Mark's Cathedral. It'll be packed with people tonight. Easier to blend in among the living."

Grace's hands trembled; Matt placed his hands over hers. "We're almost there. We're almost through this."

Grace nodded. "For better or worse." She smiled. "One last time."

"Yeah." Matt and Grace stood. "Slowly."

The two moved from headstone to headstone until they reached the edge of the cemetery. The trees and shrubbery made for good cover as they slid down a short embankment onto a neighborhood street.

Both sides of the road were lined with cars as people braved the storm to make it to Christmas Eve service. Kids with sleds and inner tubes ran by, ready to make full use of the fresh powder at the nearest hill they could find.

Then the familiar sounds of sirens rang out in the distance.

"They're widening their search," Grace said, as the two reached the road in front of the cathedral.

"Come on," Matt said, as the two turned right. Blue and red flashing lights illuminated the night no more than a half block down the road.

Matt and Grace turned to go in the opposite direction. Flashing lights now illuminated that side of the road as well.

Grace looked behind her. Flashlights swept the street where she and Matt exited the cemetery.

"Where do we go?"

Roberts shook the snow from his wool coat as he and Sanders entered the front doors of St. Mark's Cathedral. A volunteer offered them brochures. They both declined.

Matt and Grace quickly turned away from the front door and walked down a side corridor toward a group of robed boys standing outside the sanctuary.

Three police officers entered the church; Sanders gave them directions and the small group of five spread out.

"Here, put this on," Matt said, handing Grace a robe from a nearby storage cabinet. The two slid the choir attire over their heads.

An officer made her way toward the choir. Matt and Grace excused their way through the group of singers. Grace finished putting her hair in a bun as she and Matt exited the mass on the other side. Another officer made his way toward the choir from the opposite direction.

"Matt?"

"I'm thinking."

Just then, applause from inside the sanctuary sounded. A door opened and the group of singers funneled their way toward the cheers. Matt and Grace took no time to join the flow of choirboys into the sanctuary. The two walked past Roberts and made their way toward the stage.

There, in front of a packed sanctuary, Matt and Grace mouthed the Christmas song as best they could as the detectives walked toward the front. Sanders eventually met up with Roberts. "Anything?"

"No. But they couldn't have gone far."

Roberts scanned the room. "We'll make sure the perimeter of the building is covered. If they're in here, we'll catch them."

As the detectives exited the sanctuary, one of the choir members walked to the pulpit and led the congregation in prayer. With all other heads bowed and eyes closed, Matt and Grace made for the nearest exit.

"There has to be a back door to this place," Matt said, as he and Grace disrobed and walked down a hallway lined with massive stained glass windows.

"Hold it right there!" a voice yelled out from behind them.

Grace and Matt looked back. Roberts was already in full sprint.

The two ran down the vaulted corridor and up a small flight of stairs, which brought them to a smaller hallway. Offices and classroom doors lined the walls. The two made for the green glow of an exit sign at the end of the hall. Matt was just about to go through the door when Grace stopped him.

"Wait!"

"What?"

"It's an emergency exit."

Matt looked back down the hall at Roberts.

"I think this qualifies."

Matt pushed the door open. An earsplitting alarm instantly sounded as the two stepped out onto a roof.

Grace quickly shut the door behind them and scanned the area. "Toss me that piece of wood." Grace lodged the wedge under the door handle.

Roberts threw his weight from behind the door. Grace's makeshift lock held.

"It won't hold him long," Grace said, as she turned and joined Matt at the edge of the roof.

Matt looked down the wall to the parking lot. A mass of people exited the building. He looked farther down the church property. The kids with sleds were not deterred by the alarm as they continued their assault on the sloped parking lot. Matt then spotted a fire escape. "Come on."

The wood jamming the door cracked and then shattered as Roberts broke through. He ran to the nearest edge and looked down the side of the building. Matt and Grace were halfway down the flight of fire stairs and then seamlessly blended into the crowd below.

Roberts descended the stairs and joined the mass of people. A young couple caught his attention through the crowd. The general description of the young fugitives, along with the unmistakable trapper hat, made it a virtually unquestionable positive ID. Roberts closed the distance. He spoke into his radio, "Be advised, the two suspects are walking back toward the front of the church."

"I'm here," Sanders said. "I don't see them."

Roberts and Sanders made eye contact. Roberts pointed. "They're right in front of you now."

Sanders scanned the area. "I don't see them."

"They're right . . . they're running. In pursuit." Roberts bumped and shoved his way through the mass of people as he overtook the two.

"Gotcha," Roberts said, as he grabbed and turned the two around. "Who are you?"

"Who are you?" one of the kids replied.

"Where did you get that hat?"

"A couple of kids back there asked to switch."

"And what else?"

The two kids looked at each other.

Roberts showed his badge. "Do you really think it's a good idea to lie to me, kid?"

"They also paid us for our snow racers."

38: Planes, Lanes, and Snowmobiles

Matt positioned his sled's front ski near the edge of a massive hill. Grace did the same.

"You see those three intersections along the way?" Green and red traffic lights illuminated portions of the hill all the way down to the bottom. "We're going to be picking up a lot of speed, so be sure to use the brake, especially where the hill flattens out at the cross streets."

"Are you sure about this?"

"Get to the plane, save the kids. Besides, the cops can't drive their cars down these hills."

"Matt?"

"Yeah."

"Do you hear that?"

Matt's expression turned bleak.

"Is that—"

Matt looked down the street to his left. The approaching sound of a motor was accompanied by two growing sets of headlights.

"Snowmobiles." Matt looked at Grace. "Remember what I said about brakes?"

"Yeah."

"Forget it."

"Great."

"Ready?"

"Does it matter if I'm not?"

"No, not really." Matt gave Grace and her sled a push down the hill; he then jumped onto his sled, racing not far behind.

Grace couldn't help but smile as she gained speed and her stomach inched its way up her throat.

Matt looked behind him. Two snowmobiles raced around the corner and screamed down the hill in pursuit. He looked forward just in time for the first intersection.

"Hold on!"

The two sleds hit the crossroad and went airborne as the hill continued on the other side of the intersection. Matt and Grace landed hard but remained upright. The snowmobiles landed not far behind.

Grace looked back. "They're catching up!"

The snowmobile's headlight grew on Grace's back as everyone approached dangerous speeds. The engine revved as the snowmobile cut between Grace and Matt. The rider reached out, grabbed Grace by the back of her coat, and began pulling her from her sled.

Grace fought the tight grip as she neared the snowmobile's tread. She felt herself being lifted from the sled when the rider suddenly let go. Grace steadied herself as she flew into the second intersection. She held on as the four launched from the hill.

Grace floated in the air and then slammed onto the road. She almost bounced off the sled but was able to remain upright. She looked over at Matt. The second rider gained on him. Grace's pursuer revved his engine and narrowed the distance between them.

"Matt!" Grace pointed down the hill.

Two police cars positioned themselves as far up the hill as possible—just short of the last intersection. Blue and red lights flashed. One of the officers spoke through the PA system telling Grace and Matt to stop.

The hand reached out again and took Grace by the coat. This time, Grace was pulled completely from her sled and onto the snowmobile.

Matt placed his boot onto the front of his pursuer's snowmobile, which pushed him faster down the hill.

The officer with the loudspeaker continued to shout orders.

Grace struggled for freedom as the final intersection quickly approached.

"Stop!" the voice sounded over the loudspeaker.

Grace fought with the rider as he applied the brakes. The snowmobile slowed until Grace elbowed the rider in the face sending him tumbling to the ground. She reached for the throttle and gunned it. The snowmobile jolted forward into the intersection.

Matt's pursuer braked and skidded to a stop, shoving Matt forward into the intersection.

Grace's snowmobile and Matt's sled sailed through the air like they were built for flight. The police below ducked as the two flying objects cleared the parked vehicles with distance to spare.

The snowmobile landed awkwardly sending it fishtailing side to side. Grace skid to a stop.

Matt stopped his racer a little farther up the street.

Grace drove up next to Matt. "Need a lift?"

Matt jumped on the back of the snowmobile as the nearby police vehicles turned on their lights and raced toward them.

"Do you know how to drive this?" Matt asked.

"Just hold on."

❦

The small chain securing the linked fence was no match for the snowmobile as Grace used it as a battering ram.

Grace slid the snowmobile to a stop. "Which slip is it?"

"Eighteen," Matt replied, as the two ran onto the dock.

A line of police vehicles sped through the broken fence. Officers raced onto the dock, weapons in hand.

"Where'd they go?"

An engine sounded from inside a nearby structure.

The thin wooden door splintered into a thousand pieces as the plane's propeller tore through like tissue paper.

"Go, go, go!" Grace yelled.

Matt taxied the plane north toward Gas Works Park. He looked at all the gauges, switches, and levers, and mentally ran through the necessary steps for flight. Matt then gripped the throttle and pushed it forward. The plane sped forward with greater and greater speed. Chunks of ice knocked the pontoons.

"Matt?"

"I see them."

Ahead, flashing lights sped toward the plane.

"We need more speed," Matt said, as he gave the plane full throttle.

"We need an icebreaker."

A fleet of harbor patrol boats and the seaplane sped toward each other.

Grace looked over at Matt. "You do know how to fly this, right?"

"Just hold on."

Matt reduced the throttle and increased the engine's rpm, causing the plane to lift off the water. The two yelled with excitement as a spray of water showered the patrol boats below.

39: On Thin Ice

Two headlight beams pierced the night as Chet drove his SUV down the middle of the snow-blanketed road.

"You better get me my money."

"You'll get it."

"How?"

"You'll get it."

"Oh, and the fee doubled."

"Doubled? Why?"

"Emotional distress."

"From what?"

"Leaving my ex on the side of the road in the middle of a snowstorm."

"You didn't put up much of a protest."

"I was in shock."

"Fine. Whatever."

"And the homework?"

"What about it?"

"You better make it believable."

"Tell you what; I'll just imagine a baboon trying to write an essay, and then I'll dumb it down a bit."

Nate slapped Logan in the head from the back seat.

"I can still find a bridge to throw you off."

"I have a feeling you'd rather have the money and grades."

"Guys?" Nate said, looking out the back window. "What's that?"

Logan looked at his side mirror. Not far above the vehicle, blinding lights and an engine roar descended upon them.

"Is that going to hit us?" Nate asked.

Before Chet could reply, a seaplane buzzed the Land Rover's roof and skimmed the road in front of him. Chet slammed on the brakes as the aircraft disappeared into the night.

"Was that a plane?" Chet asked.

"Follow it," Logan said.

"There it is," Logan said, pointing toward wreckage under a canopy of trees near Green Lake's amphitheater.

Chet turned on his high beams. One of the seaplane's wings was missing, and a dim orange glow was visible from inside the cabin.

"That's fire," Logan said, as he opened the door.

Chet got out of the vehicle but stayed by the open door.

Logan rushed toward the plane as the fire grew. The pilot's side door swung open and Matt spilled out from his seat.

"Matt!" Logan said.

"Help me get your mother out."

Matt limped over to the passenger's side door and the two dragged Grace from the smoky cabin.

Chet looked behind him as the sounds of sirens grew. "Hey, Logan! I'll be seeing you." Chet put the Rover in drive and made for the nearest darkened side road.

"You're hurt," Logan said, as he noticed red snow spreading beneath Matt's foot.

Matt looked around at the low-hanging, snow-heavy branches. "Stay here. I'll be right back."

"Where're you going?"

Matt limped to the spot where Chet had parked and then walked backward to Logan.

"Good thinking," Logan said.

"Hopefully, it'll buy us some time." Matt grabbed a loose piece of twisted metal from the damaged plane. "Help Grace over to those trees and bushes over there. I'll be right behind you."

Logan placed Grace's arm around the back of his neck and made for the covering.

Following close behind, Matt used the piece of metal to hit each low-hanging branch along the way forcing every tree within reach to drop its collection of snow and conceal the bloody tracks.

Logan lowered Grace to the ground as police and emergency vehicles approached the wreckage.

"You okay?"

"I'm alright," Grace said.

"Where's Rebecca?" Matt asked.

"We got separated."

"How?"

"It's a long story."

Matt winced with pain. "It's time to stop this. Things are now officially way out of hand."

"You're right. You should definitely wait here," Logan said. "Take care of that foot, and look after Mom."

"No, we need to find your sister."

"She's fine. She has a gift for looking out for herself."

"May not matter," Grace said. "Look."

Matt pulled Logan down as flashlights swept the park. "We may not have fooled them after all."

Logan picked his backpack up off the ground. "I have an idea." He looked at Matt and Grace. "I need your hats and jackets."

"So you can do what exactly?" Rebecca said. "They're looking for *two* fugitives, remember?"

"Bec? How'd you? I . . ."

"Later." Rebecca placed Grace's wool hat snug on her head and zipped her jacket collar over her nose. "Well, come on then. What's the big plan? And quickly. If I found you, they certainly will too."

⁓⁓⁓

Roberts and Sanders approached the burning wreckage. The fire steadily grew.

"Do you think they made it out?" Sanders asked.

Two figures wearing police jackets ran by the plane.

"Freeze," Roberts yelled.

The two figures ran toward the lake as additional officers moved in from both the left and the right. They slowed as they approached the dock, and then turned.

"Remove your face masks," Sanders said.

"You have nowhere to go," Roberts said, as he and Sanders moved forward.

Just then, the orange glow inside the cockpit sparked into a fireball sending a plume of fire into the night sky. The explosion drew the attention of both detectives as they shielded their eyes from the heat.

"Where'd they go?" Roberts said, seeing that the two were now gone.

"There. At the lake's edge."

"Matt and Grace Stevens, or whatever your names are, it's over." The two detectives walked the length of the dock.

Rebecca looked across the lake seeing nothing but darkness. She looked back into the brightness of flashlights.

"Now what?" Rebecca asked.

"We keep moving forward."

"Logan, what are you doing?"

"Not giving up." Logan stepped onto the frozen lake. "It'll hold."

"You don't know that."

"Do not go onto the lake!" Roberts shouted through the wind.

"Come on back," Sanders yelled. "We'll figure all this out somewhere safe."

"Maybe they're right," Rebecca said. "This is crazy."

"What will they be able to figure out?" Logan said, shielding his eyes from the light. "Suffering, perseverance, character, hope. Remember? You want to know why I think Mom and Dad are divorcing? Because they gave up when it got tough. They stopped somewhere between suffering and perseverance."

"I think that's different," Rebecca said.

"Do not go onto the ice," Roberts said. "Come back here and we'll make sense of everything."

"Nothing's made sense since the night we found out Mom and Dad wanted to split. Back there, every decision will be made for us. This may be our last chance to do things our way. Right now, we decide what happens." Logan sighed. "Like you said, whoever has the antidote, has the power."

"Do not go on that ice; I repeat, do not—They're on the ice." Roberts and Sanders ran down the dock toward the two.

"Spread out a bit," Rebecca said. "We want to distribute the weight as much as possible."

"Alright, come on back," Roberts said, standing at the dock's edge. "This won't end well if you keep going."

"It won't end well if we stay," Logan said.

"We can work through this," Sanders said. "Nothing is worth the risk you're taking."

"I think that's a matter of opinion," Rebecca said.

"Alright, that's it," Roberts said to himself as he took off his wool coat. "Chasing kids around the city on Christmas Eve. Crashing my car. Getting electrocuted."

"What are you doing?" Sanders asked.

"What's it look like I'm doing?" Roberts stepped onto the ice.

"I thought you said that it wasn't safe."

"I know that's what I said. I grew up in Michigan. It'll hold."

Logan looked back. "Uh, Bec? We have company."

"It's fine," Roberts said, as he stomped the ice with the heel of his shoe. "See?" A loud cracking sound suddenly echoed through the air.

"I really do hate those kids."

A second later, Roberts broke through the ice. The hole created by Roberts' fall sent large cracks streaking toward Rebecca and Logan.

"Sanders!" Roberts managed to say amidst his splashing. "Give me a hand."

Sanders knelt down. "Come on." Sanders pulled her partner onto the dock and then grabbed her radio. "Officers, be advised. Suspects are walking across Green Lake. Be ready for interception between"—Sanders looked at her phone's GPS—"North seventy-eighth and . . . Sunnyside Avenue."

Two headlamp beams shone at the center of the lake as Rebecca and Logan made their way to the other side. All light surrounding the frozen wasteland was now out of sight—street lamps and porch lights were no match for the snow and fog separating Rebecca and Logan from their light's reach.

"When you think about it, it's pretty fortunate that I was able to catch up with you again," Rebecca said.

Logan kicked a small snowdrift to the side.

"Sort of an interesting story," Rebecca continued. "I had just made it to the other side of the bridge when this low-flying plane, I swear, almost landed on me. Soon after, a line of police cars followed. I flagged an officer down, and she gave me a lift. When I heard over the radio that tire tracks near the crash led away from Green Lake, I figured it was a decoy."

The two shuffled along a little farther as the wind whistled and howled.

"Logan, what happened at school . . . what I did . . ."

"I have an idea; let's give talking a break for a while. A little silence might be nice for a change. Besides, we should really save our energy. We're almost there."

Sanders stood against the blowing snow as she looked across the lake. Roberts, wrapped in a foil blanket, stood beside her; his hands shivered around a thermos of hot coffee.

"You shouldn't be out here. You're going to get hypothermia. Besides," Sanders looked around at the additional officers standing ready, "I think we're covered."

"I'm fine. I'm not going to miss them again." Roberts tilted the thermos in his shaking hands, promptly burning his mouth. "Son of a—!"

"There," Sanders said, pointing into the darkness. Two small lights broke through the fog.

Roberts dropped the thermos and drew his gun.

"Put that away. You're a shivering mess." Sanders looked back toward the lights. "Probably end up shooting me."

Roberts looked at his gun dancing around in his shaking hands. He placed the sidearm back into its holster.

The two lights grew in size and brightness.

"Here we go," Roberts said, as the lights emerged from the darkness. Roberts shielded his eyes as if looking toward the sun. "They're moving fast." Roberts and Sanders glanced at each other.

"Yeah, too fast. I don't think those are headlamps."

"Look out!" Roberts ducked just below a small flying object.

"What was that?"

Roberts and Sanders approached a small machine, downed by low-hanging, frozen willow branches. Roberts took the drone in his shivering hands and inspected it for a moment. He calmly set it on the ground, retrieved his gun, and unloading his clip, fired shots at the machine, never hitting it once. "Move out!"

Rebecca and Logan stepped onto a dock a few hundred feet down from the plane wreckage.

"That should keep them busy," Logan said, as he and Rebecca returned to the spot where they left Matt and Grace.

"Where's Matt?" Rebecca asked.

"He left."

Rebecca pushed aside a group of low-hanging branches. A thin trail of blood stretched from the brush out toward the homes in the distance.

40: Growing Up

Only the crunch of snow broke the heavy silence as Rebecca, Logan, and Grace approached the only house on the block without Christmas decorations. The house was void of any light except for the glow of a single lamp shining out a second-floor window. Rebecca looked at Logan and Logan looked at her.

"This can't be right," Rebecca said, looking at the address on the envelope. "Aunt Beth's house? What are we doing here?"

"It wasn't always her house," Grace said.

Rebecca looked to the second-floor window. "Why weren't we allowed to go upstairs? Who's up there?"

A fresh set of bloody footprints led around to the back of the house.

"Come on," Grace said. "Around to the back."

A crooked porch light illuminated the back door and the small patch of snow-covered patio. Next to the door, where a welcome mat once laid, was a square piece of dry cement.

The door slowly opened. From inside the darkened room, the three stood beneath the single light as tiny snowflakes swirled around them.

Logan quietly closed the door behind him as Rebecca walked to the other side of the kitchen.

Rebecca placed the palm of her hand against the kitchen door and opened it ever so slightly. She turned a small knob on the neck of a low-lit lamp inside the living room. The light slowly grew, illuminating the room's features. Rebecca picked up a framed picture from an end table.

"That was taken on my tenth birthday," a voice said from behind Rebecca.

"Aunt Beth!"

"What on earth are you doing here this time of night, Rebecca? And in the middle of a snowstorm no less?" The two hugged.

"I'm not sure anymore. We started off looking for answers, but now that everything's led us here—"

"We?"

Logan and Grace entered the room. "Logan," Beth said, as she gave her nephew a hug. "And who is this?"

"This . . . is our friend, Grace."

"Nice to meet you, Grace. Have we met before?"

"Our paths may have crossed," Grace said.

Rebecca looked at a few more pictures hanging on the wall. "These are of you and your parents, right?"

"They are."

"I don't know why I never took the time to really look at them before." Rebecca looked at the wall a few moments longer. "Why isn't my dad in any of them?"

"He was." Beth took one of the pictures from the wall and removed it from its frame. She handed it to Rebecca.

"When our parents divorced, he cut himself out of every picture in the house. Except for the photo in your hand. He missed that one."

Rebecca ran her finger down the frame's side.

"What happened?"

∼✦∼

Matt stepped cautiously as he ascended the stairs toward the second-floor light. The ice packed in the treads of his boots began to melt. The steps beneath his feet were familiar, the handrail beneath his fingers reminiscent of a time long passed. He stopped for a moment. Perhaps it was the fading adrenaline, or perhaps it was too much time spent outside on a cold night, but Matt's body felt like a sandbag. All of a sudden, his legs were not as strong as they had been. The pain in his foot throbbed.

Matt grasped the end of the rail and pulled himself atop the last stair. Like a dream where every movement feels like slow motion, Matt struggled to move toward the light coming from a half-opened door at the end of the hall.

Beth looked at the picture and then took it in her hands. "The divorce changed something in him that day; it changed something in me too." She set the picture aside. "It was just before Christmas when our mom left. I remember seeing Mom packing her suitcase like she was in a hurry. I didn't understand what was happening, so I hurried to Matt's room and asked if I should start packing my suitcase too. He just sat there holding a family picture in his hand, so I asked him again. He looked at me with sad eyes and said, 'no.'

"I was pretty young at the time. All I knew was that if the family was going on vacation, I wasn't going to miss out. So there I was packing my Care Bear backpack when Matt saw me. He sat me down and told me that Mom was the only one leaving and that the rest of us were staying behind. He did the best he could to explain to me why Mom and Dad weren't going to live together anymore, but looking back, I don't think he understood either. I started to cry, and that's when he told me that he had a plan to make her stay."

"What was the plan?" Rebecca asked.

"A gift. I wiped the tears from my eyes and saw a present in Matt's hands; it was wrapped just how you'd expect a thirteen-year-old boy to wrap it, but I thought it looked so nice. He told me he spent every last dollar he had to get it because Mom needed something extra special this Christmas. Mom wasn't happy for a while and I think Matt knew it. So maybe, just maybe, the right present would make her stay."

"So what happened?" Rebecca asked.

"We heard the front door open. Mom only had a couple of bags packed; I think she was more concerned about leaving than making sure she had everything. She was out the door and she hadn't even said goodbye.

"Matt rushed down the stairs and caught her just before she closed the door. I think the moment took Matt by surprise because after he called out to her, all he could do was wish her a Merry Christmas."

"What did she do?" Rebecca asked.

"She asked if the gift was for her. Matt nodded. She looked at the small box and then told him that he should give it to someone special. And she left. She left and never came back. No explanation. No goodbye." Beth placed the picture on the table and straightened it. "I never did see what was in the box."

Grace closed her eyes and held her hand over the necklace Matt had given to her so many years ago.

The floorboard at the end of the hall creaked beneath Matt's boot.

"Is someone there?" a weak voice called out. Matt looked around as if someone else might answer the question for him.

"Matthew? Is that you?"

A nurse opened the door, ushering Matt into the light.

"Cynthia? Who is it?"

Matt removed his hat and held it tightly in his hands. "I uh . . ."

"Let him in."

"Are you sure, Wendy?"

"That voice."

Cynthia stepped aside, giving the woman in the bed an unobstructed view of the boy standing in the doorway. For a moment, the two just looked at each other.

"Hi, Mom."

A flashlight illuminated a bloody footprint in the snow. "They came back," Roberts said, as he followed the trail with his light away from the brush.

A young officer quickly approached. "Reports of a home invasion four blocks from here. Description matches the kids we're looking for."

"Give me the address."

Wendy lay for a moment just looking at Matt. She then reached over and took her caretaker by the arm. "Cynthia, what exactly is in those pills you gave me?"

Cynthia looked at a picture next to the bed—a duplicate of the one downstairs. Seeing that the boy in the frame matched the one standing in the room, she took a step toward the door. "I'm just . . . I'll just be . . . right outside if you need anything."

Matt stood still as Cynthia exited the room.

"How is this happening?" Wendy asked.

"I don't know."

"Am I dreaming this?" Wendy asked.

"No."

"Then how?"

"I think it has something to do with the gift you sent," Matt said.

"Gift? What do you mean?"

"The bottle. With the note?"

"If you received a gift, I'm sorry, but it wasn't from me."

"It had to be."

"It did?"

"Your nurse. I saw her buy it."

"Are you sure it was her?"

Matt looked at the prescription bottles on the nightstand. "Maybe you forgot."

"Do me a favor." Wendy sat up a little. "Open the top drawer of the desk over there in the corner, would you?" Matt turned and walked to an old oak rolltop desk. He pulled the brass knob and opened the drawer to find dozens of unopened letters. Matt took one in his hands; it was addressed to him. The writing was crossed out. In its place, the words "return to sender" were written in dark ink.

"Open the drawer below it."

Matt placed the letter atop the others and opened the second drawer. More unopened letters, each one returned to Wendy.

"And the one below that."

Matt placed the letter down. "I get it."

"Matthew, the first time my letter was returned, it hurt. Junk mail or spam, you just throw away, delete. But you didn't just throw my letters away. You took the time to return it. You didn't read them—any of them. You wanted to be sure that I knew it. Every return hurt as much as the first, and while I believed I deserved the pain; there came a time when I just couldn't do it anymore. It was death by a thousand cuts. Sweetheart, the point is, I remember every item I've ever given you."

"I hurt you?"

"I know—"

"I was just a kid and you left!"

"I never thought in a million years that we'd grow so far apart—"

"Because leaving is such a great way to stay close. You know what? It doesn't matter. It really doesn't. I didn't come here to dig up old skeletons." Matt walked over to the window. It was snowing again. "Buried is better." Matt took a breath. "Everything led here though."

"And what were you hoping to find?"

"Answers."

"Answers to what?"

Matt turned to his mother. "Isn't it obvious?"

"I'm not so sure. More often than not, I've found that the answers we want and the answers we need are two different things entirely."

Matt looked at his watch. "Well, what I need is to know how to get things back to normal."

"And what would normal look like?"

Silence again hung between the two. "What would normal look like?" Matt sat on the window bench. "So all this was for nothing."

"I suppose that depends on how you look at it. Do you know the prayer I've prayed for the past ten years? The plea hidden between the lines of every letter I wrote?"

"I'm sorry, but I don't care."

"God, please send my baby back to me. Give us the opportunity to make things right before it's too late."

"Well, if you prayed any harder, I may have actually become a baby."

"Sweetheart, you may not have found what you were looking for, but please don't let this moment slip past."

Matt looked his mother in the eye. His heart began to beat a little harder as a dormant weight was brought to life. "So God answered your prayer. That's great. And at my expense."

"Matthew."

"Hey, as long as it makes you happy." Matt looked down and twisted his gloves; he then slapped them in his hand. He closed his eyes and took a breath. "I wasn't sure what it would be like to see you after all this time."

"I know."

"No you don't." Matt twisted his gloves again.

"Then help me to understand."

Matt smiled. "I've been mad at you for a long time. I've thought about this moment for so long, and I'm about to screw it up. Like a million words through a funnel."

Wendy remained silent.

"There's been something . . . deep inside of me." Matt took a breath. "For so many years, it was more than just some simple emotion. It was . . . the only thing I had control over. When you left, and then you and Dad divorced, it was like losing gravity. From that moment on, nothing felt grounded and I was just floating. Out of control. As a kid, you already feel out of control—it comes with the territory, I think. But there's a ceiling to all the chaos. As bad as it gets, as weightless as you feel, you won't float away because there's this"—Matt softly pounded the air above his head—"invisible roof keeping you safe. Your family—mom and dad."

"Matthew, I—"

"Please, let me finish. And then a day comes around that shakes your world to its core. The roof collapses and you feel yourself slipping away—slipping away from everything you thought you knew about life. You're reaching for something to hold onto. Anything to keep you from fading into that dark unknown. But there's nothing to hold onto and no outstretched hand to pull you back. You're slipping away. The places and people you knew become difficult to recognize. All of a sudden, you're further than you've ever been in a world you're not prepared to enter."

Matt continued, "At this point, you start to understand the reality of the situation. You're lost. And when you're lost and alone, you eventually check to see what you have with you—anything that will help you survive." Matt sighed. "And that's when I found it: my anger. It wasn't much, but it was mine. So I put it in my pocket and carried it with me wherever I went. In the beginning, we'd get sent to the principal's office, get detention. Every once in a while punch something that couldn't hit back—a desk, a wall.

"And then there came a day when it didn't fit in my pocket anymore, so I started carrying it around in my hands. In those days, we'd get suspended, and we started punching things that could hit back.

"But it didn't stop there. It got bigger, and I started to lose control of it. So I found ways to dull it. Not exactly therapist recommended ways, but it did the trick." Matt sighed. "But I found out that no matter what I did, the anger was always there waiting for me." Matt lowered his shoulders. "I've carried my anger for a really long time, and I swear, no matter what I do, it's never stopped growing."

Wendy swallowed. "What would happen if you were to let it go?"

The expression on Matt's face weakened. "It's all I have." Matt's eyes reddened as he looked to the floor. "But it's ruining my life. It's ruining everything I love, but I don't know how to stop it." Tears streamed down Matt's face. "I'm tired, Mom. I'm tired of carrying this around. I'm tired of it controlling my life."

"I'm sorry, baby, but I can't take it from you. You're the one that has to let go of it."

Matt looked up. "I don't want to hate you anymore."

"Sweetheart. Come here." Matt took a step forward, lowered his head, and leaned into his mother's arms.

"I never meant for things to end the way they did. I never wanted this for any of us. Matthew, I am so, so sorry."

Matt held tightly to his mother.

"I forgive you."

41: Lost Time

Matt raised his head from his mother's shoulder. Wendy looked into her son's eyes. "I've missed you."

"I've missed you too, Mom." Matt didn't recognize his own voice.

"Welcome back."

Matt stood up from his mother's side. He looked at his reflection in the window. His clothes, a few sizes too small, clung to his full-grown frame. A creak at the door drew Matt's attention.

"Sorry," Grace said, as she wiped the tears from her eyes. "We haven't been here for too long."

"It's okay," Matt said, as he wiped his face. "Mom, I'd like for you to meet my family. My wife, Grace. And these are our children, Rebecca and Logan. Your grandchildren."

Wendy took Matt by the hand and gave it a squeeze as Rebecca and Logan approached the bed. "Thank you."

Matt met Grace halfway. Grace looked down at her clothes. "Do I look as ridiculous as you?"

Matt raised her chin with the tips of his fingers. "Not in the least. I should have told you every day that I was fortunate enough to be called yours. You're beautiful. Nothing ever changed that."

Grace turned her head slightly, returning her gaze back to the floor. Matt lifted her head again. "Nothing changed that."

Grace smiled. She mouthed the words "Thank you." She then made her way to Wendy's side.

Matt turned to Rebecca. The two looked at each other from a distance before Rebecca took a few quiet steps away from the bed.

"How do I make it better between us?"

"Asking the question is a good start." Rebecca looked down for a moment. "Remember that picture of us on your desk?"

"That's my favorite picture of you and me."

"Mine too. Why haven't we had a new favorite by now? When I'm all grown up, I don't want that to still be my favorite."

Matt looked at the picture atop his mother's bedside table. "Me neither. Bec, I'm so sorry."

Rebecca thought about her father's words for a moment and smiled. "Finally." The two embraced as if reunited for the first time in years.

Matt brushed Rebecca's hair from her face. "The things I said to you outside my office. If I could, I would take them all back. I was the one that needed to grow up."

"Looks like you finally did."

"You are an amazingly smart, strong, independent young woman." Matt looked at Grace who was kneeling at Wendy's side. "You take after your mother."

"What's going to happen between you and Mom?"

"I don't know. I don't know if she'll still have me."

"I don't think you give her enough credit."

"No?"

"She's amazing, remember?"—Rebecca smiled—"Like me."

"That's a beautiful necklace," Wendy said. Grace unhooked it from her neck and placed it in Wendy's hand.

"I think this was meant for you."

Wendy looked at the necklace for a moment and then handed it back to Grace. "You shouldn't give something that precious away so easily. I told Matthew to give it to someone special." Wendy cupped Grace's hand back around the piece of jewelry. "It looks like he did." Her hand then gently slipped from Grace's, onto the bed.

"In here, in here," Cynthia said, leading Beth into the bedroom.

"Criminal? That's my brother."

"Wait, where is the other young one?" Cynthia asked, looking at Matt. "The one from the news? The one from the picture."

"I didn't hear you come in," Beth said. "Whoa, Matt, I never took you for a skinny jeans kind of guy," Beth said. "I'm glad you decided to come over."

Matt walked to his sister. He removed the stopwatch from his neck. "I think this belongs to you."

Beth smiled and took the timepiece.

"How'd you know?"

"The initials scratched on the back. Not too many athletes would engrave B.S. into their equipment if they didn't have to."

"I ran out of ideas on how to get you here."

"And you thought giving alcohol to an alcoholic was a good idea?"

"That would never be a good idea. Matt, it wasn't alcohol."

"Then what was it?"

"Juice, mostly. For what it's worth, I thought you'd just dump it down the drain. But I also knew that it would get your attention."

Matt took the poem from his pocket and handed it to his sister. "And this?"

"Finally put that writing minor to good use. It wasn't too on the nose was it?"

"A little, maybe. So how'd you do it?"

"I try to focus on the words that rhyme."

"No, I mean how'd you do *it*?"

"Do what?"

"You know. How'd you make us young?"

"I don't know what you're talking about."

"Come on. Seriously? The day after receiving the gift, Grace and I woke up the same ages as Bec and Logan."

Beth put her hand to Matt's forehead. "Are you feeling alright?"

"Then what was with all that stuff in the poem about the risk of remaining young forever?"

"Like I said the other day, if we don't deal with our past, we run the risk of staying there."

"So . . . the stopwatch?"

Beth lowered her voice and looked to the bed. "You knew Mom's time was short. Doctors said she wouldn't make it to Christmas."

"Matt," Grace said. "You need to come over here."

Rebecca watched as Matt went to his mother's side and took her by the hand. They spoke softly. Her eyes were then drawn to the window where red and blue lights flashed through the frosted glass.

"Matthew," Wendy said through tired breaths. "There's so much I want to tell you. So much I haven't said."

Matt swallowed the lump in his throat. "Mom, you already have."

"No. I'm afraid I haven't."

Matt went to the desk and took a letter from the drawer; he placed it in his mother's hand. "Please, open it."

"Matthew, it's okay."

"Please." Matt handed her a letter opener. "It's important."

Wendy slid the opener across the envelope. She then pulled out the letter and opened it.

The page was blank.

"I don't understand. How is that possible?"

Matt ran his finger along the envelope's side. A thin layer of clear glue held it together.

"Because I read it. I read all of them. I was just so . . . It's not you who has so much to say. It's me."

"Police are here," Logan said, as he walked to the window.

Unfazed by the information, Matt kept talking in low tones with his mother.

"This looks like your handiwork," Logan said to Rebecca.

"Wasn't me this time."

Logan looked at Cynthia. "Really?"

"When I saw the young one from the news . . ."

"You're the worst." Logan walked out of the room toward the stairs.

"They'll be at the front door soon," Grace said, as she followed behind Logan.

Rebecca also walked toward the bedroom door. She looked back. Wendy's breathing was shallow and slow.

Matt gently rested his mother's hand on the bed; he kissed his mother's forehead as she slowly closed her eyes.

42: All Is Calm

Roberts and Sanders stood behind their respective car doors. Roberts raised his radio to his mouth. "Everyone in position?"

"In position."

"They won't be getting away this time," Roberts said, as he and Sanders walked toward the house. "I try to keep emotion away from my work, but I have to admit, I'm really going to enjoy this." The two were now just feet away from the front door. "Here. We. Go."

The front door opened and out stepped Grace. "Is there a problem, officers?"

Roberts stopped. "Good evening, ma'am. We, uh, received a call that there was a break-in at this address."

Grace turned her head. "Matt? Did you call the police?"

Matt stepped outside. "Now why on earth would I do that? Hello, officers. Merry Christmas. Wow, look at all those police cars."

"Are you okay, Miss?" Roberts asked.

"Fine. Why do you ask?"

"I just noticed that you were limping."

"Oh, car accident. It was a while ago."

"A call was made from this address saying that someone had broken in."

"Well, it certainly wasn't me," Grace said.

Roberts looked at Sanders and then back at Matt and Grace. "Tell me, do you have any children?"

Matt looked at Grace. "Sure. Rebecca? Logan? Would you come outside, please?"

Rebecca and Logan stepped outside.

Roberts looked down at them. "You two? What are you doing here?"

"You told us to go home," Rebecca said. "Remember?"

"Is there anyone else inside?"

"Hello, officers," Cynthia said, as she stepped outside. "It was me. I'm the one who called. What I had thought was someone breaking into the house was really just a surprise visit from family."

"You're all related?" Sanders asked.

"No," Cynthia said with a smile.

"And you are?"

"The nurse."

"For whom?"

"Wendy."

"And she is?"

"Upstairs."

"No, I mean who is Wendy?"

"My mother," Matt replied.

Roberts shook his head. "Would you mind if we come inside? Have a look around?"

"Of course," Matt said. "I only ask that you keep your voices low."

Roberts spoke into the radio, "Hold positions."

Roberts and Sanders stepped inside the house. Roberts shook the snow from his coat as he walked slowly across the living room.

"Christmas cookie?" Beth asked, holding a tray of frosted trees and snowmen.

"And who are you?"

"Bethany Stevens. I live here. I'm Matthew's sister."

"Is there anyone else in this house that I should know about?"

"Just my dog, Pavlov." A golden retriever entered the room, tail wagging.

Roberts took a cookie.

"That's a beautiful necklace," Sanders said to Grace.

Grace subtly tucked the necklace under her shirt.

"I saw one just like it on a young girl earlier today."

"Really?"

"A young girl who claimed to be you, as a matter of fact."

"Claimed to be me? Must've been an unbelievable story."

"As unbelievable as a virgin birth. But that happened, didn't it?"

"Well, I certainly would've reported the necklace stolen if it had been. It's been with me the whole time."

Roberts scanned the wall of pictures. As he did, Rebecca quietly slid the only picture of young Matt behind a couch pillow. Roberts looked at Rebecca who stood smiling innocently.

Roberts walked into the kitchen, opened the back door, and inspected the frame. He looked down across the patio. The freshly fallen snow covered the boot tracks. Roberts reentered the living room. "And Ms. Wendy? She's upstairs?"

"Yes, but it would be better if you didn't bother her," Cynthia said.

"I'll be quiet." Roberts took another bite of his cookie.

Roberts walked upstairs and peeked his head into the only room with a light. The woman in the bed breathed slowly yet steadily. Cynthia entered the room and walked to the other side of the bed. As Roberts looked at Wendy, Cynthia slowly turned the framed picture of Matt and his mother away from his sight.

Roberts started to walk toward Cynthia.

"Please, sir," Cynthia whispered. "She needs her rest." Cynthia looked at the picture, still slightly in view.

Roberts walked closer.

"But since you're here, perhaps you can help me with the bedpan." Roberts stopped. "If you wouldn't mind reaching under and pulling it out."

"I uh . . . she looks like she needs her rest."

Roberts inspected the other rooms and then descended the stairs.

"Anything?" Sanders asked.

"Nothing. They're not here." Roberts put his hands in his pockets. "There's something strange happening here." Roberts looked at Rebecca, Logan, Matt, and Grace—all sitting on the couch. "I'm having the strangest feeling of déjà vu." He looked at the four again. "I have a feeling that I'm not getting the whole story."

"You're right," Logan said. "You don't have the whole story. There's something else you should know. We met a guy a little while back with the name A'houle."

"His name is A'houle?" Sanders asked.

"No, it's Benjamin. His last name is A'houle." Logan sighed. "The 'u' is silent."

"If ever there was a time for a letter to speak up."

"Right?"

"And you would like us to do what about it?" Roberts asked.

"I don't know. If you see him, give him a hug or something." Roberts just looked at Logan. "Just figured anyone with a name like that could use one."

Roberts spoke into the radio, "Everyone move out. They're not here." He walked toward the door. "Just do me a favor. Stay away from the pier for a while, alright?"

"Besides taking the ferry back and forth between Seattle and Bainbridge," Matt said, "you have our word."

Roberts sighed and opened the front door.

"Merry Christmas," Sanders said, as she exited the house behind Roberts.

"Merry Christmas," Matt said, as he closed the door and turned the deadbolt.

Only the sound of the fireplace was heard as the four stood silent and at a loss for words.

"So," Logan finally said, "this guy walks into a lounge, and there's this pianist with a small pet monkey."

"Logan," Grace said. "Maybe later."

"Don't worry; it's a holiday joke. So this guy walks into a lounge, and there's this pianist with a small pet monkey. The guy orders a drink and the monkey immediately runs over and dunks his butt in the glass. The guy says to the pianist, 'Hey pal, do you know your monkey put his butt in my drink?' The pianist says, 'No, but hum a few bars and I'll give it a shot.'"

"And how exactly is that a holiday joke?" Rebecca asked.

"The monkey was wearing a little Santa hat."

"And on that note," Matt said. "It's been a very long day. Why don't we settle in for the night? We can try to make sense of things a little better after a good night's sleep. Rebecca and Logan, you can stretch out on the couches down here. I'm going to spend some time with my mom upstairs."

Grace looked at Matt. "Do you want me to stay with you?"

"I do."

43: Home for Christmas

"**I**t's freezing out here."

"Mom, you don't ride a ferry and not stand out on the deck," Rebecca said. "You just don't."

The still waters of Puget Sound mirrored the Seattle skyline in a perfect reflection as the ferry distanced herself from downtown. A handful of people bundled in heavy coats and wool hats shared the observation deck alongside the four.

"It looks so small," Rebecca said of the city as it shrunk in the distance.

Logan closed one of his eyes and captured the skyline between his thumb and index finger.

Rebecca looked at her brother. "Do you hate me?"

"Do I hate you? Nah."

"Why? I would."

"Well, I left you on a bridge in the middle of a snowstorm, which in hindsight wasn't very cool. Plus, you did say that you were sorry. I assume you meant it?"

"I just don't know if I'd be that quick to forgive me."

"Well, you obviously take after Dad. Kidding . . . sort of."

"Even though I like to think that I make good decisions, I realize that I'm not going to get it right every time."

"You mean like with the video?"

"Yeah."

"And when you left us at the monorail."

"Uh-huh."

"And sneaking into Dad's office."

"Starting to ruin the moment, Logan. Yes, I'm a screwup sometimes, alright? I'm not perfect." Rebecca looked down at the rail. "Not even close."

"Oh, Bec." Logan put his hand on his sister's shoulder. "This isn't a surprise to anyone. Seriously, we all know this." Rebecca shrugged her shoulder out from under Logan's arm. "As for me," Logan said, "I think I'm retiring from 'getting even'—both active and passive forms of it." He took a breath. "Besides, look what happened to Dad and Mom. When I'm an adult, I intend to stay that way."

"Oh, Logan." Rebecca placed her hand on Logan's shoulder. "It's cute that you think you'll someday be mature enough to be considered an adult." Rebecca furrowed her eyebrows. "Say, Dad, Mom. Both of you changed back after Dad got right with Grandma. Why?"

"For better or for worse, I think," Grace said. "What affects one of us, affects both of us. That's part of the deal. No one should suffer alone in marriage."

"That's right," Matt said, as he looked at Grace. "We should be equally miserable." Grace shoved Matt's shoulder with one of her own.

"And your decisions affect both of us," Rebecca said.

"And if anyone should've known that, it's me," Matt said. He looked at Grace again. "I think for some time now, you've been the better and I've been the worse."

"I'm not sure that you can take all the credit," Grace said with a smile. "Most of it, maybe." Grace looked to the ferry floor. "It was real, wasn't it?" Grace said. She looked at Matt. "Us."

"Of course."

"We had our problems along the way, times we drifted apart, but we always found our way back to each other. How didn't we this time?"

"Because I lied to you. The day we married, I said I'd always be there for you, and I wasn't. I don't think we drifted apart; I think I pushed you away."

"Why?"

"Every time I saw you with that cane, it was another reminder of what I did to you. I couldn't look at you without hating myself. And I couldn't ask forgiveness because I think I knew that deep down inside I didn't deserve it. I couldn't forgive; how could I expect to be forgiven? So I did what I knew best. I started building walls. And the more I pushed you away, the more I was that little kid all over again—scared to death that I was going to lose another woman I loved, but convinced that it was somehow inevitable. Grace, I am so sorry for what I did to you."

"Someone once said that suffering produces perseverance, and perseverance produces character. Do you think that can be the same for a marriage?"

Matt's phone began to sound. Mr. Cartnight's name appeared in the caller ID. Matt sighed. "I really should take this."

Rebecca's shoulders sunk as she made eye contact with her mother.

"Mr. Cartnight. Merry Christmas, sir . . . Yes, I know and I apologize . . . I know, it was a once in a lifetime opportunity . . . Yes, right down the toilet, sir . . . I understand . . . Why throw it all away?" Matt looked at Grace. "For another once in a lifetime opportunity . . . Yes, you heard that correctly . . . Because I've found something else that drives me . . . Hope."

"His strong arms and piercing eyes are like that of a Greek god. I wished time stood still . . ." Logan read from a small book. "This *is* a diary?"

"It is a journal. Where did you get that?"

"Oh, it was zipped up in your backpack just sitting there for anyone to read. First came across it last night. It's also how I knew you meant it when you said that you were sorry. Your entry the night of Mom and Dad's Christmas party? Very self-loathing. That meant a lot. Greek god though? Were you talking about Chet?"

"Give it back."

"It's like a sad version of WikiLeaks."

"Logan." Rebecca reached for the journal.

Logan stepped away. "'When he says my name, it's like hearing the laugh of a newborn.' What does that even mean? I literally can't even right now."

"Add that phrase to the list, and give me back my journal, you exasperant."

"Add that word to the list."

"Tell me what it means and I will." Rebecca reached for the journal again.

Logan stepped away and then moved toward the front of the ferry, all the while continuing his narration.

"I'm going to kill you," Rebecca shouted as she chased after her brother.

Matt and Grace turned to see their children race away. Matt apologized to an elderly couple as he and Grace walked past them.

"Oh, to be young again," the elderly woman said.

Matt and Grace simply smiled as they entered the cabin—side by side, hand in hand.